Deep Kill

DEEP KILL

A Micah Dunn Mystery

M. K. Shuman

St. Martin's Press   New York

DESIGN BY JUDITH A. STAGNITTO

Library of Congress Cataloging-in-Publication Data

Shuman, M. K.
    Deep kill / M. K. Shuman.
        p.   cm.
    ISBN 0-312-05854-3
    I. Title.
    PS3569.H779D44   1991
    813'.54—dc20   91-4487
                                                            CIP

First Edition
10 9 8 7 6 5 4 3 2 1

This book is dedicated to the memory of my parents.

Deep Kill

One

"*M*olesting kids is the lowest thing anybody can do," the man in the chair said. "And that's why when that detective came—" His voice caught, and I dropped my eyes, because I don't like to see a man cry. Especially if the man's a friend.

I'd known Calvin Autry for almost all the years I'd been in New Orleans. The first time I met him was when my old Buick was stopping on me and four other mechanics had given up. So I took it to his garage just off Esplanade, and he listened and shook his head and said he was too busy to work on it that day. When I told him about the other mechanics, his faded blue eyes narrowed, and I could tell he was getting mad. He told me to leave it, and when I came around at five he told me it was a hairline crack in a resistor. He wasn't mad anymore, because he'd locked horns with the son of a bitch and had beaten it. Calvin Autry loved a good fight. But right now, slumped across the desk from me in my little walk-up office on Decatur, he didn't know who to confront.

"I know the kid they're talking about," he said. "Little black boy came in looking for work a couple of days ago. I gave him a dollar to sweep up." His lined face begged mine for understanding. "Hell, that ain't molesting, is it?"

"Not in my book," I told him.

He raised a pair of gnarled, grease-smudged hands. The tip of his left index finger was missing, and his nails were split.

"Look, Micah, I do honest work. I ain't no saint; I ain't saying I ain't never played around with women, especially since Marie run off. But I'm a normal man. I stick to grown women, not kids, and not boys."

"I believe you," I told him, shifting in my chair. Calvin Autry was more than my mechanic, he was my friend. But even friends can lie when the chips are down. If not, I wouldn't be in business. "But why would somebody make this up?"

"Shee-it." He fished in the pocket of his blue uniform shirt for a pack of Camels, took one out, and lit it. Calvin Autry had emphysema, but in the part of Oklahoma he hailed from you did what you wanted as long as you didn't complain about the consequences.

"Mechanic's got a shitload of enemies," he said, exhaling. "Every third customer thinks you screwed 'em. I got a Ford pickup sitting there now man won't come get, claims I'm charging too much. Bastard had a cracked engine block when he brought it in. Some people'd rather call up the Better Business Bureau than give you the time of day. I been took to small claims court. Damn crooked judges around here always side with the money. Man that owns my building, he'd like to run me out and rent it to some friend of his. I ain't sure he ain't behind this. And there's that lying bastard, Frazier, down the street; sent more cars to the junkyard than the wreckers has. He's been telling people not to go to me, I know that for a fact, and I'm about ready to go down there and shove a spanner up his ass."

"What about the boy?" I asked. "Does he have any reason you can think of?"

Autry shrugged. "Probably. He came back the next day, wanted to work some more, and I run him off." He flicked ash in his empty Coke bottle. "Hell, I ain't no public relations outfit. I asked him why the hell he wasn't in school. Pissed him off."

"Well, that might be the reason," I said.

"Christ," he spat. "To ruin a man's life?"

"I've seen people ruined for less," I said truthfully.

He licked his lips. A rawboned man of fifty-odd, it didn't come easy for Calvin Autry to show vulnerability, but here he was, and it was killing him almost as much as the accusation was.

"Look, Micah, whatever I have to do . . ." He ran out of words, and I smelled the fear. It wasn't a smell I like.

"You're a friend, Calvin. But it'll cost money; I'd better tell you that straight out. It'll cost a lot of money."

He nodded, his expression bitter. "I figured that. How much?"

"Two or three thousand. And I can't guarantee anything. What I'll do, I'll do as cheaply as I can. Mainly I'll just charge for the expenses. But you'll need a lawyer. The lawyer will almost certainly want to do a background check on you, which will mean contacting an agency in Oklahoma to build a file on you. I can find somebody to do that." I looked him in the eye. "If there's ever been anything like this before, it'll come out."

"God as my witness," he said, raising a hand, "Micah—"

"I know. I just thought I'd mention it. It may never come to the law, of course, it may be I can talk to the kid, or develop something that shows somebody put him up to it. But if it does come to your being arrested, the lawyer will want to go in loaded."

"But I told you I never—"

"It's not just this; he'll need a picture of your character in general. No lawyer wants to know less than the other side."

Autry sighed. "I'll have to sell my little piece of land across the lake. I was saving that for my grandkids. I was going to build a pier and a boathouse on the river. Marie and me used to go up there."

"And that's another thing," I said. "There'll be a lot of digging about Marie."

Another shrug. "What can anybody dig up they didn't dig up five years ago? Anyway, I'm not the first man whose old lady left him— the bitch."

It was my turn to nod. Marie was a sore spot with him. One day he'd come in and found a good-bye note. She'd taken their '86 Olds and her clothes and the household cash. Neither woman nor car nor money had ever been seen again, but a few days later she'd sent him a postcard from the West Coast, no return address. I had a feeling that despite his claims, he hadn't tried too hard to find her: it isn't easy for a man like Calvin Autry to admit he's been weighed and found wanting.

I handed him a sheet of paper and a pen.

"I want you to write down the names and addresses, phone numbers, whatever you can come up with for the people you mentioned, anyone who might have a grudge against you. And the name of the cop that came to see you, if you can remember." I pulled out another form. "And you can sign this. It's a waiver of privacy, allowing me to check your accounts and your credit rating. And I want a list of your accounts, by bank. Include your mortgage."

"What the hell?"

"Forget your privacy," I told him. "From now on you don't have any. Just think what it'll be like if it ever gets to court."

He took out his wallet and consulted several bank cards, and while he wrote I picked up my phone and hit the autodialer for John O'Rourke's number.

"John," I said when O'Rourke answered, "I've got a friend in trouble. I'd like to send him over. But he doesn't trust lawyers, so don't skin him."

O'Rourke's muffled snort erupted from the earpiece, and I managed a smile. "His name is Calvin Autry. Yeah, like the cowboy. It's a criminal case."

I hung up as Calvin was finishing the list of names.

"I want you to go over to see this man," I told him, fishing one of O'Rourke's cards out of my desk drawer. "It's on Gravier; you could walk if you wanted. He's a good man and an honest lawyer." I held up my one good hand. "I know, but trust me: he's one."

"Are you coming?" His eyes sought mine, hopefully.

"No. You're a big boy. And the time I'd spend listening to you tell him about it all over again I could be spending here doing some good." I hesitated. "Like I said, Calvin, it'll cost you some money, but you won't find it cheaper anywhere else, unless you've got a lawyer in the family."

"No such luck," he mumbled. "My kid's a damn construction worker, when he's got any work at all. Hell of a lot of good that does me."

I rose and patted his shoulder. "I guess it could be worse."

"Think so?" He started for the door and then turned. "Micah, it ain't no secret. Whenever anybody gets accused of something like this, people believe it. Maybe I need to call my best customers and let 'em know, but some people are gonna believe it no matter what I say. I'll probably lose my business. But Micah, I don't want *you* to believe it."

"I don't," I assured him, and when we shook hands I had the feeling I was holding onto a drowning man. I watched him go down the steps and then went back to my desk.

There was a picture of the platoon on one wall, and the VC battle flag we'd taken on the other. It had been a dirty little war, where people you thought were friendly sniped at you and kids tossed you grenades. I'd come back with a useless left arm and a bitterness it had taken a few years, a divorce, and too many bottles to work through. Now Calvin Autry was facing a dirty little war. I wanted to help him. But we'd lost the dirty little war in Nam, and I wondered if I would be any more successful here.

Because another memory was intruding on my thoughts now. It was the memory of two men sitting inside a concrete building one New Year's Eve, passing a bottle of Black Label between them, while a space heater pumped warm air to combat the chill seeping in from outside. Two men, pouring each other drinks to celebrate the end of one year and the beginning of another, knowing the last car had been repaired and sent on its way two hours before, and that no further work would be done that day. Two men exchanging confidences, in the intimacy of male bonding, knowing nothing would be repeated beyond those doors. And one of the men, more drunk than the other, talking aloud to himself about the wife who had left him the year before, staring through the bottle as he made his admission.

"Maybe she had cause. Maybe there's things a woman shouldn't have to put up with. If a man's a little different, if he can't help it, you can't hold it against him, can you? But a woman doesn't have to put up with it, either."

Cal had never again referred to his difference and I'd forgotten until this moment. But now I remembered and wished I hadn't. Because sooner or later I would have to return to that New Year's Eve and dredge up what he'd spoken of in confidence. And I was afraid of what I would find.

Two

*C*alvin Autry lived in Metairie, a suburb hugging the west side of the city. Two years ago they'd sent an ex-Klansman to the state legislature because the other candidate was too dull. They loved God, America, Saints football, and Dixie beer, not necessarily in that order. The houses were a mixture of white frame and red brick, nothing pretentious. The lawns were kept mowed, and you weren't afraid to walk the streets at night.

It was late morning, but I figured I might catch a housewife or two at home if I was lucky. Sal Mancuso hadn't been at the detective bureau when I'd called, and driving out to Calvin's neighborhood seemed like a good investment of time.

I'd never been to his house, because our friendship had started with business and gone from there, instead of the other way around. To date, our socializing had been restricted to an occasional six-pack at his garage at day's end, after my car was fixed, so I felt it was worthwhile to check out his home ground and talk to the people who knew him when he wasn't at work. Maybe somebody would let slip something that would change my image of him and show him for a liar. I hoped not. I preferred to believe somebody might hand me a lead about his enemies.

As I pulled to a halt in front of his house, I could glimpse cars whipping past on the interstate a block and a half away. Once it had been a quiet neighborhood; now there was a racetrack as backdrop to the sleepy oaks and camphor trees.

Cal's house was a bungalow type dating from the twenties, one story, with red brick pillars framing a front porch. There was a rose trellis, and the roses were blooming; somewhere I remembered his telling me he liked to play in the garden. The house had been freshly painted, in contrast to the homes on either side. I recalled Calvin saying he'd spent August sanding off the old paint and applying a new coat. The people you hired these days, he explained, did a crappy job.

I considered the houses on each side. There were cars in both driveways, so there was a good chance somebody was home whichever way I went. I went left, stopping on the porch to take out my card, which read GRAND GULF CREDIT and had a phony name and address. Sometimes it worked and people wanted to talk, and other times they'd just had a round with their own credit card company and slammed the door in my face.

A sign on the porch said THE BONCHAUDS: VIRGIL & MABEL, and I silently prayed Mabel would be a talker. It was early October, and dead leaves pirouetted across the walkway in front of me. In the next block somebody was burning brush, and my mind flashed to boyhood images of football on front lawns and Friday night games. I'd been fast, very fast. In high school I'd been a star receiver. But that was a few lifetimes ago.

I went up the steps onto the porch and had just raised my hand to knock when the door opened and a man appeared. He wore a jumpsuit, and a toolbelt dangled from one hand. A patch over his right pocket said BIG V PLUMBING.

"Lady of the house in?" I asked.

"Nope." The man had steel-colored hair and a roman nose. "What you want?" he asked, eyes wary. Then I saw the stitched name, *Virgil*, over the other pocket, and realized that he lived there. I showed him my card.

"I don't want any," he said.

"I'm not selling anything," I told him. "I'm running a credit check on your neighbor, Mr. Autry. He's applied for a gold label credit card from our company. Of course, we have his complete credit record, but we always like to talk with a person's neighbors, to see if there's anything we missed."

The man looked down at my card again and then back at me. "I never heard of you," he said.

I shrugged. "You'd be helping Mr. Autry if you could answer a couple of questions. I promise it won't take long."

He looked at me like he knew what my promise was worth. "I don't feel worth a shit," he said, sniffing to emphasize his point. "That's why I'm late. But I can't miss much more work. I got five calls to make. What you wanta know?"

I cleared my throat in my best official fashion. "Well, would you consider Mr. Autry a reliable, steady sort of person?"

My informant hawked and spat. "As reliable as anybody."

"Would you say he lived a quiet life, or does he entertain a lot?"

"Entertain? Oh, you mean parties. No. When Marie was around—that was his wife. They broke up a few years back. I guess you already know that."

"He mentioned he was divorced," I said.

"Divorced. Yeah. She lit out on him. Nice-looking woman, Marie."

"Do you have any idea why?"

He squinted at me. "You ever *met* Cal Autry? Got a personality like a hemorrhoid. I don't know how she lived with him as long as she did. But it ain't my business."

"Is he planning to remarry?"

"I never heard it if he is. But we ain't asshole buddies, okay? I mean, yeah, in the old days we came over for a barbecue once in a while, but you can't be around Calvin for very long without having to put up with his bullshit." He hawked again. "Hell, I said too much. Now don't go putting all that down. He ain't a bad sort. He keeps his grass mowed and he don't bother nobody."

"He have any other friends?"

"How would I know? Ask his kid, Melville. I don't see him here much, but Cal talks about him a lot."

I decided to change my tack. "Would you know if he had a problem with alcohol or drugs?" I asked.

The plumber chuckled. "I was waiting for that one. They all ask it nowadays. Didn't you all make him piss in a jar?" He seemed to think it was funny. "I can just see Calvin doing that." He shook his head. "Man has a few beers. I never seen him too fucked up, except once on New Year's Eve, but everybody gets fucked up then. Now I gotta go."

He started off the porch. "Look," he said, turning back, "what I said about his personality and all. Man, don't put all that down. He's rough as a rock, but he's good-hearted. Man would have to be, to like kids that much."

"Kids?" I asked, my mouth going dry.

"Sure. His clown act. He goes to hospitals and schools. I hear he's a scream. Calvin the Clown, he calls himself. And he's always hiring some kid off the street to mow his grass. There's been times he had a whole gang of little nigger boys in the yard. I never been too crazy about that. Too many houses robbed in this neighborhood. But Calvin, he's a soft touch."

"Right," I said, and thanked him.

I went back to my car, my feet leaden. Calvin the Clown. It was a side of Calvin Autry I hadn't seen, or even suspected. A man who loved children, went to the hospitals, hired kids off the street to do his yard work. He wouldn't be the first person who could change character by donning a wig and a rubber nose. The trouble was, what kind of character did he change into?

Wishing now that Calvin had never come to me, I drove back to my office. I didn't like no-win situations, and this felt like one. I went down Decatur onto Barracks and turned into my courtyard, going back to close the big wooden door behind me once I'd parked. As I climbed the outside steps I caught a glimpse of Henri LaVelle in the voodoo shop on the first floor. He sat on his stool, looking glum now that the summer tourist season was over. I opened my back door from the balcony, heading through the kitchen to the front room that served as my office. The red light on my answering machine was blinking, and when I played the message, Mancuso's voice said he was back in his office at homicide. It was just before noon, so I called him, hoping there hadn't been another killing in the meantime to pull him away.

"Micah," he sighed when I identified myself. "Good to hear from you. Ruin my day."

"I wouldn't do that," I told him. "I just need a little favor. There's a case I need some info on." I told him about Cal Autry and heard him sigh a second time.

"It's open season on child molesters, Micah. You know that."

"Sure. But a man's got a right to a trial. And kids do lie."

"*Everybody* lies," the detective said. "That's the problem. Look, I'll have to find out who's handling this and get back to you. But for Christ's sake, don't try anything heavy. I can't have you fucking with an ongoing investigation—especially one involving a kid. That'd be worth my job. Kids' names are supposed to be privileged in this kind of case."

"But Cal Autry will get his name splashed all over the *Picayune*, and he'll lose his business, even if he's acquitted six months later."

"Man, I don't make the fucking rules."

"I know. And I'll be grateful for whatever you can come up with. And any past raps, of course."

"Of course." There was a pause. "Look, is this guy a special friend of yours or what?"

I thought of Cal. I probably saw him every three months, tops, but ever since he had trusted me with the story of Marie's flight I'd felt like I'd enjoyed his trust, whether I wanted it or not.

"Yeah, I guess he is," I said.

"Then you got a feeling for this one?"

I thought about Calvin the Clown, and the kids doing yard work. "Too early to call," I said.

"Yeah. I'll talk to you later."

I suppressed an urge to avoid the job at hand by flipping through my album of famous yachts and called John O'Rourke for an update on Cal.

"How did it go?" I asked.

"What am I supposed to say?" O'Rourke answered in his lazy drawl. "Man's scared to death. Can't say I blame him. He thinks a hell of a lot of you, though, Micah. He seems to think you can pull the fat out of the fire if anybody can."

I groaned. "That's all I need to hear. Look, I told him the usual things, that you'd order a background on him and all. Is there anything else, anything that came through in your talk with him?"

"You mean anything you missed because he's your friend? Answer's no. I'd like to tell you he's innocent, but as the Bard said, 'There's no art to find the mind's construction in the face.' Do you know who's got the case?"

"Mancuso's checking on it."

"Okay. Lemme know when you find out. I don't want him talking to anybody besides you and me right now. I told him if they want him, they can go get a warrant. There's a pretty fair chance that'll stop it cold. Unless the kid has a witness, it's his word against Autry's. And when we find out who the kid is, we may be able to find out whether he's on the up-and-up. If he's from a project, if he's got a juvenile record—"

"We can hope," I said.

"I'm just dreaming out loud. I'll probably have to make a formal request. But call somebody in Oklahoma City and have them check out Autry's family and childhood friends. Find out why he came to Louisiana, and when."

I started to tell him about the construction business, how Cal had come in with Brown and Root and had gotten caught when the unions lowered the boom, back in the days when labor had the state in its pocket, but I caught myself. It was what I'd heard from Cal; there were ways to prove or disprove it.

"How much should I tell them?" I asked.

"Fifteen hundred," O'Rourke said. "He wrote me a check for that much. I called the bank. It's good."

Of course it's good, I thought. Cal Autry probably never bounced a check in his life. But then, I reminded myself, bouncing checks wasn't what this was about.

"Anything else?" The lawyer asked.

I thought about the clown act, but again I didn't say anything. After all, it wasn't evidence of anything but a good heart.

"No," I said finally.

He must have sensed my state of mind, because when he spoke again his voice was gentle. "Micah, you know, there are some people who lead their whole lives as upstanding, wholesome people, but there's one little corner, a little closet, like, where they keep something dark hidden. Every once in a while it gets out, and they have to run and grab it back. Afterward, they manage to convince themselves it never got out at all."

"That's still a poor excuse for molesting children," I said.

"I'm not the judge, I'm the lawyer. And I'm just trying to explain how it could happen. Autry may be like that, is all I'm saying. That could explain why he's so sincere. Or he may just be telling the truth. We may never know."

"No," I said, realizing he was right. "Well, I guess I'll check out some of the names of people he thinks hold a grudge against him."

"Right. Let me know how it goes." He changed to a more light-hearted vein. "Look, how's Katherine?"

"Fine. This is her second year, you know. She still feels strange, taking classes at a place where she used to work and knows all the professors."

"Could be worse," O'Rourke opined. "Give her a kiss."

I replaced the receiver and spread out the page with the names of people Calvin Autry considered suspects. The first name was Morris Frazier. Beside it Cal had written, *Crooked mechanic who also drinks on job, probably sells stolen parts, waters his gas. Told people I was overcharging. Dishonest bastard.*

I smiled in spite of myself. The address was scribbled in at the side. I looked at the rest of the list.

*Herman Villiere. A greedy son of a bitch if there ever
was one. Never worked a day in his life. Got my building
by inheriting it from his aunt, who he talked into leaving
everything to him. Wants to raise my rent so he can put
some friends of his in here, probably to sell dope.*

*George Guidry. Brought me a BMW that needed a
valve job and new piston rings. Wouldn't let me do it
because he said it just needed a tune-up, so I did one.
Then he drove it till the engine burnt up. Wanted me
to fix it free. I wouldn't do it. Took me to court and got
the crooked judge to take his side. Got a friend to lie
and say I told him he could drive around with it like
that.*

Beside this he had scribbled, *Don't know where this bastard is
and don't care, but used to live in Algiers.*

*Sam DeNova. Gave me $150 deposit on a used Chev-
rolet, then came back and wanted to call off the deal
after I lost somebody else who wanted to buy it. I kept
the money. Said he'd get me. Told him to bring his
momma. That was last year. Haven't seen him but once.
He cussed me.*

The final entry was *NOPSI. Rates too damn high. I complained
and called them blood suckers.*

That was one I didn't copy into my notebook. Somehow I couldn't
see New Orleans Public Service, Incorporated, setting out to get
him; they had a whole city to torture.

I read over the names again. It occurred to me that they were all
business related; there were no personal enemies, no neighbors, and
no members of his wife's family. I made a note to check these areas
and put his list into a new folder. I started to type out a label with
his name, but the thought of him lost among the other folders with

their impersonal little red tabs got to me, and I just scribbled his initials at the top and slipped the folder into my drawer. Then I called the agency in Oklahoma City.

For the next two hours I did paperwork, which meant collating my notes into a long, tape-recorded report for a homosexual pro football player who was jealous of his artist-lover. My assistant, Sandy, would type it up when she in came the next day. It was just after three when Mancuso called.

"Listen, I got what you wanted. O'Rourke called and they had to cough up the name, so I guess it doesn't really matter. Got a pencil?"

"In my hand."

"The boy's name is Arthur Augustine. He's fifteen, and he lives down on Marais, a couple of blocks from Esplanade." He read me the street address. "No juvenile record. Boy lives with his mama and her mama; you know the deal. He's supposed to be in high school, but he wasn't that day."

"When are we talking about, Sal?"

"Let's see; it was Friday, September twenty-eighth. Kid and his mama came in yesterday, Monday, to make the complaint."

I rubbed my eyes, wishing I didn't have to hear it. But there was no way out now. "What does it allege?"

"Kid says at about four o'clock on Thursday, the twenty-seventh he rode by on his bike and saw Calvin Autry sitting in his chair, just inside the door to his garage. To quote, 'He seen me and wave me over. I gone over and he asked did I want to make five dollars to work for five minutes. I said sure. He give me a broom and told me he was finished for the day and I was to sweep up. I sweep up and he ask does I know some tricks. I don't know what he mean and he say can I watch a card disappear. Then he asks can I see how to make a ten-dollar bill out a five. He got a little machine like a cigarette-paper roller, and he put in a five-dollar bill he say he going to give me and out come a ten. Then he say I only got to do one thing for the ten.' "

My stomach started getting queasy as I visualized the scene.

" 'Then he take and put his hand down my pants and feel my thing. He look scared like somebody maybe coming and he pull out his hand and tell me to come back tomorrow, he give me twenty and show me a good time. I left and gone home. Next day I come back about five o'clock and he tell me to get away, he done change his mind.' "

The image of the red-faced Calvin lingered for an instant longer. I forced it away because, I kept telling myself, none of it had happened.

"That's it," Mancuso said. "I've got to admit it isn't exactly iron-clad."

"No, but it's enough to ruin a man if it gets printed in the paper." I thought for a second. "Sal, doesn't it seem strange that the kid was willing to come back the next day and then only complained because Autry reneged?"

The policeman snorted. "Strange? In this job? Micah, I admire you for standing up for a friend, but you know as well as I do people'll lie, cheat, or kill over the wrong color shirt." He sighed. "Look, so far it's just an unsubstantiated complaint. Nobody's going to push it too hard without some kind of corroboration. But we have to go through the official motions."

"And meanwhile a man's in hell because he doesn't know what will happen."

"What can I say? You can talk to the investigating officer if you want."

"Later maybe. Thanks a lot, Sal. I appreciate it."

I spent the rest of the afternoon finishing my report, and then I drove over to Katherine Dégas' place, on Prytania. In the heart of the University District, it was an old Victorian two-story that she rented from a retired physician. I'd met Katherine a couple of years before, on another case. She'd been working as a secretary for the head of Tulane's Middle American Research Insitute, trying to forget the husband killed in the war while she put a son through college. At the time, she'd had a fixation on the chairman of the institute, but somehow in the middle of the investigation we ended up to-gether, and we'd been together since. She was beautiful, mature, and made me feel a way I'd never felt with a woman before. My physical disability didn't matter to her, and so after years of sensitivity, I had come to realize it was ceasing to matter to me. She's that kind of woman.

I let myself in and got a beer from the refrigerator. She was still in class but home any minute. I took a seat on the sofa and tried to sort out my thoughts. Soon her key turned in the door and she came in, smiling.

We kissed, and I nuzzled her auburn hair, for just an instant forgetting the sordidness of my day's work. She put down her notebook and went to the kitchen for some wine. When she came back she stood in the doorway for an extra instant, assessing me, and then walked over and took a seat on the sofa beside me.

"So what's wrong?" she said.

"Is it that obvious?"

"After all this time?" She traced my lips with her finger. "You look like the Sad Sack."

"Kind of the way I feel." I told her about Calvin. She listened thoughtfully, frowning slightly. "I remember when his best friend died, a couple of years back. He went to the hospital every day, and then to the man's house, and when it finally happened, he gave the family money for expenses until they could get on their feet again."

"You don't want to think he did it," she said. "But deep down you wonder."

I told her what O'Rourke had said about people who keep an evil locked away inside themselves. "And he's right," I told her. "It could be that way."

"That bothers you, because then you have to deal with a human being and not a label."

I nodded. "Exactly. Child molesters are supposed to fit labels, just like terrorists. It isn't true, but it helps to pretend."

Katherine took a thoughtful sip of her Chablis. "Poor Micah. Your job is being suspicious of people."

"Shitty job," I said. "I should've turned him down and sent him to somebody else. Somebody who wasn't his friend."

"It's too late for that now. Besides, he was coming to you for help; he expected you to help him. And look at it this way: maybe he didn't do it."

"That's what I keep telling myself. And then I keep thinking about the clown act. Baby, if the kid was making it all up, how did he know Cal knew magic tricks?"

"Maybe Cal showed him some tricks. That doesn't mean he molested him. Have you asked Cal?"

"I've put off calling him all day. I didn't know what to say." I shook my head. "It's a hell of world where you have to suspect people because they do nice things."

Much later, I held her tightly in the big bed upstairs where we'd first made love and tried to blot Cal Autry out of my thoughts. But my mind struggled against sleep, and even when slumber overtook me, my dreams were filled with images of clowns.

Three

Katherine had already left for the university when I roused myself. I didn't really want to go back to my office, but there wasn't any choice. Sandy Gibson, the tall, attractive black woman who was fast becoming indispensable to me, would be in at nine to see if I had any assignments for her. It had been a thin couple of weeks so far, ever since we'd wound up a custody case, and I'd been handling the business of the football player on my own. But today would be different. Today I had something for her to do.

I parked in the courtyard at eight thirty and stood there beside the fountain for a minute, enjoying the fine spray as it feathered down against my face. I was just starting up the outside stairs when LaVelle stuck his head out the rear door of his shop.

"Hey, Micah, seen my latest?" A thin, dark man in his thirties with a spade beard, Lavelle professed to be an expert on voodoo, but tourists were the only ones who fell for his act, and lately there hadn't been too many of them.

"Your latest?" I asked, glancing at the object he held in his hand.

"*Absolument*," he said, holding up a withered piece of root with a fleur-de-lis tag hanging from it. "This is my Saints gris-gris. I plan to market it to Saints fans all over the country. I mean, what do you think of when you think New Orleans? The Saints, right? And voodoo, right? It came to me yesterday, while I was sitting there all by my lonesome, why not combine 'em? Get a mailing list from *Sports Illustrated*, okay? Take everybody in Alabama, Louisiana, Arkansas and Mississippi, and everybody else with a French name, which means going for all the ex-Louisianites everywhere else in the country. With me so far? You send out a blurb, telling them this is a way to make the Saints win, only it gets its power through numbers. Everybody sends ten bucks for a New Orleans Saints John the Conqueror Voodoo Root. For fifty thousand faithful, which is a conservative number, understand, that's half a million bucks." He waited. "Well?"

"Well, what? Sounds like a postal inspector's full-employment guarantee."

"Jesus, Micah, you're a wet blanket. Don't you see? It's a *joke*. I *market* it as a joke. It gets to be an *in* thing, like, well, like *Mardi Gras*, for Christ's sake. Every Saints fan has to have one, that sort of thing. A symbol of solidarity with the mystical team."

I started up the steps. "Well, what the hell?" I said. "I don't guess voodoo can hurt. The Saints've tried everything else."

I had a bowl of cereal and debated taking out my percolator. The rich smell of New Orleans coffee was drifting in from the French Market, but for me the promise was always greater than the fulfillment; my taste for coffee had been ruined by too many night shifts in Nam, when the brew we'd had to drink was more like something you'd use to cure baldness. So I stuck with orange juice and waited.

At ten after nine I heard her footsteps on the stairs.

She was wearing a gray pants suit that quietly advised the arrival of fall. Her high heels told me she didn't expect to be doing any leg work today, and her alligator handbag suggested that she was going to confine herself to the decent parts of town—if there still were any. She wore pearls that on any other woman would have been *faux.* On Sandy, though, I knew they were real, and that she was daring any of the various lowlifes who inhabited the Quarter to make a grab for them. It had happened once before, and a low-power junkie had found himself inhaling a short-barreled Smith & Wesson and begging her not to pull the trigger.

"Micah man," she said, closing the door after her. "Sorry I'm late, but traffic in this city is hell. Did I miss the big case?"

"No, I've been waiting, actually, to put you on it."

"Are you serious?" She seated herself in the same chair Calvin Autry had used the day before. "Not another custody, I hope. I get so tired of these no-win deals. Give me a good old-fashioned embezzlement any day."

"How does child molesting grab you?" I asked.

She shook her head. "Dirty, very dirty. Are we prosecuting or defending?"

"Prosecuting," I said. "At least, for practical purposes. We need to find everything the prosecutor's going to have. And we have to find it before an arrest is made, if possible. Because after that, it's all over, even if the charges get dropped."

She frowned slightly. "You got a personal stake in this, Micah?"

"Yeah." I told her about Calvin. "I want him to be innocent, but we have to go with whatever we find."

"We may not find anything," she said. "You know these cases, Micah: one person's word against another's."

"I know. But all we can do is check everything out. I'm going after his enemies to see if I can find a connection; I need you to check out the boy. See if he's really clean, or whether there's something else going on there."

"I'll do my best," she promised, rising again like a jungle cat. "But I've got to go home and change first. Can't hardly go looking like *Mademoiselle*."

I watched the door close behind her and was just reaching for my notebook when the phone rang.

"Micah?" It was Calvin's voice, but there was something in it I wasn't used to hearing.

"I'm here, Cal. Is everything okay?"

"Yeah. Sure. I'm down at the garage now. I finished the first job. I was just thinking I'd call before I started the second one, since I hadn't heard nothing from you. . . ."

"I'm sorry, Cal. I should have called. But I've been working on it. And these things take time."

"Sure. I understand. Look, did you talk to the cops? I mean, is there anything they didn't tell me?"

"You know as much as I do," I reassured him. "No hidden punches, so far as I can tell. Listen, how did you like O'Rourke?"

"The lawyer? Oh, all right. Sure, I mean, he seemed like a straight shooter. He wanted money like you said, but—"

"Believe me, it'll be money well spent," I promised.

"I know. It's just, hell, Micah, a man shouldn't have to put himself in hock just because some fucking little bastard lied on him."

"No," I agreed.

"I'm not complaining," he said quickly. "I mean, I don't expect nobody to work for nothing. It's just the system that ain't worth a damn." There was a pause. "Look, Micah, my day ain't that full. If you happen to be around here about four or four thirty, I still got that bottle of Black Label from the Fourth of July."

"Sure. But you've got to understand, Calvin; I may be on the job. So just keep a couple of swallows for me." I replaced the receiver and tried to tell myself that I'd given him the truth and that it had nothing to do with not wanting to have to sit next to him and wonder.

I took out my notebook and then got out the city directory and began to match names to addresses and telephone numbers.

I already had Morris Frazier's address. He owned a service station on Esplanade a few blocks from Cal's garage. Herman Villiere was harder to pin down. There was no listing for him in either the city directory or the telephone book. I considered calling Cal, but I thought it would be best to keep him out of it for the time being. So I started through the Villieres in the phone book, calling each and asking for Herman. I hit pay dirt on number three. She told me that I had the wrong number and that Herman lived across town. She didn't see him much, but she had his business card somewhere. After a minute she came up with it, so I thanked her, entered the information in my notebook, and went on to the third name. There were about two dozen Guidrys in the phone book. I'd call them all if I had to, but it would be easier to drop by Calvin's and get what I needed from his records.

But first I'd see what I could find out about Frazier and Villiere. That there were unresolved complaints against Morris Frazier and the Esplanade Full Service Center I was able to find out just by calling the Better Business Bureau. I slapped on enough cologne to set a hound baying, threw on a jacket and tie, and donned a pair of glasses. Making sure my Rotary pin was on my lapel, I grabbed the attaché case Sandy called my "nerd prop" and went down the steps to the courtyard. When I'd loosened the clamp on my car's radiator hose and let my engine run for a while, I headed out onto Barracks and over to Esplanade. I drove past Frazier's to get an idea of his operation. It was an old-style service station, with a young black man to pump gas while a grease monkey in a gray jumpsuit worked on a car inside one of the two repair bays. A hard business to keep going these days, I thought as I made a U-turn in the next block and came back to slide in beside the pump island. Close up I could see paint flaking on the walls of the office, and the window needed a good cleaning.

I got out as the pump boy ambled over. "Your mechanic busy?" I asked. "My temperature light's on."

The pump boy rubbed his nose and went back into the office. A second later a plump little man in his fifties came out, walking pigeon-toed. His red face and veined nose made me wonder if he drank his profits, but I'd often thought running a filling station these days would make anybody drink.

"Yes sir?" the man asked, trying a little too hard with his smile. "You got a problem?"

"Red light's on," I said. "I don't know what's the problem. I just paid somebody three hundred bucks for a new water pump. I don't mind paying money, but I expect to have the thing fixed. I'm never going to that place again."

"What place is that?" the man asked, and I could see the wheels already turning in his mind.

"Garage down the way; what's the man's name? Same as some old cowboy star."

"Autry," the man breathed, and leaned back against one of the pumps. "Calvin Autry. You shouldn't have gone there. He don't know what he's doing. Should've come here to begin with."

"Somebody recommended him," I said. "Poor recommendation, I must say."

The man signaled for me to release the hood. I reached in, pretending to fumble for the inside lever. His head disappeared inside the engine space, and I knew he was checking the new water pump Cal Autry had put in two weeks ago, for a hundred dollars, not three hundred.

"Start her up."

I got in and complied, watching the red temperature light go on. I knew the water would be coming out of the upper hose where it joined the radiator, something anybody could see. When the man came back around the car shaking his head and wiping his hands on a rag, I knew he'd taken the bait.

"Water pump again," he said. "Have you looked at this pump since he put it in?"

"I just told him to do the work," I said. "I don't know anything about water pumps, or care. He told me it had a thirty-day guarantee."

"When was that?"

"In August, I think. Yes, August, because I remember we had the accounting convention then."

"Well, you need another one," he said. "But it won't cost you anywhere near three hundred. I can get it for two and a quarter."

"And is it guaranteed?"

"A full ninety days. But they generally last a couple of years. I imagine you got cheated on this one. Doesn't look like he put one in at all. My guess is he just poured some sealant in, to hold it for a little while. And that's another problem."

"Oh?"

The man's expression became mournful. "Sure. No matter what they claim in the ads, those sealants they use mess up your cooling system. I wouldn't be surprised your radiator's so gummed up it'll have to be pulled and flushed out." He motioned for me to cut off the engine and then gestured for me to come and look under the hood with him while he poked his penlight at the backside of the radiator.

I made a face, as if the worst thing that could happen would be to get some grease on my jacket.

"Now see there?" he said, his flashlight beam hitting the wet part of the engine block, where water from the leaking hose had thrown it. "That's radiator water. Coming right out the core. We're gonna have to send it to a radiator shop."

I touched the wet spot on the hose where it entered the radiator. "What's this?" I asked.

He squinted at me for a second and then chuckled like I was a little too backward to understand. "Water from the radiator's getting flung up every which way after it hits the fan."

"Oh." I straightened up. "And how much will all that cost?"

"Pull your radiator and repair the damage? Two hundred. But we'll flush the system for nothing. And add antifreeze."

"What about that other mechanic?" I said irritably. "I have a good mind to report him. I mean, he simply can't be allowed to cheat people that way."

The man shrugged. "Happens all the time. Lot of crooks in this business, and you picked one to deal with."

"You've had other complaints about him?" I asked.

"Yes, sir. Many's the car I've had to straighten out after that man's had his hands on it. We get a lot of our best customers from him, you know what I mean."

"But he should be put out of business!"

"Man like him puts himself outta business, sooner or later."

"But how long has he been down there? Surely not very long?"

"Ten, twelve years. I been here longer. But I stay in business 'cause I treat people right, see; he stays in business by cheating old ladies and people that don't know—" He stopped, realizing he might have said too much, but I went on as if I hadn't noticed.

"And another thing," I said, leaning close to him and dropping my voice to a whisper. "When I was in there, he had these little colored boys sweeping out the place. Now I don't know about you, but I didn't like the looks of it. Never know when something'll turn up missing."

But he only looked blank. "Yes sir. Well, we can take care of you, and nothing'll be missing." He checked his watch. "Walter's just changing a set of shocks on that car now and he can get to you in fifteen or twenty minutes."

A light seemed to go on in his mind. He turned around and gave my front fender a shove. "Come to think of it, you could stand some new shocks yourself. We could put 'em on while the radiator's being fixed."

"Really?" I said. I glanced at my own watch. "I have a meeting in half an hour. Very important meeting. The assistant auditor will be there." I let my brow rise a half inch. "Can I come back this afternoon, say?"

"You won't get very far like this," he warned, sensing the fish starting to slip away. "I'd hate to see you stuck on the freeway."

"I just have to go downtown."

"I can put some water in," he offered, quickly adding, "but it won't last long. That radiator's like a sieve, and the water pump bearing's shot."

"I'll make it. If I don't, I'll call you. Do you have a card?"

He stumped into the office and come out with a dog-eared square of pasteboard with ESPLANADE FULL SERVICE CENTER, MORRIS FRAZIER, OWNER printed on it.

I watched them fill the radiator from a watering can, and when they'd finished, I thanked him again, promised to come back, and chugged off into the traffic, leaving him with a perplexed expression. I'd seen that look before: he'd sized me up for the handicapped brother-in-law of somebody high enough in the city bureaucracy to give me a meaningless job, which meant I wasn't really good for anything, and so why was I escaping from his net?

I'd let him figure that one out. But I had to admit I hadn't come out much better for my trouble. I'd confirmed the fact that he didn't like Calvin Autry, and that he was a crook. But if he'd put the boy up to complaining, Frazier had resisted the temptation to rise to the bait and let something slip. And somehow I didn't have the feeling he was smart enough or had the will power to let such a chance go by.

I decided to pay a visit to Herman Villiere. I chose my financial consultant's card and, after tightening my hose clamp, drove over to the address I'd been given.

It was an office building on Elysian Fields, near where Gentilly crosses it, a low, modern one-story that formed a U around the parking lot, like a corporate motel. The aunt hadn't told me which office in the honeycomb belonged to her nephew, but when I'd checked the directory board outside and eliminated the psychologist, the travel agency, the bookkeeping service, and the lawyers, the only tenant left was MVP Properties. I knew I was taking a chance by not calling first, but I didn't want to give anybody an opportunity to turn me away. This way I could at least get an idea of the layout. And then, if necessary, I could wait until the man himself appeared.

The office was twentieth-century impersonal, with furniture that might have come from a rental agency and prints on the wall that probably came with the lease. The receptionist's desk seemed exceptionally tidy, and I had the feeling I hadn't interrupted anything more pressing than her daydreams of next weekend. She was pretty, but I suspected the red hair came out of a bottle, and the long nails must have played hell when she typed.

"Can I help you?" she asked as if she thought I had the wrong door.

"Is Mr. Villiere in?" I asked.

"No, he's not here," she said. "Does he know you?"

"No, but I think he might like to. I have a client who may be interested in some property he owns."

Her penciled brows went up a fraction. "He'll be in this afternoon," she said. "Do you want him to call you?"

"I'll check back," I said, and started out.

Her voice caught me at the door. "Maybe I can get him in his car."

"That would be fine," I told her, coming back to the desk and handing her my card.

She dialed. "Hi," she said into the phone, cupping her hand over the mouthpiece, but not enough to keep me from hearing. "There's a Mr. Hudson here to see you about some property. No. Just said he's interested." She looked up from the phone. "What property is that?"

"I'd prefer to discuss it with him in person." I wrinkled my nose. "You know these car phones. Never can tell who'll be listening."

"Okay," she said, and hung up. "He'll be here in a few minutes. He's just leaving one of our properties on St. Bernard."

I thanked her and took a seat. For the next few minutes I watched her don fresh makeup and admire herself in the mirror. The phone didn't ring and nobody else appeared until a quarter to eleven, when I heard a car skid to a halt outside. A door slammed and a few seconds later the office door opened and Mr. Herman Villiere walked into the room.

He was young, late twenties at the oldest, with fine features and dark slicked-back hair. His blue blazer was open, showing a silk shirt underneath, and in lieu of a tie he wore gold chains at the neck.

"Hi," he greeted me, sticking out a hand. "You wanted to see me?" He smelled like a whore's boudoir, but his grip was firm and I could tell from his muscles that he placed a high value on fitness.

"Carl Hudson," I said, handing him my card. "I'm here at the request of a client. He was interested in some property you own."

He gave his gum a few chews and put my card in his top pocket. "Yeah? What property is that, Carl?"

I gave him the address. "I think it's being used as a garage now."

He nodded. "That's one of our properties." He motioned for me to follow him into the office at the rear. I noticed his desk was clear, except for a small gold model Ferrari that would have served as a paperweight if there had been anything to hold down. The walls were hung with the same kinds of pictures as were in the front office, and as he slumped into the big chair behind the desk, I wondered how much time he actually spent here.

"So who's your client, Carl?"

"I'd rather not say at this point," I told him, taking the chair across from him.

He gave a single nod. "What does he want with it? Going to open another garage?"

"I doubt that." I let him have what I hoped was a winning smile. "He frequently invests in areas he thinks have potential. Old neighborhoods that could be renovated."

"He looking to raise a new River Walk in the ghetto? What is he, a one-man HUD?" Villiere's laugh had a nasty tone.

"He doesn't always explain these things," I said. "But he might be willing to make an offer. Now, if the person in there's got a lease—"

"No lease," Villiere said. "But he's been a renter for more years than I can remember. Rented from my aunt before she passed away. They were big friends. I can't say he's a special friend of mine, though."

"Then you might be willing to sell?"

"I didn't say that, Carl. If I sell, your client's going to evict him. I'm not sure that would be right. Man's got a right to make a living."

"Couldn't he go somewhere else?"

"Maybe he's used to where he is now. Location's a lot in that kinda business."

"Admirable attitude," I said. "I'll tell my client you aren't interested."

"Tell him that, Carl." He tapped his pocket. "But if I change my mind, I've got your card."

"Right." I rose, and he extended a hand without getting up.

"Thanks for your time," I told him, shaking hands.

"Right."

I turned and started out, feeling distinctly uneasy. Maybe it was his eyes on my back. Or maybe it was the fact that Herman Villiere didn't seem like the kind who was interested in renters' rights. Whatever it was, it was catching, because the girl at the desk had put down her magazine and watched me like a cat as I went through the front office and out the door.

I noted the license number of the red Ferrari at the curb and then got into my own slightly battered Chevrolet. I'd learned to sense when a situation wasn't right, and every part of my body was vibrating a warning. Maybe, I told myself, Villiere is the man.

But I still had to check out the other two, Guidry and DeNova.

I got a burger and some tea at a Burger King and took them with me to Pontchartrain, where I sat in my car and watched the gray waves roll in with the inevitability of disappointed dreams. I'd barely begun the investigation, but I wanted Villiere to be the villain. I wanted to find that, for whatever twisted motive, he was trying to ruin Calvin Autry. It didn't matter that he didn't have to falsely accuse the man to get the building: maybe, I thought, he was afraid Cal would kick up a stink if he evicted him. This way, Cal would be on the defensive. Maybe he was afraid of Cal. God, I wanted to believe that. Anything but the memory of that New Year's Eve.

Maybe she had cause. Maybe there's things a woman shouldn't have to put up with. If a man's a little different, if he can't help it, you can't hold it against him, can you?

A little different I thought. Is that all we're talking about? An idiosyncrasy?

Four

I spent the next two hours in the clerk of court's office, going through the conveyance books. I found a judgment from 1988 giving all the worldly goods of Mrs. Gladys Villiere Dejean to her only surviving relative, her nephew, Herman Patrick Villiere. Her worldly goods were fairly considerable: house in Gentilly, valued at $75,000; an apartment building on Camp near the river, which had a value of $60,000; some property in East New Orleans, which had been swamp twenty years ago but was now part of a subdivision; and the building which she'd rented to Calvin Autry as a garage. There was also a savings account worth a hundred thousand dollars and another $220,000 in CD's. The property descriptions all bore the same probate number, and when I looked it up I saw that the real estate had come from her late husband, along with most of the other assets. When I ran Herman Villiere through the vendor and vendee files, I discovered that he had not bought real estate in his lifetime, but just a year ago he'd sold off his aunt's house at a ten-thousand-dollar loss. I wondered if he'd run through the cash, and if so, why he'd want to hold onto a worthless garage.

I left the clerk's office at three thirty, with the traffic already building toward rush hour. I made my way through the narrow streets with my window down, enjoying the first hint of fall after a searing summer. From somewhere came a scent of baking bread, blotted out quickly by the odor of bus exhaust. When night came, the streets would change and the predators would be out, high on crack and willing to take a life for a one-dollar bill, but right now it was an autumn day, and people looked grateful for the crisp weather. I thought of Katherine's son Scott, now a senior at Tulane, and wondered if he'd gotten me a ticket for the next home game.

I found Cal under an '83 Caddie, cursing some part that wouldn't come loose. When he slid back out and saw me, his face showed relief.

"Damn, I thought you wasn't never coming."

"I told you I was busy," I said. "I've been trying to check out anybody that might have a grudge."

He wiped his hands on a rag, his face hopeful. "And?"

"Nothing for sure. Right now I need you to look in your records and get me the addresses for DeNova and Guidry."

Cal hawked and walked into the little glassed-in office. He took a seat in his swivel chair and began to open drawers in his filing cabinet.

"Let's see, it was 'eighty-eight. Or maybe 'eighty-nine. Here it is." He produced a yellow invoice. "Right here. George Guidry. Lives on Canal Boulevard, the son of a bitch." I copied down the address and phone number.

"Was he a customer of yours before?" I asked.

"He was in here a few times. If I'd of known then what he was like, I'd of told him to go somewhere else."

"Okay. What about DeNova?"

"I ain't seen him since." He fished in his files. "Here's the receipt I give him. Lived in Gentilly." Autry squinted at me. "You reckon maybe it was him? He said he'd get me."

"I don't know," I told him. "People say a lot of things." I started up from my chair.

"Hell, Micah, you don't have to go already do you?"

"Pretty soon." I answered. "You called your customers about this yet?"

He looked away. "Not just yet. I wanted to wait and see what you came up with."

"Right." I sighed. "Cal, you never told me you were a clown."

He blinked and then tried to laugh. "Hell, I guess it just never came up. Why?"

"Because there are those that would say . . . " I let the sentence trail off.

A look of horror twisted Cal's face. "You mean, that I . . . Micah, for God's sake, you don't think—"

"I don't think anything," I said, trying to keep my voice neutral. "I'm just trying to tell you what a prosecutor would think."

"Christ, is anything I ever did going to go against me? Micah, I was a clown because I like kids. I always liked kids. But I haven't done any clown shows for a couple of years, not since Melville was out of the Scouts. Just haven't felt like it. That's all there is to it." He looked away, voice choking. "Micah, I swear to God . . . "

"It's okay. I'm just doing my job," I said. "I have to prepare you for what they may say. If there's anything at all . . . "

"I told you there wasn't," he mumbled, and tugged a bottle out of the lower drawer. "You want a couple of swallows?"

"I'll pass today. I'm tired."

He nodded, his expression rueful. "Micah, I want you to know that, well hell, it means a lot knowing you're on this. I laid there all night, thinking about things, wondering why it was happening, half out of my mind, to tell you the truth, and then I thought,

Micah's on it. He'll take care of things. It made me feel better."

I patted his shoulder. "Keep up the spirits," I said.

As I walked toward my car I saw a black kid circling in the street outside on his bike. It cast a pall over the drive back to my office.

There was an angry message on my machine from the football player, who'd expected a call from me about his report. I called him back and got his answering machine. I could hardly complain.

Then I looked up the names in the phone book again. There was a G. Guidry listed at the address on Canal Boulevard, but no DeNova at the address Cal had given me.

If DeNova had left the city, he'd probably long forgotten his promise to get Cal. What about Guidry? He might bear Cal hard feelings, but from what Cal said, Guidry had won the court case and so had little reason to take the issue further. I decided to call Guidry and see what happened.

He wasn't home, but his wife gave me his business number, an exchange in the downtown area. The woman who answered identified it as a law firm. I gave her my true name and business and said that I wanted to talk to Mr. Guidry about a past case. She put me on hold, and I listened to elevator music for a couple of minutes. Then a male voice came on.

"Hello?"

"Mr. Guidry, my name is Micah Dunn. I'm looking into some things for a man named Calvin Autry. I think you know Mr. Autry?"

"Who?" There was a pause. "Oh, you mean the mechanic. I'd about forgotten him." His voice was deep, with a hint of humor. "There was a time when I didn't think I ever would. That man caused me a lot of trouble."

"I understand you went to court over a car of yours?"

"That's right. But what's this about? He's not sueing *me* now, is he?"

"No, sir. Some threats have been made against him, and—"

"And I'm on his enemies list." Guidry laughed. There was a faint touch of Cajun accent in his pronunciation. "Well, I can't say I blame him. But he made me so damn mad. I went to him with my car knocking, and he wanted to overhaul the motor. I couldn't see

that, so I told him to try a tune-up first. He claims he warned me
I'd damage the engine, but I don't remember that. Besides, mechanics love to tell you what'll happen if you don't buy their estimate
lock, stock, and barrel."

"But the engine *was* damaged," I said quietly.

"Yeah. But legally he shouldn't have done the tune-up if, in his
professional judgment, that wasn't the problem. And that's what the
judge held."

"Kind of a fine point, wasn't it?" I asked. "Especially if you asked
him to do it."

"Maybe so. But the law says a professional is supposed to know
what he's doing and refrain from things that are inappropriate." He
sounded like he was quoting from a lawbook.

Before I could respond, he chuckled again. "But maybe he did
have a point, looking back. I was mad then. The car was fairly new;
I thought I was saving by avoiding the dealer. So when that happened
and he refused to work on it for nothing, I sued him on principle.
But it wasn't any big deal."

"No," I said, visualizing him in his big padded chair, BMW
parked outside, a handful of unpaid parking tickets in the glove
compartment.

"But all he had to do was put in the gasket and he could have
avoided the whole thing. After all, how much does a gasket cost?
It's nothing but asbestos. There's such a thing as customer relations."

I would have disliked George Guidry, too. He was a big man who
for the sake of a principle had ground a little man under his heel,
except that I knew this had never occurred to him, and had I told
him he would have been shocked.

"You haven't seen him since then?" I asked, keeping my voice
level.

"Not since that day in court. I thought he was going to have a
stroke when the judge gave his decision."

Maybe, I thought, there was more to Cal's claim that the judge
was crooked than I'd originally credited: how do you insure an
impartial hearing when one of the parties attends all the same social
functions as the judge, maybe even contributed to his campaign?

"Well, thank you for your time, Mr. Guidry."

"No problem. Hey, is old Autry in trouble, then? I hope not. I don't wish him any bad. I'm not one to hold a grudge."

"Nice of you, Mr. Guidry."

I hung up and made a mental note to ask O'Rourke to find out what kind of law Guidry practiced, and how successful he was, but in my heart I knew he wasn't the man I was looking for, just as I'd known I didn't need to look further with Frazier.

It kept coming back to the middleman, Herman Villiere. All I knew about him was that he'd inherited money he seemed on the way to squandering, drove a fancy car, and didn't want to consider dumping the kind of property that was a glut on today's New Orleans market. I called Mancuso and asked if he'd ever heard of Herman Villiere, knowing it was an off chance.

"I'll run the name, if you want. You want to tell me what this is about? Not the child molesting?"

"No, I don't suspect him of that," I said ambiguously, and heard the policeman sigh. "But I'd like to have a home address for this license plate," I said, and read him the number of the Ferrari. He put me on hold and came back a minute later with a location on Crystal Street, in Lakeview. I wrote it down.

"By the way, anything new on the case since the last time we talked?"

"Don't know. It ain't my case, Hoss. I've got all I can handle with the last homicide in the French Quarter."

"What about my man Calvin Autry? Turn up any criminal record?"

"Oh, yeah, I meant to call about that. Answer is no, not here, anyway. I guess that's good."

"I'd say so. Thanks, Sal." I hesitated. "Oh, a couple more names, if you wouldn't mind." I gave him Frazier, Guidry and Sam DeNova.

"I thought you said a couple. That's three."

"Please."

"Okay, if you put it that way. I'll call back when I find out anything."

I thanked him and hung up.

I went out to the porch overlooking the patio fountain. I'd done all I could, hadn't I? Checked the names Calvin had given me, started a background check with an agency in his home state, had Mancuso run everybody remotely connected through the police computer. I'd even sent Sandy after the complainant. So why didn't I feel better?

Because experience told me that in cases like this, there was often no resolution. Accusations were made and left to fester unproven, and action was sometimes deferred indefinitely. In the end, almost nobody knew the truth except the accused person, and sometimes after all the mind games and psychological stress, even *he* didn't remember what had occurred.

In Nam I'd know men who'd blanked on the entire six months before they'd stepped on the mines that blew off their limbs. And one of the best NCOs I'd ever worked with called in artillery on a peasant hamlet, and afterward he swore he'd seen a reinforced NVA platoon take cover there. I hadn't found a sign of one anywhere, and neither had anybody else, including him, but the mind reacts oddly under stress, and he was able to describe in detail their weapons and positions. It was necessary for his sanity, because some errors are too terrible to admit.

I thought about going inside for a beer but decided not to. I'd been drinking too many of them lately, and exercising them off was even harder for me than most people, because running with one arm strapped to your body throws you a little off balance, just as one-armed push ups are more difficult than the regular kind. Maybe, I told myself, I'd call the Captain. Then I decided against it: I loved my father, but I wasn't in the mood to hear about people from years ago in Charleston. He'd reconciled himself to my going into the marines rather than the navy a long time ago, and more recently, even to my profession, but there was always a wistful element in his conversation, an unspoken hope that someday I might give it up here in New Orleans and come back to live near him during his remaining years. We both knew it wouldn't work, because the Captain was accustomed to command, and I wasn't eight years old anymore and awed by gold braid. But there was still the silent *if*. I was still thinking about it when the phone inside shook me out of my reverie. I picked it up to hear Sandy's voice.

"I didn't feel like driving all the way over there," she said. "But I knew you wanted to hear what I had to say."

"You're right, and I'm all ears."

"Well, I went down to talk to the boy, but he was at school. Just his auntie and his mama and his uncle."

"What cover did you use?"

"None. I thought about it, but Micah, these folks know jive when they hear it. Better to come straight out."

"Your call," I said. "So what happened?"

"Well, the boy's a little wild, cuts school, runs with some older kids that'll end up in Angola, but he hasn't done anything yet."

"No father," I hazarded.

"No." There was a brief silence, and I knew she was thinking of her own childhood on these streets, a subject to which she seldom alluded. "Anyway, I asked what they understood about all this. The uncle, the mother's brother, is a man named Taylor Augustine. He did the talking, for the most part. He's an ex–equipment operator for the city, retired on disability. I trust him."

"Go on."

"Well, the boy skipped school last Thursday, and his uncle gave him a hiding when he got home. Boy said he'd been working, but they didn't believe him."

"That was the afternoon he was supposed to be sweeping up for Cal Autry," I said.

"Right. Well, he cut school the next day, Friday, probably because he was mad at them for the beating," Sandy said. "He came back at about six-thirty, almost dark, but this time he said he'd been trying to get work from the same white man as the day before, but this time the white man tried to molest him. He was pretty shook up."

"That was when they called the police?"

"They talked to their minister, first. He recommended it."

"Anything else?"

"Yeah; matter of fact, there is."

"Well?"

"Micah, the boy knew Autry before. He told his family he and some other boys were hired by Autry to work in his garden once. He said Autry tried something then."

I took a deep breath. "Is there any chance he's lying?"

"Well, he told them Autry had a house in Metairie."

"Oh, Jesus."

"Amen."

I tried to think of something else to say, but there wasn't a whole lot. When I spoke again it was hard to push the words out.

"Thanks, Sandy. We'll talk tomorrow."

"Night, Micah." There was a pause. "I'm sorry."

I replaced the receiver in the cradle and stared at the wall for a few minutes. It was rush hour, and traffic was lined up outside like beads on a rosary. Logic said I should call it a day, throw on my shorts and jogging shoes, and work it all off with a run. But I wasn't feeling very logical, so I went downstairs to where my car was parked next to the patio fountain. Five minutes later I was headed west on Esplanade, on my way to Wisner, which would lead me north, through City Park toward the lake.

It took me half an hour, with the traffic bumper to bumper, horns blaring and tempers raw. By the time I got to Robert E. Lee the rush had thinned somewhat. I turned right, toward the lake, and into the exclusive Lakeview subdivision. The homes here were expensive and tasteful, and the cars were BMWs, Volvos and Audis. I found the address I'd written down for Herman Villiere and cruised past slowly. It was a two-story neo-Spanish with a tile roof and palm trees out front. The lawn looked like Astroturf, though a sprinkler kept it wet. There was a Porsche in the drive, but the red Ferrari was nowhere to be seen.

I made the block, then parked two houses down and settled in to watch, turning over possibilities in my mind. Villiere didn't own the house, or I would have found a record of the sale in the conveyance files. Nor did he seem like the kind to rent; that was for ordinary people. Even as I watched and considered the possibilities, the door of the house opened and a blonde came out. She was wearing shorts and no shoes, and as she sauntered through the spray to collect the newspaper from the front lawn she seemed a little spaced out.

The answer hit me then: she was the owner, of course, and Villiere was living with her. And if her place was listed as his domicile with the Department of Motor Vehicles, the arrangement was of some duration. But I wasn't surprised; what would have surprised me more would have been to learn that Villiere was paying the mortgage.

The blonde wandered back inside with the paper and the door closed behind her. A few seconds later the red Ferrari zoomed into the driveway and Villiere got out, blazer slung over his shoulder, and headed inside.

I waited, keeping my eyes on the front door. Katherine had a night class, so she wasn't expecting me until late. Darkness fell. A snort of nose candy and a quickie, I told myself; Herman Villiere wasn't the kind to stay at home, even on a Wednesday night. Sure enough, at eight the door opened again and the pair emerged, the girl leaning heavily on Villiere as he steered her to the car. He let her open her own door like an old married, and a moment later the engine roared and the headlights stabbed the blackness. The car slid backwards into the street and headed away from me. I pulled out, did a U-turn, and started after them.

He took Robert E. Lee west, then headed south on West End to Vets Boulevard. We passed Causeway and he opened up, his tail-lights barely visible as he wove through the traffic. I gunned my engine and tried to follow and just as I was beginning to think I'd lost him I almost shot past him, plodding along in the right lane, almost as if he'd waited for me to catch up. I settled in four cars back and watched him slide right onto Clearview. On Clearview I started to catch up again, then saw a light change to yellow ahead of him and hit my own brakes as his taillights went bright. The signal went green and he drove another block, and turned right into a shopping center. I followed, and when they parked I slid into a space in the parking area a hundred yards away. They got out and headed for a flashing neon sign that said PLAYTIME. I waited before walking across the blacktop after them, passing through several knots of people in the parking lot. Everybody seemed to be waiting for something and I wondered what.

When I got to the door, they'd already been inside half a minute. I let a foursome precede me and then followed.

My ears were assaulted by loud music, if you could call it that, and flashing lights strobed my vision. An outline of moving shapes mingled and diverged on the dance floor.

A shape came out of nowhere and a hand grabbed my arm.

"Five," the owner of the hand said.

I fished out five dollars and the voice said, "Hold out your hand."

I did and the doorman stamped something on the back of it in fluorescent ink. I started through the doorway and felt the hand grab me again.

"You carrying?"

That should have been the tip-off, but I let it slide. "No," I told him, wondering how he'd picked me out.

"Better not be," he said. "This is a clean place."

"I'd never have guessed," I mumbled, and slipped into the cluster of black forms.

Villiere and his woman were nowhere to be seen, but now I knew what the people outside were waiting for: it didn't take too long to spot the dope deals going down. Nothing spectacular, just money changing hands, a little envelope palmed here and there.

I threaded my way through the crowd and hit the men's room, interrupting a furtive conversation between a man in a leather jacket and a yuppie in a silk shirt. They eyed me suspiciously as I used the urinal, and I felt their eyes on the back of my neck as I went out.

I seldom carry a gun. Except when you're in a project or on the streets at night, there's no need for one, and the cops don't take kindly to citizens packing firearms, even if they have the obligatory honorary sheriff's commission, as I do. Without a pistol, you're betting the worst that will happen is a punch or two in the gut, or a broken nose. When you carry a pistol you've already drawn the line. Right now, though, I was half-wishing I'd stuck my .38 into my belt. The place had that kind of feel.

Another slow pass around the room and along the bar, and I knew Villiere and the woman had slipped out. I went back, past the doorman. They'd gone out the back, which meant they knew the layout. And Villiere had told him who I was, or he wouldn't have asked about the gun.

I headed back to my car. The parking lot was more crowded now, and none of the people standing around outside smoking paid any attention to me. I passed the first row of cars and stopped, trying to orient myself.

The Ferrari was gone.

Swearing under my breath, I hurried the rest of the way to my car. I got in quickly, checking the back seat out of habit even though the doors had been locked, and started the engine.

They'd slipped me, damn it. But was it intentional, or just dumb luck? I put the car in gear and a second later had the answer.

My tire was flat.

Twenty minutes later I'd managed to replace it with the spare, not the easiest of jobs when you only have one arm that works. I found a filling station on Causeway with an attendant who said he could fix it, but when the man rolled the tire into the light of the arc lamps he only shook his head.

"Looks like it's been cut to me," he said. "This tire ain't no good."

I looked at the slash marks, sucking in my breath. He sold me another one for sixty bucks, and half an hour later I was on my way again.

I had part of the answer, and the answer was white and came from a country far to the south. The question that remained was whether Villiere was only using or dealing. And what, if anything, that had to do with a mechanic who rented a building from him on Esplanade.

After a quick shower I called Katherine, but she wasn't home yet. Probably, I thought, she was holed up in the Tulane library doing research. I lay down on the bed with my hand behind my head, determined to blank my mind and let the thoughts flow on their own, like a stream, until I was asleep. It must have worked, because sometime during the night I heard a phone jangling from nearby and I fought my way back from oblivion to pick it up.

I started to tell her I couldn't make it tonight but it wasn't Katherine's voice, it was Mancuso's.

"Micah, are you asleep?"

"I was trying," I said, forcing myself awake. Surely he hadn't called just to tell me about the results of the record checks. I glanced over at the dial of the clock radio. It was ten-fifty.

"Sorry to bust in, man, but I thought you'd want to know this as soon as possible."

"Know what?" I asked him, awake now to the tone in his voice. "What happened?"

"That boy, Augustine?" he said. "The one who accused your friend?"

"Yeah?" I asked, my belly doing a flip-flop.

"Well, they just found him on the batture in Algiers, near the naval station. Somebody beat his head in, Micah. He's dead."

Five

*I*t was eleven thirty at night when I crossed the river on the Greater New Orleans Bridge. The lights of Algiers twinkled ahead of me like so many luminescent fish in a dark sea. Even this late, life went on unabated, and I slid through the traffic on the four-lane, past the short-order joints and shopping centers. I went left off General de Gaulle onto MacArthur and a few blocks later came to Holiday, where I turned left again.

What the hell was the Augustine boy doing on this side of the river? Somebody must have taken him there and dumped him. But he hadn't been missing when Sandy had questioned his family a few hours earlier, so he must have been taken that afternoon, after school.

When had I seen Cal? Four o'clock, when school was already out. The boy hadn't been around while I was there. Then I remembered the kid on the bike. I didn't know the Augustine boy, and I hadn't paid much attention to the boy in the street. Surely Arthur Augustine wouldn't have gone back to Cal's after lodging a complaint?

I crossed General Meyer. Two blocks on, in a neighborhood of quiet, middle-class houses, was the levee, a twenty-foot-high embankment of grass-grown earth that snaked along the river from its mouth at Head of Passes to above St. Louis. Levees were one of the first things the flood-conscious French built when they founded New Orleans in 1717. They were constructed by Bienville's engineer, de La Tour. I suspect the first body was found on a levee shortly thereafter.

I stopped at Patterson, which was the name given to the river road at this point, and looked left. I was about a mile below the naval facility, but Mancuso hadn't been precise, and there was a lot of levee. About a half mile away I saw a blink of blue light, up near the top of the levee, and then a pale streak, as from a flashlight. I drove toward the activity, and as I approached, the lights defined themselves as a couple of police flashers and some men with flashlights. I pulled into the quiet neighborhood, parked on a side street, and walked across the river road and up the slope.

The heavy mud smell of the river hugged the air. When I reached the top a stiff breeze from the water slapped me in the face. A flashlight beam picked out my face and held it.

"Who are you?" somebody asked.

"I know him." It was Mancuso's voice. "I asked him to come."

The light held me for a second longer, to let me know I didn't carry any particular weight, and then dipped away.

Mancuso guided me away from the others, who seemed engaged mainly in a game of standing around while the essential personnnel worked down by the water's edge.

"So what is it?" I asked. "Are you sure it's the boy?"

The policeman nodded. "He had a school ID on him. The mouth over there, who splashed the light on you, that's Fox. He's the detective in charge of the case; he talked to the boy when he filed the complaint. He gave a positive ID."

"I know Fox," I said. "He tried to get my license lifted once."

I felt cold all over and knew only part of it was from the wind. We started down the batture toward the water. The willows waved back and forth in front of us like warning fingers, and the *lap-lap* of the waves on the mud flats sounded like some night beast licking its chops. Out in the stream a huge tanker lay anchored, dominating the blackness. As we walked I heard voices, distant yet clear, and recognized them as the sound of seamen talking on the ship a quarter mile away.

The men at the water's edge were measuring and taking photos, and I realized the body had already been removed.

Mancuso shoved his hands in his pockets. "A guard at the station saw somebody up on the levee a couple of hours ago and walked down to investigate. When he got close, whoever it was ran away and got into a vehicle that was parked right about where you are, in that side street. He flashed his light around and found the boy down by the water."

I looked at the debris of bottles and other trash nibbling at the shore. The mud smell was mixed now with the odor of human feces and the chemicals dumped by the ships. I wondered what kind of mutant fish must swim in the river's depths and then I wondered if they could be any worse than the ones you found breathing air, in the city streets. I turned away.

"Any idea how long he'd been dead?"

"He was still warm. Probably been killed less than an hour before."

"Anything else?"

Mancuso's simian face screwed into a grimace. "Yeah. He'd been hit in the head, it looked like. We figure it was to subdue him, probably when the killer approached him first. Then he tied the kid's hands behind him with wire, took him out, and finished the job."

I flinched inwardly. We trudged back to the top of the levee, and I felt the eyes of the other men on me. Fox detached himself and put his face in mine.

"Listen, Dunn, I don't know what stake you got in this case, but I'm warning you not to fuck up my investigation." He had short graying hair and pig eyes, and his breath smelt of garlic. "Mancuso here says you've helped him before. That's his business. But if you try to screw with my investigation—"

Sal tried to get between us, but Fox slapped away his hand and stepped around him.

"You go for the bright lights and the TV cameras. You play that one-arm shit for all it's worth, and you get a lot of free advertising for your transom-peeking."

"Jake," Mancuso protested, embarrassed that the others were looking on, "let's save it for the bureau."

"Bullshit," Fox snorted. "I just want it on record that I don't want this civilian fucking things up. And if he tries," he said bringing his face as close to mine as he could, "his dick will end up in a wringer."

There was a time when I might have slugged him, but there was also a time when I drank too much, and smoked. He'd had his say, and he knew I was too careful to punch a cop. I turned away from him and started back down the slope toward my car.

Mancuso hurried after me. "Micah, listen, don't pay any attention to him. He's like that with everybody."

"I doubt it," I said, reaching the paved roadway. "He's got a hard-on because I messed up a case for him once. I had to go to the newspapers and TV stations."

"Oh, yeah," Mancuso said. "I remember: the guy wasn't guilty."

I nodded, turning to the detective. "Tell me something, Sal. You say this guard saw somebody drive away; did he get a look at the car?"

Mancuso nodded. "Just a glimpse. No plates. All he could see was that it was a light-colored van."

I thanked him and shook his hand. I tried to tell myself that it could be a coincidence, or that somebody was setting Cal up, that when I talked to him he'd have an alibi for the time after I'd seen him. But there was one thing I couldn't ignore, which I knew the cops would seize on immediately.

Calvin Autry owned a white Ford van.

I came onto de Gaulle, heading back toward the bridge, but I stopped at the first convenience store to use a pay phone. I tried Cal's home and on the second ring someone lifted the receiver, but there was no response to my "hello." I hung up, not liking the feel of it, and got back into my car. I crossed the bridge and stayed on the freeway, curving past the bald cupola of the Superdome on my right and then heading north, toward the lake.

The question was whether Herman Villiere would have had enough time to snatch the kid and bring him over here while he was playing games with me. It was a nice thought, but I had to face up to the fact that the killer had not used a red Ferrari.

I got off at Causeway and headed south, toward the river.

My gut told me I was going to be too late, but I had to try.

When I reached Calvin's house all the lights were on, and there was a DA's evidence van parked in front. They'd gotten a warrant in record time. So it hadn't been Cal who'd picked up the phone when I'd called; it was a cop.

There was a trio of people on the sidewalk watching, two men and a woman with her hair in curlers. I got out to talk to them. One was the plumber, Bonchaud, in his bathrobe.

"What's going on at Cal's?" I asked. "Is something the matter?"

"You tell us," Bonchaud said. "We got woke up." He nodded toward the woman with her hair in curlers. "All them damn radios and doors slamming."

"Not to mention that dog barking in the back yard," the woman said.

The other man, who was leaning on a cane, shook his head. "I asked 'em if something happened to him, but they just wanted to know had I seen him."

"He isn't there?" I asked.

It was the plumber's turn to shake his head. "I think I heard him in the driveway right before I went to bed, but who pays attention?"

"Any idea where he is?" I asked.

Bonchaud shrugged. "Beats me. You know, oughta be the cops could do this quieter." He squinted in my direction. "Hey, don't I know you?"

"Maybe," I said noncommitally. "I meet a lot of people in my work."

His eyes went to my left arm and then his mind made the connection. "You're the credit card guy."

"That's right."

"What the hell are you doing out here this time of night?"

"Part of the job," I said. "We like to know we're dealing with reliable people."

"Goddamn if that don't beat all." The plumber spat on the sidewalk. "Damn credit people know everything nowadays."

I left him ruminating over the wonders of the information society and drove away. I had a hunch; it was only that, but it was worth playing.

I pulled into an all-night convenience store and took my packet of maps from the holder on the seat. I had road maps, tourist maps, parish maps and even some topographic sheets for New Orleans and the surrounding parishes. What I was looking for now was the tourist commission map of Tangipahoa Parish. I found it and tried to remember what Cal had told me. The problem was that I'd only been half listening, and the name of the place hadn't really sunk in. Pinewood Estates? No, Pine *Hills* Estates. I traced my finger along Highway 22, which runs from Madisonville to Ponchatoula, and there it was, just on the west side of the Tickfaw River. I knew it would be easier to find the place in the morning, but I wanted to talk to Cal before the law found him. So if I was going to have a chance, I knew I had to go now, because sooner or later the investigators would ask the plumber or one of the other neighbors, or find a marked map or a bill of sale, and send a local deputy to check it out.

Two minutes later I was back on I-10, headed west across the swamps, the black expanse of the lake to my right, a cup of coffee in the plastic holder on the seat. I was tired, but the adrenaline was keeping me awake, so far. I knew that wouldn't last, though, and I was counting on the coffee to help.

Ten miles after civilization ended was the sign for I-55. I turned right, alone now except for the trucks.

Twenty-odd years ago, when they'd built the interstate system in Louisiana, it had been a modern miracle: four lanes of elevated concrete arrowing across a state that had once been a disconnected series of communities, with New Orleans sitting in proud isolation at the far end. They'd sunk pilings into gumbo mud and carved rights-of-way through sucking swamp. It had cut almost half an hour off the time it took to get from Baton Rouge to New Orleans. It had also made it easier to kill somebody and be miles away before the deed was discovered. The stretch I was driving, running north for thirty deserted miles between Lakes Maurepas and Pontchartrain, is the dumping ground of the state. Some of the crimes are drug related, but it's also a convienient place to leave a wife, a mother-in-law, or a girl who won't say yes.

What if Cal wasn't there? Then I'd have made a long trip for nothing, and I'd end up paying a motel bill. But after a while in this business, you tend to pick up on things: nuances of meaning, comments made in unguarded moments. Cal had described his cabin in the woods as the place he went when he wanted to lower his blood pressure.

I finished the last of the coffee and tried to get my thoughts together. What if he was there? What did I mean to do? Hold a midnight interrogation? Trap him into some damning admission? My God, why was I so willing to believe he was guilty? I'd known the man for nearly ten years; that had to be worth something.

The lights of Pass Manchac blurred by on the right. I was leaving the swamps now, and soon I'd be in the pine woods. I cracked my window to get some fresh air and flinched as the cold breeze hit me in the face. It was going on one-thirty, and sane people were asleep.

Which proved all the people in Ponchatoula were sane. The only sign of life was the traffic light, a bloodshot eye that held me at the crossroads like a dare, flashing green in its own good time. I turned right, heading east along a two-lane. Ahead of me lumbered a lop-sided car with one taillight, which seemed to have second thoughts and pulled to the side as I approached. For the next ten minutes, except for two trucks coming from the other direction I saw no one.

How the hell was I going to know where to turn? It wasn't like I could ask at the local filling station. But then I saw it ahead of me, a big sign that had been new five years ago but now sagged badly: PINE HILLS ESTATES. An arrow pointed right. I slowed and took the road indicated. I'd had my radio on, to catch an all-night jazz station from New Orleans, but now I turned it off and rolled my window all the way down. Crickets chirped, and my tires made slick sounds on the blacktop. The road deteriorated as I went, and I slowed to a sedate ten miles an hour. Three miles after the turnoff I came to another sign, this one with an arrow indicating a dirt road to the left. I left the pavement, and the slick sounds changed to the crunching of gravel. The night closed around me, the road becoming a tunnel through the trees.

All at once I glimpsed a cabin on the right. It was a two-story, with a Jeep wagon in the drive and reflectors on the mailbox, and I knew it wasn't Cal's place. The road ended in a T intersection, and I saw other cabins in both directions. I halted. Straight ahead there was a blackness even more profound than the night itself, and when I listened I heard frogs croaking. I had come to the lake.

I turned right and cruised slowly pass the lakefront properties. There were only a couple of cabins, I realized, the rest of the lots being unimproved. Some of them had For Sale signs, and I guessed the development had pretty well gone bust with the oil crash of 'eighty-six. I reached the end and turned around, headed back in the other direction.

I came to the crossroads, wondering if anyone had been awake in the cabin with the Jeep parked outside. The other places didn't seem occupied, but it only took one person to call the sheriff about a suspicious car.

The first cabin on the other side of the crossroads was apparently unoccupied. I was beginning to think I'd struck out when I came to the turnaround at the end and saw Cal's van. It was pulled up beside the last cabin on the far side, away from the road, and there were no lights on in the place.

I took my flashlight and got out, walking over to the van. The engine cover was cold, but he could have killed the boy at ten-thirty and gotten here by twelve, and the motor would have had nearly two hours to cool.

I moved carefully around the van, my feet sinking silently into the pine needles. The air smelled of ozone, fresh and tingling, unlike the heavy mud smell of the city. Somewhere in the darkness a fish plopped in the water, making me freeze for a second. I made my way to the side of the cabin and looked through the window.

It was dark inside, too dark for me to see if he was there, so I came around the side to the back and put my hand on the door handle. It was unlocked, and I pushed the door open carefully, an inch at a time.

I found myself in the kitchen, I could make out some canned goods on a low shelf, barely visible in the gloom. The air smelled of stale cigarettes and something sour. I started to risk the overhead light but thought better of it. I made my way across the kitchen to the doorway and started through, and my foot came down on something hard and slippery. A bottle shot out from under my foot, rolling against the wall as I lost my balance and tumbled against the doorframe, the flashlight falling out of my hand to crash onto the board floor. I swallowed a curse and bent to pick it up, and that was when I hard the noise behind me and felt the cold gun barrel poking the middle of my back.

The lights blazed on and the man behind me muttered an oath. "Micah, what the hell?"

I turned slowly, exhaling. "Cal. Where the hell were you?"

Calvin Autry tried to laugh. "I was outside, down by the lake. I drunk that bottle there and went down to the lake to think. I guess I musta passed out, and when I come to I heard somebody up here breaking into my place. Damn, Micah, I could've shot you." He lowered the pistol. His hair was uncombed and his clothes were disheveled. When he talked his words slid out on fumes of whiskey.

"What are you doing out here, Cal?"

"What?" He swayed a little. "I could ask you the same thing. Fact is, I come over here to get away and think. This is where I always come to think. And since I ain't gonna have it much longer, I was taking advantage. How the fuck did you know I was out here, anyhow?"

"I just figured it," I said. "You weren't at your house, so it seemed a good bet."

He nodded like it made perfect sense, but his mind, slowed by the liquor, was busy trying to make the connections. Finally the gears meshed and he licked his lips.

"What was you going to my house for at this time of night?"

I tried to think of a way to break it to him gently, but there wasn't any good way to say it. "There's been trouble, Cal. That boy, Arthur Augustine? They found him dead."

He blinked and then cocked his head to one side. "Dead? the one that accused me?"

"That one. Somebody beat his head in and dumped him on the levee at Algiers."

Cal exhaled heavily. "Shee-it." His mind made another connection then, and his mouth dropped open. "Christ, they don't think I . . . ?"

"Whoever did it was driving a van."

"A van? So what? Half the goddamn world drives vans. Did they get the license number?"

"No, it was too dark."

"So they got nothing."

"Maybe. But they were searching your house when I went there. It's pretty sure you'll be a suspect. If you've got an alibi, though . . ."

"Alibi? For when?"

"Between about four and ten, I'd say."

He laid the pistol on the counter, turning suddenly to stagger to the back door. I heard him retching outside. I picked up the pistol. It was a Ruger Single Six, .22 caliber, mid-fifties vintage, before they added the nylock screws. A westerner's weapon, the kind of gun I'd have associated with Cal Autry; the kind, I tried to convince myself, he'd have used if he really had planned to kill the boy. I unloaded the cylinder, pocketed the five rounds that came out, and stuck the revolver in my belt

From outside I heard Cal give a final, weak heave. He came unsteadily back through the door.

"Oh, shit." He sighed. "You reckon they'll come here?"

"Sooner or later," I said softly. "Best thing would be for you to go to them first."

"Fuckers," he spat, suddenly defiant. "Why the hell should I? I didn't do nothing."

"Do you have an alibi?" I asked.

He turned slowly to look at me through red-rimmed eyes. "Hell no, man. I closed up right after you left and I come up here. Wasn't nobody home at that house up at the head of the road, so they didn't see me pass. I been down here ever since. Damn, do I have to have a fucking picture or something? Jesus, this is America, ain't it?"

"This is America," I said.

"Yeah." He turned around suddenly and barged into me. I stepped back. "Shit, I might as well finish what I started." He reached into one of the cabinets and took out a full bottle. I started to say something but decided against it.

"Come on," he said, jerking his head toward the door. I followed him back out into the night, a few steps behind his weaving form. The light from the kitchen splashed a dull glow on the grass, and ahead I could just see the placid surface of the water. He slid down with his back against a pine tree and opened the bottle. I sat down across from him and waited.

"Here." He passed the bottle to me, and I took a mouthful and handed it back. The liquor burned my tongue and the roof of my mouth, and I closed my eyes.

"So you found anything yet?" he asked after he'd taken a long pull.

I told him about my visits to Frazier and Villiere and my talk with Guidry.

He snorted. "Any one of 'em could've done it."

"But to have killed the boy?" I asked. "Why?"

"Shit, man, why do any of it? People'll do things when they put their mind to it. A man that's mean in his gut'll be mean in business, in his private life, and to strangers."

I took another swig. "Cal, they're going to try to claim you lured the boy with magic tricks. That you knew him before, when he worked at your house."

"Let 'em claim what they want. Maybe I did know him. Hell, I don't keep track. I like kids. I was a scoutmaster once, before I came to this goddamn place. Is every scoutmaster a child molester?"

I stared out at the lake. "Cal, you've got to promise me you'll go back."

"You mean, let 'em lock me up?"

"If there's no better evidence than they have now, we'll get you out. John O'Rourke's a good lawyer. They can't hold you without giving you a chance to make bail."

"And then my name'll be splashed all over the fucking *Picayune* and on the six o'clock news."

I reached for the bottle. "Cal, your name's going to be in the news now no matter what." There was a long silence. I heard a plop as he threw a stick into the water.

"Shit, Micah, what am I going to do? I can sell this place; I've had offers. But if I have to pay for a long trial, I'll lose my house and everything."

I didn't know what to say. For a while the only sound was the frogs.

"Right out there," he said, getting up on shaky legs and pointing. "That's where my pier was going to go, and the boathouse. My neighbor and me was going to put it in. I was going to bring out the grandkids. I told 'em their grandmother's dead. They believe it. They like to come up here. Water's deeper on this side, and there's some big fish in there."

I forced myself to stand and look him in the eye. "Cal, why did Marie run away?" I asked.

"What?" He blinked and looked away.

"Was it another man? Were you two having problems?" There was another question I wanted to ask him, but I didn't have the nerve.

"What the hell's that got to do with anything?"

"Everything. They're going to make it sound like you had some kind of sexual hang-up that made her leave you."

"Oh Christ," he spat. "You're shittin' me."

"I'm not. They'll do everything they can to find her, too, and get her testimony. Do you have any idea where she is?"

He kicked at the ground. "West Coast, I reckon. That's where the postcard was from. But if she's in hell it ain't hot enough." He wiped his mouth with his hand. "Damn it, Micah, I was good to that woman. There was no cause for her to make a fool out of me the way she done. Yeah, we fought sometimes, but everybody fights. You mean they have to rake all that up?"

"I'm afraid so."

"Well, it ain't right." He spat. "Hell, the bitch even took my car."

"Is there anything you can think of that might have made her do it? Some argument you had just before it happened, say?"

"Well . . ." He was looking into the past, and I could see that I'd scored.

"What was it about?" I asked.

He shrugged. "Money. I never had enough for her. I . . ." His voice trailed off, and he drank from the bottle. Then he turned and looked me in the eye.

"Hold on, Micah. Are you telling me you believe what they're saying?"

I swallowed. Somehow I'd known it would come to this. "I'm not saying anything. I'm just telling you what they're going to claim."

"I ain't talking about what they claim." His voice was angry now. "So don't bullshit me. I'm asking you man to man, friend to friend: do you believe I had anything to do with this?"

I hesitated, then shook my head. "No, Cal. I don't." The words sounded hollow to me, but they seemed to mollify him.

" 'Cause I didn't," he said.

"Fair enough," I said. "Promise me you'll come with me to-morrow to O'Rourke's office and let him call the police."

"Oh, man." He shook his head and took another swig. "Yeah, okay. If you think I ought to."

"I do."

He sighed. "Okay. But that's tomorrow. Lemme just set here for tonight and look at the lake. I ain't gonna see it again for a long time."

"Sure," I agreed, and accepted the bottle. I'd been keeping my intake down, but even the few mouthfuls had made me warm inside and had given me a light-headed feeling. What the hell, I thought. I hadn't done such a great job for Cal up to now. The least I could do was have a few swallows with him on his last night of freedom.

Sometime before dawn he passed out against the tree, and I went inside, got a blanket from one of the beds, and threw it over him. Then I went back inside and lay down on the bunk and dozed off.

When I awoke the sun was coming through the windows. I forced myself up and stumbled groggily out to where I'd left him.

The blanket was still there, but Cal was gone. When I looked in the drive, his van was missing too.

Six

There was a scrawled note on my front seat: *Sorry, Micah, but I couldnt let them arrest me like a killer. Ill pay you whatever I owe you after I get rid of this place meanwhile Im going hide out til you or somebody can prove I didnt do nothing they accuse me of.* His full name was signed underneath with a flourish, *Calvin Russell Autry, Jr,* and at the bottom was the postscript *You was sleeping so I didnt want to wake you. I took my sixshooter from out of your belt.*

I swore under my breath. There wasn't anything to do now but get back to the city. I picked up the empty bottle from outside and made up the bunk. Then I stood behind the cabin for a long minute, staring at the quiet lake. A terrible notion crept into my mind. I tried to ignore it, but it wouldn't go away: I wondered if he'd ever brought boys up here.

Then I flashed on his face as it had been last night, half indignant, half terrified as he swore to his innocence.

I turned my back on the lake and drove away, down the gravel road and away from the unanswered questions.

As I reached the highway a sheriff's cruiser turned in and headed in the direction from which I'd come. Good thing I hadn't lingered; I didn't need any complications at this point.

I headed east through Madisonville and Chinchuba, instead of back the way I'd come, taking the Pontchartrain Causeway south for twenty miles over the gray, roiling waters of the lake. In the distance I could make out the buildings of the city, hovering in a pall of smog. Below, occasional boats bobbed and twisted on the waves, and I wished I were out yachting. It had been a hobby before my injury, and I still do it occasionally. But mostly I collect the pictures of famous yachts, the way some people collect stamps. Suddenly I had a passionate desire to go home, immerse myself in my album, and forget about Cal Autry and his problem. He'd had his chance, hadn't he? I'd done what I could and he'd broken his promise. What more did I owe him?

And then his words came back to me: *Jesus, this is America, ain't it?*

It was nearly eleven when I got back to my office. I snuck up the rear stairs, avoiding LaVelle, who was occupied with some tourists, and locked myself into my apartment without checking my answering machine. I showered, brushed my teeth, and downed half a quart of milk. Then I dressed and went into my office.

The red eye of my answering machine told me I had been missed.

The first message was from Katherine. She'd expected me last night and hoped everything was all right; there was no hysteria in her voice, because she was accustomed to the kind of work I did and knew that if I hadn't called I was probably following some lead. But she'd feel better if I touched base as soon as possible.

The second message was from a man named Burris, who identified himself as an insurance executive; maybe he was just trying to sell me a policy, but there was also a good chance he wanted me to find somebody who'd gotten killed locally after insuring himself for big bucks. I wrote down his name and number.

The final message was from Mancuso: "Micah, where the hell are you? Gimme a call when you get back, okay? And look . . . Oh, never mind."

I called Katherine first, got her own machine, and left a message that I was back. Then I called Mancuso. After a two-minute wait he came on the line, his voice anxious.

"Where the hell've you been?"

"Working," I said. "I don't get paid by the city, remember?"

"Real funny. Look, they know you were at Autry's house last night, and now your buddy's missing. Damn it, Micah, if you've been screwing with Fox's case he's going to do what he said."

"Relax," I said. "You didn't call me just to tell me that, did you?"

"No, I didn't, matter of fact." He cleared his throat. "I just wanted to pass along something, but you don't let on where you got it."

"Agreed." I could tell from the tone of his voice it wasn't something I wanted to hear.

"They turned Autry's house inside out, okay?" The sick feeling started to radiate out from my stomach. "It was behind the house, in his garage, what they found."

"Which was?"

"Wire. A spool of the same kind of wire that was used to tie the boy up. It wasn't even hidden, either."

I breathed out. "Is that all?"

"Isn't it enough? It can send Autry to the chair."

"What about books, films, the usual porno crap that child molesters keep?"

"Well, there were some girlie books in his shop. Pretty hardcore stuff."

"Grown-up females?"

"From what I saw. Men, too, doing their thing with the girls."

"Doesn't sound like child molesting to me."

"Shit, Micha, you know as well as I do that doesn't prove anything. He might've gotten rid of any kiddie porn. Or he might never have bought any, because it would force him to admit what he is. It's the wire that counts."

"Maybe so," I said. "What about those names I gave you yesterday? Frazier, Guidry, and DeNova?"

"Oh, I almost forgot." There was a silence, and I figured he was fishing out his notes. "Let's see. Morris Frazier. Used to be a wrestler, twenty years ago. Got thrown out for being even crookeder than professional wrestling will put up with. Has a bust for brawling. Nothing big; paid a fine. Guidry is superclean, unless you count traffic warrants, but everybody's got those. He's a big backer of city hall, so nobody's likely to bust him for a few speeding tickets. He practices criminal law; right now he's defending a yuk named Sawyer who tried to take over a Central American country."

"I hope he gets his fee," I said wryly.

"And that just leaves this DeNova. But the only Sam DeNova I could turn was a bookie seventy-eight years old. I don't think that's your man."

"No," I said, and thanked him.

I sat silently thinking about it. Mancuso was right, of course: finding the wrong kind of porn wasn't evidence in anybody's court, and the wire was what really counted. But for the first time I felt a faint, irrational flicker of hope.

I returned the call from the insurance man.

The man who answered sounded black and had a deep voice with a hint of a Caribbean accent, and I realized it wasn't the man who had left the message.

"I was asked to call a man named Burris," I said.

"Mr. Burris isn't available," the voice said, "but I can handle the matter. We'd like to meet with you as soon as possible to discuss something of mutual interest."

"I don't need any insurance," I said.

"No, of course not." The man chuckled. "This is something different. We would like you to undertake an investigation for us."

"I see. May I know who recommended me?"

He gave Sandy's name. "She said you were very good."

I mentally ran through the things I could do for Cal and decided that at this point there weren't many.

"Where would you like to meet?" I asked. "At my office?"

"There's a church on Thalia, near Erato. It's called the Church of the Deliverance."

"I know the place."

"Knock on the front door, at one o'clock. Ask for the pastor."

I started to ask for details but the line went dead.

I tried Sandy's place, to ask her what she knew about the Church of the Deliverance, but I got only her answering machine. It was Thursday, her morning to be in class at UNO. She was taking an art course, just why I hadn't figured out, except that she had eclectic tastes, and I'd seen her use even a small amount of outré knowledge to pass herself off as an expert.

There was nearly an hour and a half before my meeting, not time enough to do anything much, beside which I felt dragged out from my late night with Cal. I took out my notebook and made a little list of things to do: *Talk to Cal's son; Check with the agency in Oklahoma City; Put Sandy onto Frazier and Guidry.*

And it might be worth my while to pay a visit to my downstairs neighbor, Henri LaVelle.

His real name was David Erickson, though he hated to be reminded of it. He'd set up shop to fleece tourists, but these days the tourists were fewer in number, driven away by the crime that infested the Quarter. His thing was voodoo, but I doubted he'd recognize it if somebody dropped him in Haiti.

When I came down the front stairs and passed through the hanging beads into his shop, I almost sneezed from the mixture of incense and exotic herbs in the air. He got up from behind his counter and put aside an issue of *Sports Illustrated*.

"Well, why am I so honored? Or did you run out of cooking oil again?"

"If I did I wouldn't ask. That last stuff you gave me said Corpse Oil on it."

He shrugged. "Poetic license. It was Wesson oil, and it worked, didn't it?"

"Well enough." I took a seat on a nearby stool. "Tell me something, David—"

"Henri, damn it."

"Henri. What do you know about kiddie porn?"

His dark brows arched up in pretended amazement.

"You tired of women finally?"

"Right. If you wanted to get some, where would you go?"

He snickered. "Anywhere. They clamped down on it a few years ago, but that just means it isn't openly advertised. What kind you want? You can tell me. I'm discreet."

"Good man. What about rings, groups of child molesters?"

"Ah. Pedophiles, you mean. They exist. Even in New Orleans, with its active DA and Neighborhood Watch."

"Imagine that. Is it likely somebody who engaged in that kind of behavior would be known to others?"

LaVelle's lips curled cynically. "Of course. One does not practice it alone. At a minimum there is the victim, who may be victimized by other adults. And since victims often talk, that means that even if person A and person B have never met, they may know of each other's habits."

"And I guess preferences come in all shapes and sizes?"

"Absolutely. Ages, builds, colors. You'd be amazed how some of these people have specialized." He squinted at me. "But you're asking all this for a reason. You're working on a case."

"More or less. If I was interested in black boys, where would I make the connection?"

He pursed his lips. "Micah, there are things I have done in my time that do not fill me with pride. But pedophilia is several light-years from my experience. What I know I've picked up second- or thirdhand from people who, well, rub elbows with the slimebags in question. Anything I know is strictly hearsay, and I do not wish to be connected with it."

"Understood."

"It has to be more than understood. I seem to remember giving you the name of a certain immigration lawyer, and you ended up shooting him."

"I felt real bad about that," I said.

LaVelle rolled his eyes. "I can tell. Look, some of these people are *very* well connected. We're not just talking about a blue-collar sport. If you make them angry with you, you'll wish you hadn't gotten involved in this."

"I'll try not to make anybody mad," I promised.

"Sure." He leaned toward me. "I hear the person to see is the Spiderwoman."

"Who?"

He shrugged. "I didn't give her the name."

"You mean a woman is running this?"

"Well, it isn't like the Mafia, for Christ's sake. I'm just saying she's one of the names I hear dropped. And second, why not a woman? It's time Louisiana got with ERA."

"Where do I find her?" I asked.

"There's a spirits shop on Magazine, near Napoleon. You go in and ask for a rare wine. She feels you out and does some checking." He sniffed. "No offense, Micah, but you'd never make it through the preliminary."

I nodded. He was right. My lame arm made me easy to trace.

"You ever met this Spiderwoman?" I asked.

"No. I told you, I just heard the name. I'm told she keeps books with pictures of available kids in them."

I thought for a moment. Sandy wouldn't do for this one. I needed a male. I thought of LaVelle and then dismissed the possibility.

"Well, thanks a lot, David—I mean, Henri."

"You're welcome," he said. "And Micah . . ."

I turned on my way out. "Yeah?"

"You were right. I wouldn't have done it."

"Done what?"

"Been your stooge on this one. No matter how much you paid me."

"Touché, Papa Doc."

I got an oyster loaf at Frankie & Johnny's and then drove over to the Church of the Deliverance. It was a square white two-story, all brick and concrete, and it looked more like a fortress than a place of worship. The downstairs door, which faced Thalia, was oak, and looked to be about a foot thick. It was the only church door I'd ever seen with a peephole. The windows had bars instead of stained glass. The only concession to convention was an iron cross on the top, but even it had a spear blade on the end.

I was about twenty minutes early, and I made the block a few times. It was a black section, but not what you would call a ghetto. Before the freeway had run through the center of it, it had been a respectable neighborhood. New Orleans still has neighborhoods; the projects are the ghettos. I found a parking place on the street and slid in.

Sandy would have told me if she'd referred me to someone for an investigation. This had to be something else. I wasn't sure I liked it, but there wasn't enough yet for warning signals to go off.

I went up the broad steps and knocked on the door. The panel slid back and a face stared out at me. I held up my card.

"You were told one o'clock," the face said accusingly.

"I can leave."

The panel slid closed and the big door creaked open.

"Come in." The man facing me was dressed in a green dashiki and highly polished black shoes. He stepped aside and once I was inside closed and bolted the big door behind me.

"This way," he said, leading me down a narrow hallway filled with African art. The floor was hardwood, but somehow his feet made no sound. The air held the fragrance of incense, and somewhere inside the bowels of the building I heard a deep, mellifluous laugh. We came to another oak door and he knocked twice. The door opened and he stood aside for me.

The room I entered was vast, with a ceiling twelve feet high. The walls were hung with animal skins and the floor was covered by a bamboo mat. At the back of the room was some kind of altar, and standing before the altar was a man dressed in white.

"Mr. Dunn," he said, coming forward, and I knew he was the man I had spoken to on the phone.

He was an inch taller than I was, with skin the color of chocolate and a thin mustache. I judged his age to be forty, but he could have been five years either way: he seemed to be in good condition, with muscles that bulged under the white fabric of his long-sleeved guayabera.

"You know my name," I said, "but I'm afraid I don't know yours."

He thrust out a hand. "It's Condon. The Reverend Gabriel Condon. I am the spiritual adviser of the Augustine family."

Condon. Of course; Sandy had mentioned the name. "I didn't think this had anything to do with insurance," I said.

"Actually, it does." He pointed to a pair of cushions and sat down on one. I ignored the offer and took a chair across from him. "You see, we provide members of the congregation with a small life insurance policy as part of their tithe."

"Interesting idea," I said.

"Vital, in today's world. So many of our people have nothing."

"The Augustine boy was insured, then."

"Most definitely. It will be enough to bury him and provide his mother with a few miserable dollars for the next few months." His tone was suddenly bitter. "Certainly not enough to purchase the services of a private detective to find the man who killed him."

"The police are supposed to do that," I said.

He laughed. "Yes, the police. I spoke to them this morning, and they tell me the man who committed the crime has escaped."

"If you mean Calvin Autry, I don't know that he committed the crime. But I can promise you he will be found."

"Of course. And his high-priced attorney, Mr. John O'Rourke, who once defended antiwar activists, will now defend a child molester and murderer and buy his client five to ten years in Hunt Correctional. Justice."

I was sure Sandy hadn't mentioned O'Rourke's name, which meant Condon had a pipeline in the police department.

"Reverend Condon, since I'm here you must know that I've been hired by Calvin Autry. But you also know I can't withhold evidence. If you've got some evidence that either implicates or exonerates him, I'd like to know."

His lips curved into a thin smile. "Of course you would."

"Why did you ask me here, Reverend Condon?"

He got up quickly like a spring uncoiling. " 'Blessed are the meek,' " he said with sudden vehemence. "That boy, his family, and all the people in this city like them are the meek, Mr. Dunn. The downtrodden. The persecuted. The ignored." Turning away, he walked over to the wall and then wheeled again to face me. "If that boy had been white, don't you think the district attorney would have called the chief of police, and that a dragnet would be combing this city right now?"

I exhaled. "A dragnet *is* combing this city. And the mayor is black, as was the mayor before him."

He chuckled. "Ah, yes. I forgot. The Oreo aristocracy. And what do you think their attitude is, Mr. Dunn? Do you want me to tell you? It is not, why did a depraved homosexual attack and kill a defenseless child? It is, what did that child do to provoke him? It is, what can be gotten on that boy and his family to excuse the killer? It is, one more little nigger boy dead, so who cares, he would've grown up to be a criminal anyway."

"That may be the attitude of some. It isn't mine."

"No? Then why did you send your assistant to the family to pry and peep? Why are you taking money to try to make the boy out to be the criminal, instead of the victim? Is it that a man with your infirmity cannot get any other kind of work?"

"I think I'll be going now, Reverend." I rose and started for the door.

"Wait," he called. I heard his steps coming across the mat behind me. I turned. "I'm sorry for what I said. Here." He reached under his shirt and came out with an envelope. "Look inside," he urged.

I did and found myself staring down at a sheaf of hundred-dollar bills.

"What's this for?" I asked.

"To find the truth about the molestation and murder of Arthur Augustine."

"I already have a client," I told him, handing back the envelope. "The rule is one client per investigation at a time."

"Too bad," Condon said ruefully. "I was hoping we could do business."

"Not today, Reverend."

I went back down the hall and out into the cool October sunlight, taking a deep breath. There was something going on, and I didn't like it.

Seven

I drove for half an hour, trying to put it together, but nothing came clear. Did Condon want to buy me off because he had a political ax to grind, or was there something more to it, like guilty knowledge?

Finally I stopped and called my answering machine from a pay phone. The only message was from Katherine, reminding me that we were on for dinner at seven-thirty and asking me to confirm. I dialed her number, left an acknowledgment on her machine, and then called Sandy, but Sandy still wasn't home. I hung up in frustration. Then it came to me: I was almost all the way uptown, only a few blocks from the wineshop where the Spiderwoman hung out. It must have been in my unconscious all along, prodding me in this direction, so I decided to give in. I drove to the address and went in.

It was an old house, converted about ten years before, from the looks of it. It smelled of cheese and nuts, and from the tasting table floated the slightly fruity aroma of wine. The racks were filled with different vintages, from the ordinary to the esoteric, and a wide range of liquors. They even had a line bottled under their own name. The cheeses came from most countries in Europe, from Wisconsin in the U.S., and there were even some from the Orient and the Mideast. It was yuppie heaven and I wondered what would happen if anyone came in and asked for Mogen David. And, of course, I knew: he'd get it with a smile. The smirks would come later.

I was still pondering the choices when a woman appeared from behind the counter and asked if she could help. Blonde and maybe twenty-five, she was too fresh-faced and collegiate to be the proprietress.

"I was looking for something special," I said.

"How special?" she asked.

I shrugged. "I'm not an expert on wines. But something different."

The clerk frowned. "What will you be having to eat with it?"

"I don't know yet," I said truthfully. "I guess I need something that can go with about anything."

She nodded and took me to a rack in the center of the room.

"What about a Martini zinfandel?" She held up a bottle.

I nodded. "If you think so."

"It goes with almost anything."

"All right." I followed her to the checkout and paid. As she rang it up my eyes went to the doorway and found a TV camera. She handed me my change and thanked me. I started out, turning at the door ostensibly to inspect their specials in a barrel just inside the entranceway.

That was when I saw the Spiderwoman.

She was standing at the rear, near a closed door that must lead into the office. Tall, she wore a burgundy dress and a necklace of pearls the color of her hair, and she was watching me like a spider watches it prey. She was a handsome woman, but she had the eyes of a killer, gray and cold. I finished inspecting the wines in the barrel and went back out into the sunlight, leaving the chill behind me.

When I got back to the office Sandy was waiting.

"I met the Reverend Condon," I told her wryly. Then I told her about the money in the envelope.

"I knew the man played rough," she said. "But Micah, in a way you can't blame him."

"Can't blame him? What he did was try to bribe me."

"He's a street fighter. He sees this as a political thing."

"It's political that a man who worked all his life is going to lose his business and his good name because of something he doesn't know anything about?"

She stiffened in her chair. "Well, what about Arthur Augustine? What did he do, except be in the wrong place at the wrong time? Your friend is alive, at least. That's more than anybody can say for Arthur Augustine."

I came forward, surprised. "Sandy, are you saying you've made up your mind already that our client did it?"

"I'm saying that just because he's our client doesn't make him, if you'll pardon the expression, lily white." Her voice dropped as she rose to lean over my desk. "And just because Arthur Augustine was black doesn't make him the instigator of all this."

Our eyes held, and I felt my heart racing. We'd never talked about race much before, and now I realized that maybe we should have.

"It sounds like you've made up your mind," I said quietly. "But I hope you don't think anything I've been doing was racially motivated."

She laughed. "Micah, you're from Charleston. You went to the naval academy. You're a good man, but how could you get away from it?"

"I don't know," I owned. "How can you? How can any of us?"

She nodded. "Yeah, you're right." She reached out and put her hand over mine. "Look, Micah, I'm sorry. I didn't mean to unload on you. Everybody's got some buttons that nobody should push. I thought mine were taped over, but I guess maybe they aren't."

"I didn't mean to push them."

"You didn't, Condon did. There's just enough truth in it to set me off. I grew up in these streets. My best friend died of an overdose when she was sixteen. Her mother ended up taking care of her two little girls. My own brother spent three years at Angola, doing the hardest kind of time they got in this state. I never met my father. When I see Arthur Augustine, I see myself. Maybe if he'd of lived another year, another month, another week even, he'd have met somebody—a teacher, a minister, even a cop—who'd have made him the one out of all those kids he ran with to make something of his life. Now . . ." She shook her head. "Just one more little black kid that didn't make it."

"Yeah." I rubbed my eyes. "Hell, I don't know, Sandy. Maybe Cal *is* guilty. But I have to check all the angles. I have to give him his best shot."

"I know," she said softly. "And I know you well enough to know you'll do your best, and the hell with Condon. I guess I was just saying you can see it from different sides, and I didn't want to see the victim turned into the villain when he can't fight back."

I squeezed her hand. "I don't want that either. And if Cal Autry's guilty, I won't cover it up. You have my promise on that."

"That's good enough for me," she said. "I don't know if it'll be good enough for Condon. He's a natural force, Micah. The man's got charisma. If I wasn't so damn independent, I could almost—"

The ringing telephone interrupted her. I picked it up and heard a nasal voice that it took me a second to identify as male.

"Micah Dunn?"

"Speaking."

"This is Abe Steiner with Big O Investigations in Oklahoma City. I wanted to give you what I have on your subject, Calvin Autry, Jr. Of course, I'll write all this up, but my secretary quit and I thought you'd rather hear it first."

"I appreciate it," I said.

"Part of the service. Now let's see." I heard him riffling pages. "Yeah. Well, born Pauls Valley, 1932. Father was a farmer who lost the place in the Depression. Kept the family alive by odd jobs. Parents both dead. An older brother, Elton, in California; an older sister, Minnie, in Pauls Valley. I talked to her. She said

Calvin was alway mechanical-minded. She also said he had problems with the other boys when he was little; wouldn't go into it
further. Calvin didn't date in high school. Dropped out of high
school and left home when he was fifteen. Didn't come back again
for nearly fifteen years, when he brought his wife, Marie, with him,
for a visit."

"That it?"

"Well, you might be interested in why he left town."

"Why?"

His chuckle told me he was about to flourish his pièce de résis-
tance. "He and another kid got into an argument, and he pulled a
gun. Told the other boy he'd fill him full of holes if he ever saw
him again." He paused to let the import sink in.

"Any idea what they were arguing about?"

"The book, as they say, closes on that chapter." He cleared his
throat.

"What did his sister say about Marie?"

"Who? Oh, you mean Cal's old lady. Well, not much. Just said
he took up with some little floozie looked no better than she should
be."

I thought for a moment. "How long did this take?"

"Not long. Better part of a day. Write it up'll be a couple of
hours."

"Okay, then I'd like for you to scratch around and see if you can
find out more about the gun incident. Check with some of the men
he went to high school with; there must be some of them still around.
I'd like to know what the friction was about."

"Of course. I should be able to have that by tomorrow."

"That'll be fine. Oh, and one other thing."

"Yes, Mr. Dunn?"

"See if there's anybody he's still close to. And keep your eyes
open: Autry's spooked, and he may show up there."

"Ah, so it suddenly becomes a bail case."

"Not yet. He hasn't been arrested. But he will be when he's
found."

"I can't protect a fugitive, Mr. Dunn. You have to understand that."

"I don't expect you to, Mr. Steiner. Just get back to me, whatever happens—as soon as it happens."

"Will do. Good-bye, Mr. Dunn."

I replaced the receiver.

"Trouble?" Sandy asked.

"I don't know." I filled her in on Steiner's report. "There're lots of reasons a boy might not get along with his classmates. The problem is, every damn time I look hard at Cal something else pops up. And yet I've known the man for ten years."

"Maybe," she said softly, "you just think you know him."

"That," I said, "is what bothers me."

She got up. "What do you want me to do now?"

I gave her Guidry's name and address. "Check this guy out and see if it looks like he could have any motive for wanting Autry out of the way. See if there's any possible connection with the Augustine boy. The man's a lawyer; has he represented anybody in that family? There's a lot you may not be able to find, but do your best. I've got to admit, it's a long shot, so don't spend more time than your gut tells you to."

"My gut," she said with a smirk: "Is that where we're at?"

"Isn't that where we're *always* at?" I asked. "Let me know what you turn up."

"Sho' nuff." She turned and left, and I sat back down heavily in my chair. It was such a long shot it amounted only to covering the bases.

I heaved myself up and went into the kitchen for a soft drink and that was why I didn't hear the footsteps on the stairs. I'd taken my seat again and was staring moodily at the model yacht on my desk when the door burst open.

Calvin Autry stood swaying before me.

Eight

*E*xcept that it wasn't Calvin Autry, I saw, as the man moved into the light from my open window: it was Calvin Autry the way he might have looked a quarter century ago, thin, with more hair, but still muscular, with an outthrust jaw.

"You're Micah Dunn," the man said.

"I am," I said. "And you're . . . ?"

"Melville Autry. Calvin Autry's my father."

"Come in, Mr. Autry." I came around the desk and offered him my hand.

His hand was wet with perspiration, and as he sat down he reached into his jeans for a bandana and wiped his face.

"Tell you the truth, Mr. Dunn, I'm scared shitless."

"Just take it easy. It'll be okay," I said, reflecting on the fact that he was in the same chair where his father had sat just two days ago. "Can I get you a Coke, or a beer?"

"No thanks," he said, removing a little tin from his shirt pocket and carefully packing some snuff between his upper lip and his gum. Then he took out a small jar and set it on the floor. "I got to dip when I'm nervous," he explained.

"Have you heard from your father?"

His eyes darted away. "Is he in as much trouble as they say?" he asked.

"Every hour he stays out there, the trouble gets worse. He'll do himself a favor if he comes on in."

"Yeah. But he ain't got no trust of the law, Mr. Dunn. And hell, I don't either. I seen the cops here beat people black and blue at Mardi Gras. And some of them nigger cops'd love to get hold of an Okie like the old man. Especially with what they're sayin' he did."

"If he surrenders I'll see nothing happens to him. The danger's in his being spotted out there. You can't expect a cop to ask too many questions when they think they're up against a murderer."

"Yeah," he nodded, bending over to spit into the little jar. "There's that. But, Mr. Dunn, he ain't nowhere they gonna find him till he wants to be found."

"Hiding a fugitive's a felony," I said.

"Christ, he's my father. They can do what they want."

I nodded reluctantly. "I understand. Then what is it I can do for you, Melville?"

He hunched his shoulders uncomfortably. "I just wanted to know have you found anything that might help get him off?"

"Is that what he sent you to ask?"

"Don't matter."

"No. I guess not. And the answer is, not yet. But I'm still looking. But there's something I need you to ask your father for me."

"Yeah?"

"Did he have any wire at home, in his garage? Baling wire, say?"

Melville Autry frowned. "Why?"

"Just ask him."

"Okay." He got up slowly, picking up his little jar.

"Mr. Dunn, you got to do something. He never done nothing. Him and me, we've had words, sure; once't I come close to clobbering him, he was so stubborn. But he's my old man. And he's been a good one, too. He's been lonely since Ma left, but he wouldn't do nothing like this."

I nodded and walked with him to the door. "Any idea why your mother left, Melville?"

"No. Except her and Pop had a lot of problems. Ma, she always wanted more than he could give. He tried, but sometimes I used to hear 'em arguing, and once, especially, when I was little, I heard her threaten to leave, and he yelled back at her, 'Go ahead, leave, see if I can't raise this boy as good without you as with you.' And that kinda quieted her down." He shrugged. "I just guess when I got all growed up she figured, what was the harm now."

"You've never tried to find her?"

"Where would I look? Pop said she went to California. He got one postcard and that was all. He said he figured she didn't want to be found, and he said that was okay by him. Wasn't nothing we could do. If I knew where she was at, I reckon I'd try to see her, but I don't know where to start."

"Was there anything else they used to argue about? Anything you can remember?"

He spat into the jar again. "Just money. He said she used to spend too much of it."

"Did he ever accuse her of being with other men?"

"I never heard that, but I wouldn't be surprised. I seen her once't when I was little, with some slick-dressed fellow. She said he was a radio announcer."

"And your father? Were there other women?"

"I never asked him." His face went red, like he'd already said too much, and I went and put a hand on his shoulder. After a moment he rose uncomfortably, and I guided him out.

He picked his way down the stairs with a slightly bowlegged gait and veered away from the entrance to the voodoo shop like a branded calf. I thought of following, but dissuaded myself: Cal was safe where he was, and as long as I didn't find him I wouldn't be obstructing justice. My time could be better spent in trying to prove him innocent. Or guilty.

I went over what I knew: Cal Autry claimed there were four people who had reason to hurt him, but so far the people he suspected seemed too self-absorbed to go out of their way just to get him in trouble. Add the murder of the boy and it seemed even more unlikely that Frazier, Villiere, or Guidry had anything to do with it, unless of course a mean joke had gone sour and the boy had been killed to prevent exposure. But what if it had nothing to do with Calvin? What if somebody was setting him up because they needed a stooge and he was available? It was an ugly thought, as ugly as the first possibility, and I played with it for a while, trying to think of possible scenarios.

And I kept coming back to the clown, and the kids he took in off the streets, and the wire in his garage. I kept remembering his secret, something hidden that he wouldn't mention, and the problems he'd had with boys his own age, when he was a kid. And I remembered the van.

Damn it, it all held together. And I didn't want it to.

I called O'Rourke and told him about Abe Steiner's report from Oklahoma.

"You think that business about friction with the other boys means something?" he asked.

"I don't know," I told him. "Look, what do you know about a Reverend Gabriel Condon of the Church of the Deliverance?"

"Gabe?" O'Rourke laughed. "We did some sit-ins together in the old days. He's from Jamaica, you know. He's younger than I am, but you'd never know it from the way he talked: all assurance, all certainty. Somewhere between Louis Farrakhan and Jesse Jackson is where I'd put him. He's a big noise in the black community. I think he'd like to get on the city council."

I told him about the money and he laughed.

"That's vintage Gabe. He's ambitious as hell and goes after what he wants. You just got in his way."

"Evidently. I didn't know he was such a big friend of yours."

"Haven't seen him for a couple of years, but last time I did he was getting into a Continental. I introduced myself and asked him if he remembered me, and all he said was, 'Bless you, sir.' Then he leaned close and said, 'Don't let the bastards grind you down, bro.' And winked."

"A man of principle," I said.

"We've all changed," O'Rourke sighed.

I let him go and sat considering my options. I'd run out of leads. If somebody was framing Cal, the only hope I had was to stir things up. I decided to pay a visit to the Augustine household.

It was a neighborhood just off Esplanade, where teenaged boys eyed me suspiciously from street corners, unsure whether I was the law or looking to buy drugs. The house itself was easy to locate, a shotgun with cars in front. Some women in Sunday-go-to-meeting clothes were talking on the front porch and on the sidewalk. A wake. I was going to stand out like a one-legged man on a tightrope. Maybe,

I thought, it wasn't a bad simile. Because that was the idea. But I hated it. Crashing a wake isn't my idea of fun, and getting my head knocked in as part of the bargain is an even less fulfilling proposition.

I parked near the corner and felt eyes on my back all the way up the sidewalk. I was going to take abuse, and I was already trying to steady myself. I just hoped somebody would be watching and it would shake them. It was the only hand I had to play.

Faces turned to look at me as I started up the walk. Bodies parted reluctantly. From inside I heard the sound of moaning, rising to a wail and then dying down again.

As I started up the rickety steps a man came through the sagging doorway. Maybe fifty, he was still powerful, despite the gray in his mustache. He wore a coat, open at the neck, and a checked shirt underneath.

"What you want?" he asked.

"My name is Dunn," I said. "I'm a private investigator representing Calvin Autry. Are you Taylor Augustine?"

"I am. We're having a wake here, mister. Don't you see that? My nephew was murdered by that man. We got no time for you."

I took a deep breath and said a silent prayer. "I have reason to think Calvin Autry is innocent. Before this goes any further, I have to do my best to see there's no miscarriage of justice."

The man advanced on me, his big fist balled. "Man, you better get outta here while you can still walk."

I raised my hand, palm outward. "I don't mean any disrespect," I told him. "But investigating things is my job."

By now all the people gathered were staring at us, women with frowns, children half hidden behind their mothers' skirts. The screen door opened and a woman emerged. Tears streaked her face, and her eyes were glazed over.

"Who this man?" she demanded. "Who this come to make trouble over my dead baby?"

"Miss Augustine," I said. "I'm very sorry about your son."

"Sorry? You say *sorry*?" Hands tried to pull her back but she shook them off. "You want to see sorry? I'll show you sorry."

Taylor Augustine was halfway down the steps, but the woman's hand reached out to catch him.

"No. I want him to see. He come here, let him see. Let him see what sorry all about."

"Miss Augustine," I began, but before I could finish hands were on me, shoving me forward, up the steps, across the porch and through the doorway.

Shocked faces glared hatred at me from the sides of the room, but I didn't have a chance to react, because I was being pushed forward, toward the rear.

"That's sorry," the Augustine woman cried, pointing at the gold-framed photograph of her son.

For the first and last time I saw Arthur Augustine. He had been a nice-looking boy, but, I reminded myself, everybody smiles for school portraits. His hair was combed, his smile real, and there was nothing to show he hadn't been a normal, happy boy for his age.

In ten years, I thought, Arthur Augustine might have ended up in the state prison, or dead of an overdose. Or he might have been on the way to stardom as a musician, a quarterback, or a heart surgeon. The odds had been against him, of course. But he'd deserved a chance to defeat the odds, just as Sandy had.

"That's my baby," his mother declared. "No use talking to him, he don't hear you. My baby dead. You got something to say, you say it to me."

I started to turn around, but the hands still held me.

"You through?" Taylor Augustine hissed in my ear. "You finished now?"

Before I could answer he jerked me around and, with the help of two others I couldn't really see, pushed me across the room and through the doorway. I reached the steps and a foot came out of nowhere; I lurched headlong toward the sidewalk, landing on my right side and rolling, judo fashion. As I got to my knees a keening wail cut the air behind me and then died away into sobbing. I stumbled back to my car, hands and arms bruised, wondering why I had chosen such a lousy job.

Nine

*I*t was early yet, not quite four, but I didn't feel like going back to the office, so I made my way uptown in the swelling traffic to Katherine's place. I let myself in and put the bottle of wine in the kitchen. I couldn't remember whether it was supposed to be chilled or not, so I left it on the counter and opened a beer.

I should have told Autry's son I was off the case. I should have told him to tell his old man that when Calvin skipped out, all bets were off. It was the sensible thing to do.

So why hadn't I done it?

Because I had the clown, the wire in the garage, the secret he didn't want to mention, and a wife who'd split after twenty years of marriage. I had Arthur Augustine, who was nothing now but a picture in his mother's house.

I had too much.

I don't know how to describe the feeling. It comes from the gut, and sometimes you listen, because you know it's composed of all the nuances and logical connections your mind senses but doesn't know how to explain. But at other times it's wishful thinking, and it can lead you into a morass. Anybody who says your gut is an infallible guide to the truth is a fool, or else he never came back from a trip that started in the sixties. The real truth is that you often never know the truth until too late.

My gut was telling me something now, but I was damned if I knew whether I ought to listen. I was still mulling it over an hour later when Katherine came in. Her son Scott was with her, and we shook hands after I gave his mother a kiss and a hug. I'd met Scott during the investigation that had introduced me to Katherine, while he was in the throes of a sophomore identity crisis. Now he was a senior biology major, with good grades and a level head. I liked him, not least because he'd managed to survive with only one parent, his mother, and would have done anything he could to protect her.

"So what happened today?" he asked, nodding at my soiled pants and shirt. "You get mugged by spies or just plain run-of-the-mill murderers?"

"No business talk tonight," I said. "I just want to enjoy your mother's cooking."

"Come on." He held up a copy of the *Picayune*. "They've got the boy's picture and everything."

I shot Katherine a glance and she shrugged. "I didn't say anything."

"Look, I've heard you talk about old man Autry: You even sent me there once," Scott explained. "When I saw his name in the paper and that he was wanted in this killing, I figured you must have *something* to do with it."

I smiled wearily at Katherine. "Can't fault your son on his brains. Well, maybe I've got something to do with it. Let's just leave it at that."

Scott went to the kitchen and came back with a beer of his own. "So why doesn't he turn himself in?"

I groaned, and Katherine smiled.

"Scott," I said, "would it surprise you to learn that not everybody trusts New Orleans' finest?"

"*No*. You mean he's seen 'em beat people at Mardi Gras?"

"Let's just say he comes from a subculture that distrusts authority," I said.

Scott nodded and took a long swig of his beer. "Probably a pretty good thing."

My eyes went to the clock on the wall and I went reluctantly to turn on the television. It was five, time for the local news.

"I thought there wasn't going to be any business," Katherine chided with a smile.

"I just want the news," I said. "That's harmless enough."

Scott and his mother exchanged amused glances. The station logo came on and then the face of one of the anchors, a blond Miss America type in her twenties.

"Charges of racial discrimination and corruption were leveled today by a black minister in the case of a murdered youth," she said airily, and I felt my heart sink.

Suddenly the room was very quiet. Katherine and Scott sat down, eyes on the television.

There followed a chain of commercials, and I cursed the ads for their slowness. What seemed hours later, the blond anchor came back on, seated beside a slightly older black man with a mustache.

"Well, Adam, the big news of the day has to do with charges leveled by a prominent minister," she bubbled.

"Yes, Karen. It has to do with the murder yesterday of a thirteen-year-old youth, Arthur Augustine."

The camera focused on the blonde's face. "The Reverend Gabriel Condon of the Church of the Deliverance said just minutes ago at a news conference that a private detective employed by the man police are accusing of the murder attempted to buy Condon's silence with money from the suspect."

"Oh, shit," I breathed. Now I knew what the last-minute offer by Condon had been about. I saw a black-and-white videotape of myself standing there handing an envelope of bills back to Condon, who flipped through them for the camera.

"The minister," the breathless anchorwoman went on, "claims that what you are seeing was secretly videotaped during a visit to his offices by Micah Dunn, a local private investigator. Dunn, he said, represents Calvin Autry, who police are looking for in a case involving torture, child abuse, and murder. Condon accused local police of dragging their feet and said their failure to find Autry was due to racial bias. He suggested that police know Autry's whereabouts and are protecting him."

"Christ Almighty," Scott swore. Katherine, instead of silencing him, only stared ahead, numb.

I got up and switched off the set. "Well, I guess I don't have to describe my current case," I said as lightly as I could.

"Micah, what are they trying to do?" Katherine asked.

"That's easy enough," I said. "Condon's trying to get me out of the way and make some headlines at the same time. And I was stupid enough to make it easy for him."

"Autry didn't give you that money, though, right?" Scott said. "I mean, was that tape spliced?"

"It wasn't spliced," I said. "What you just saw was real: a fourteen-carat fool letting himself get set up." I knew it didn't matter now; they wouldn't be satisfied until I told them everything, and besides, I could use some sounding boards. When I'd finished, Scott whistled, and Katherine looked frightened.

"The hell of it is that station didn't have the integrity to talk to me first," I said. "Condon set them up too—and close enough to airtime to make them have to fish or cut bait."

"I know the news director over there," Katherine said. "I dealt with him when I was working at the Middle American Research Institute. He's an asshole."

Scott shot a look at his mother and his mouth opened; then he smiled and looked away.

"Look," I said, "I didn't mean to drag you both into this."

"It's too late now," Katherine said, nodding at her son. "The question is how you're going to drag yourself out of it."

"Actually, I was thinking," Scott said. "Always dangerous, my teachers tell me, but it's a habit. This business about the Spider-woman: you really think the boy might have been doing this a lot?"

"It's just one of the possibilities," I said. "I've got to admit, it can cut both ways, but if the boy turns up in their files, at the very least it shows the kid was troubled and so maybe he wasn't credible."

"Or maybe just victimizable," Katherine said tartly.

"Yes, of course."

She turned to face me on the sofa. "Micah, when we talked about this, we were just talking child abuse. Now it's murder. Do you still think Cal's innocent?"

"I hope he is," I said. "That's about all I can say."

She got up without replying and went into the back to prepare the meal. Scott crushed his empty beer can and leaned forward in his chair.

"I know that wineshop," he said. "The woman you're talking about is named Francine LeJeune."

"What?"

"Sure. It's a popular place, especially with Tulane faculty and students. Lots of people go there."

"Presumably for wine," I said, but the joke didn't sound funny, even to me.

"Who knows. But I could help you, Micah. You know you're burned now, your face all over the TV and everything. But they wouldn't suspect me."

I considered the earnest face in front of me. "What are you trying to say, Scott?"

"I'm saying I'm tired of the books, and all the outlines and the chapters to read. I need a break. So why can't I try being a pervert for a while?"

"You're the least likely pervert I ever saw," his mother said suddenly from behind him. "What are you two concocting?"

"Look," Scott went on, undeterred. "I could go to the wineshop and tell her I'm looking for a kid. I could get her to show me whatever files she keeps and—"

"No you couldn't," Katherine said firmly. "You're a student, not a detective. Let Micah handle this."

"Well, I just thought . . ."

"That Micah isn't doing such a great job," I finished ruefully.

Katharine shot me a fiery glance. "Micah's a grown-up," she said. "He can take care of himself. He doesn't need my son to do his work for him."

"I'm grown up, too," he said. "I'll be twenty-one in a few months. I'm old enough for the army, and I'm old enough to get married. And all I'd have to do is find out if the boy is listed."

Katherine started to protest, but I cut her off. "There's a problem with that," I said. "If she hasn't destroyed any file on him by now, she's stupider than she ought to be. And you don't even know what he looks like."

"You could get me a picture," Scott said.

Katherine's eyes narrowed. "But he won't," she declared.

"Well," I began.

"No," she pronounced. "That's final."

I looked over at Scott and shrugged. "You heard her. Sorry."

Scott started to say something, then changed his mind and went back to the kitchen for another beer.

"I mean it, Micah," his mother said.

"Okay," I said. "It wasn't my idea, remember."

"I know. But I also know how you get involved in your cases. I don't want Scott caught up in this kind of thing."

"You mean the kind of shabby work I do," I replied.

"I didn't mean it that way." Her voice softened. "I just mean—"

"I know what you mean," I said.

She reached for my hand. "Micah, he's my son. You've got to understand. He's only twenty years old."

"He's asking for a chance to grow up," I told her. "He wants to get out from under. It's natural."

"It may be, but you're twenty years older than he is. You can handle yourself. You know the streets."

"Yeah," I admitted. "I know the streets. But I didn't always."

"No. But you *chose* to find out. You needed to, for your work. But not everybody has to. Not everybody has to get involved in the slime out there. Is it so bad for me to want my son to keep away from that?"

"It's not bad," I said. "You're just being a mother. I guess my mother would've felt the same way."

"You're good at what you do," she went on. "But Scott doesn't have the background."

I knew what she was talking about. My training hadn't been in the urban jungle but in the real one, with mortars and machine guns firing at me. When I got back home, I figured nothing they could do to me in a city could be any worse.

"No," I agreed. "He doesn't. But you never can tell when it will come in handy."

"Maybe," she said. "But I'm hoping that it won't come to that in microbiology."

I started to reply but then shut my mouth. We'd met because her former employer, a university professor, had been unwittingly involved in artifact smuggling and murder. I'd learned then that a college campus can be as big a snakepit as the ghetto.

Scott came back with his beer, and a few minutes later we sat down to eat. But conversation was muted, and what should have been a pleasant occasion was an exercise in strained civility. Katherine knew she'd stung me by attacking my profession; it was the same attitude my father, the Captain, held, and it drew the same response. I kept telling myself that if I was truly reconciled to what I did, I wouldn't be so sensitive. But I couldn't control the feelings.

Not that I'd intended to use Scott; it had been his idea. But I thought he'd had a right to express it. Then again, I wasn't his mother. I wasn't even his father. His father had died in Nam. I was only his mother's lover, and right now I wondered what that counted for.

At just after ten Scott rose to make his good-byes. I shook his hand, and he gave me a wink as he went through the door. Katherine and I watched him go down the walkway toward his car and I felt her hand creep into mine.

"Don't be angry," she said softly.

"I'm not," I said, but my words sounded hollow even to me. "Look, I'd better head back myself."

"You don't want to stay." It was an observation.

"No. I've got some things to do."

"Sure." She looked suddenly smaller, more vulnerable. "Micah . . ."

"Look," I told her, "I don't know why I do what I do. Sometimes I don't like it. I meet a lot of lowlifes. Sometimes I wonder if there's any way it won't rub off. But I can't go back to the marines, and I wouldn't be worth a damn working in an office. I try to be as honest as the next guy, and there are some cases I won't take. But most of them I do, and when everything works and things come together at the end, I feel good about it. Sometimes the feeling lasts for hours and sometimes for a couple of days. Most of my work I do at my desk, and I don't carry a gun very often, because most cases are pretty run-of-the-mill. But once in a while I run up against something different, and then, if I think it's worth it, I follow it no matter where it goes. This is that kind of case."

"Micah, you don't have to explain. I understand."

"Good. Because it may be that Calvin Autry did what he's accused of doing, and if he did, he'll pay. But if he didn't, he'll probably go to prison for life anyway, unless I stay on this thing. Don't get me wrong: I'm not powerful, I'm not a mover or a shaker. But I have one little thing that helps, and that's what I know about the streets. And if that keeps an innocent man from going to jail, then for just a little while it makes what I do worthwhile. And I think maybe that's something your son felt."

"And you think I don't?"

"I think you're a mother," I said, kissing her lightly on the lips. "And that's no sin. It's just not what will work for us tonight."

I went to the door, feeling empty. "It was a good meal," I said, turning to her. "Thanks."

All the way back I had the image of her standing on the stoop, and I felt hollow.

Once I'd thought I had a chance to rejoin the marines, but it hadn't worked out. I'd come away feeling raw, and while I'd managed to pretty much put it all behind me, there were times when the raw feeling came back. I shouldn't have taken it out on Katherine, but I knew if I'd stayed we'd only have quarreled. So it was best to get away.

I opened the wooden gate with my pass key and shoved the big doors open so I could drive into the courtyard. The fountain wasn't playing, and the only sound was the noise the hinges made as I pushed the doors shut again, closing out the Quarter.

I went up the outside stairs and let myself in. It was ten thirty, but for once there was no blinking light on my answering machine. If I did the sensible thing, I'd go to bed and work through it all in my dreams. But the rawness hurt too much, and I had an urge to pull out a bottle of whiskey and, for the first time in years, drink myself to sleep.

It was something I'd done frequently after my wife had left. I'd stopped the habit when John O'Rourke had shown some faith in me and started hiring me for some of his cases. Now I had a decent practice, enough to keep me eating, anyway, but staring at the bottle reminded me of the old days.

I'd just poured a shot into a water glass when the phone interrupted me. I went out to the office and picked it up.

"Micah Dunn."

"Mr. Dunn, this is Taylor Augustine. Look, we got to talk. Is there someplace we can meet?"

"Can you get here?" I asked.

"No way. There's a bar on Esplanade, about four blocks before the river."

"I know the place."

"Be there in half an hour. By yourself."

"Mind telling me what this is about?"

"Just be there." The line went dead.

I stood quietly for a moment, the receiver in my hand. Then I replaced it, went around the desk, and opened the top right-hand drawer. Removing a clip holster, which I stuck inside my belt, I took out the Colt Agent and checked the cylinder. I added an extra round to give it the full six-shot capacity and stuck it into the holster. Then I dropped a couple of speed loaders into my pocket.

I didn't know what Taylor Augustine had to tell me, but I was damned if I was going to be set up twice in the same day.

Ten

I parked on the other side of Esplanade, facing west, and waited. Across the neutral ground I could make out the front door of the bar, where a few men lounged. A couple of cars passed but nobody stopped. A man came walking down the sidewalk toward the corner. It was too dark to see him clearly, and he was at least a hundred feet away. I hesitated, and then, leaving my key in the ignition, opened my door and got out. I was halfway across the street when somebody called out. The voice came from behind me, and I turned to see a figure silhouetted on the other side of my car. I halted in the middle of the street, caught in the headlights of an oncoming car, and as I stepped back onto the neutral ground the figure fired.

I flattened myself onto the ground as the oncoming car rolled past, its driver unaware of what had happened. By the time it had gone I was up on my elbow, gun in hand, but the silhouette on the other side was gone. There was the sound of a car starting.

I raced to my own car. Dropping the revolver onto the seat, I twisted the ignition key and the engine roared to life. I nosed out onto the boulevard and right at the next corner, where a pair of taillights were disappearing north. I gunned my motor, catching up in two blocks. Then a truck pulled out of a side street, blocking me. I swore under my breath.

But it didn't matter, because in the few seconds I'd been close to his bumper I'd gotten a good view of his car, a late-model mud-colored Monte Carlo. Better yet, I had his tag number, and the memory of a sticker that said he belonged to the Friends of the Police, one of a myriad of phony benevolent organizations that for a twenty-dollar contribution handed out stickers to suckers who thought it would buy them out of a ticket. Or who, conversely, wanted to impress the gullible with their ties to the law.

I figured my man was among the latter. I let him go, and went back home. But I was too hyped up to sleep, and besides, I was mad. Maybe too mad to be rational, or I wouldn't have done what I did.

Which was to rummage in my drawer for the alligator clips and copper wire I'd taken from a small-time break-in artist, along with the jimmy and glass cutter and the roll of tape.

It was just before twelve, still plenty of traffic in the streets and a good chance of my being seen. So I'd have to scope out the situation and see whether the odds were in my favor.

I drove past the Church of the Deliverance. One of the second-floor windows was lit, but otherwise the place seemed quiet. The neighborhood was silent, with only a few people out. A white man would attract attention, so my best chance was fast in, fast out. I parked by the interstate and walked away from my car quickly, before some panhandler steered toward me for a handout. I had a dark coat on, and I kept the collar up to hide as much of my face as possible, likewise pulling down the dark-colored hat I'd snatched from a shelf. I seldom used it, but it had a soft felt crown, which cushioned blows, and its brim could be turned down to hide my features.

It was only a block from the freeway to the church. If I saw anybody outside it would be a no go, and my anger would have to find some other outlet. But as I drew near I saw that the big building was as silent as it appeared at first glance.

My guess was that there was a back door, and maybe some windows. I'd seen the ADT sign in front, and I doubted they'd have a different kind of alarm at the back.

I walked quickly into the shadows that hugged the side of the building and along the narrow path that I knew must lead somewhere. At the rear corner was a door, and over the door was a single safety light that had burned out, leaving the area in blackness.

I took out my penlight and played it on the top of the door. Sure enough, there was a contact alarm. I went around to the back, almost colliding with a garbage can. The air reeked of rotting vegetables, and there was a heavy odor of mold. Too late, I realized I was standing in water, and I felt the wetness seeping into my socks.

But the way out was obvious, for just over my head was a fire escape and when I pulled, the rusty mechanism came down within reach and I stepped up, out of the morass.

On the second floor was a door out onto the fire escape, obviously a fire outlet, and I was relieved to see that its top half was a glass panel. Moving carefully upward so as not to set off any creaks, I came to the door and found what I suspected: the glass was armed with aluminum strips. Working carefully, I attached one set of jumper wires to bypass the circuit and then, after taping the glass so that the panel wouldn't fall, I used the glass cutters to remove a section. I peered through into what looked like a hallway, but it was too dark to clearly see what was inside.

Reaching in with one hand, I found the lead wire to the top contact alarm. I attached one alligator clip and put the other clip on the wire leading to the second contact.

I felt inside the door and found a barrel bolt, which I slid back. Pulling from the outside, I found to my relief that the barrel bolt had been the only lock holding the door closed. In a second I was inside the hallway.

I took a few moments to assess the situation. Faint light glowed at the end of the corridor, and from somewhere far away I heard music that might have been reggae. The hall smelled musty; as I advanced the odor of incense tickled my nose. I came to a door on the right and put my ear against it, but there were no sounds from inside. I made my way to the end of the corridor and looked down the stairwell. The music was louder now, and I heard someone cough. I started down the stairs slowly, my body tense, and halfway down I froze.

There was a man seated at a table, his back to me, his feet propped up on a chair. On the table in front of him was a half eaten sandwich and a flashlight, and the radio was on a shelf at the other side of the room. He was nodding, and even as I watched his head dropped to his chest.

I backed my way to the top of the stairs and considered.

There was another door, across from the first one, and I decided to check it. When I did I heard human sounds inside.

One was the wordless voice of a woman, and there wasn't much doubt what was going on. I waited, patient, and her voice mounted to a passionate wail. Floorboards and bedsprings creaked, and I heard a sigh.

But damn it, who was she with?

Then I heard a man's low voice, speaking softly, and though I could not make out the words, I knew.

It was Condon, the man I had come to see.

I took a deep breath and slowly turned the doorknob. Not surprisingly, the door was locked. It was a simple household lock, though, the kind a dime store skeleton key would unfasten, and I silently reached into my pocket for the little felt key case I had brought for just such a contingency. I found the key I needed, slipped it quietly into the keyhole, and waited. A second later I heard the tinkle of female laughter and figured they were getting ready to start again. I twisted the key quickly, feeling it turn in the lock, and froze.

Five seconds passed and Condon's chuckle floated out from under the door. They hadn't heard.

I turned the knob again, and this time the door opened a crack. With the glow from outside behind me it was now or never, so I wedged the penlight in the strap of my wristwatch so it would shine where I pointed my gun, shoved the door open the rest of the way, and jumped inside.

Condon was halfway out of the bed by the time I reached him, but when he felt the cold muzzle of the gun against his throat he froze. The girl was gasping, and I sensed a scream coming so I shone the penlight in her eyes.

"Don't scream, don't yell," I told her. "If you do, you're dead."

She stared at me from eyes the size of saucers, not bothering to pull the sheet up over her nakedness.

"Now," I said. "Nobody's going to get hurt. I just want you both to do exactly what I say. Is that understood?"

The girl nodded, but Condon only stared at me malevolently.

I pushed the gun barrel into the flesh under his jaw.

"Is that understood?"

He exhaled slightly, and I felt the tension start to go out of the muscles in his neck.

"Whatever," he said.

"I want you, Reverend, to get down on your belly on the floor," I ordered. *"Now."* A jab with the pistol sent him down onto his hands and knees and then flat onto the floorboards. I turned to the woman. "Take the sheet and twist it into a rope and tie his hands," I ordered her. When I was satisfied, I shot my light on the other sheet. "Now that one. Tie his legs."

She did as she was told, working silently, her big breasts swinging lustily in the darkness.

"Okay," I said. "Now just stand there." I ran the light along the wall, finding a door that had the look of a closet. I walked over quickly and jerked it open. There was enough room for her and I motioned her over.

"The Reverend and I have some things to discuss," I said. "So you go inside. Don't come out until I say to."

She scampered over and fitted herself inside. I closed the door after her and then went back to the man on the floor. The room was thick with incense, but underlying it all was the pungent odor of human sweat. I sat down on the bed and regarded my victim.

"If you came here to rob me," Condon began, but I cut him off with a toe against his ribs.

"I came here to find out what's going on," I said. "And why you set me up today. I don't like seeing lies about myself on the five o'clock news." He started to protest and this time I gave him a little jab with my toe. "And I especially don't like getting shot at."

"I don't know anything—"

"Bullshit!" I kicked him again. "I guess you didn't tell Taylor Augustine to call me and set up a meeting. And I guess you didn't have some two-bit gun-for-hire waiting in the bushes on Esplanade just now."

"Man, you're crazy. I don't kill people. I don't *have* to."

"No? What do you do, just ruin their reputations?"

"That was insurance. We just wanted you off the case. We wanted justice for Arthur Augustine."

I got off the bed slowly and squatted beside him, my mouth inches from his ear. "You know what, Condon? You're a phony. All this religious crap, all this talk about justice. All you want is power. You want to be the man who deals, right? You don't give a damn about Arthur Augustine. He was just an excuse, somebody to use."

"That's not true."

"Sure it's true. Look at you. How old is the girl there? Fourteen? Fifteen? Want me to ask her? Want me to call the *Picayune*?"

"You don't know what you're getting into."

"It's too late for me to worry about that."

He raised his head slightly, and I could see the sweat glistening on his face.

"Okay, so I used you a little. Look, man, you'd do the same to me, don't tell me anything else. But I didn't try to kill you. I swear to God."

"Convince me."

But he didn't have to: the door burst open then, and light flooded the room.

"Drop it, mother!"

It was my turn to freeze. I had half a second to make my decision, and even in that fraction it was clear I didn't really have a decision to make. I let my gun fall to the floor.

Something cold and round poked into my back and before I could protest, what felt like an anvil slammed me in the head and I fell forward into nothingness.

Eleven

I watched them drag somebody downstairs, one on either side, while Condon threw on his pants and a shirt. I heard a woman screaming next, and the sound seemed to go on forever, and I wanted to tell her to stop, but then I told myself it didn't matter, no one was hurt, the man they were dragging away had just fainted and they were going to take good care of him.

They went to a van that had been pulled up to the side entrance, and I saw them toss the man in like a sack of laundry. He was limp, and I wondered for a moment if he might be dead, but then unaccountably, pain lanced up from the back of my neck and I wanted to gag and I forgot about the man.

An engine started somewhere nearby and I tried to turn my head to see where it was and found myself staring up at the roof of a van.

That was when I realized I was the man they were dragging.

The van lurched out into the street, and I felt more pain. The pain meant I was alive, but the question now was for how much longer.

I was getting careless. I had reacted out of hurt pride and anger, and as a result I was being taken on what might well be a one-way ride.

I sneaked a look through half closed eyes. I was on my back, so they were upside down in my vision, but the man in the right-hand passenger seat looked like Condon. I didn't recognize the driver, but I guessed he was one of those who had burst into the room. The man next to me seemed familiar, and I figured I must have seen him earlier, when I'd met with his boss. He was resting a sawed-off shotgun on his knees, with the barrels disconcertingly close to my face.

Somewhere above us a siren screamed, and I realized we were under the freeway. Somebody lit a cigarette. I coughed.

"You awake?" A foot kicked me, and I grunted. "He awake."

Condon turned around and looked down at me over the back of the seat.

"You got balls, you know that? Coming in like that. And with only one good arm too." He shook his head. "But you're kinda stupid. Smart man wouldn't have done that."

I tried to roll onto my side, but a foot came down, keeping me on my back.

"You know, a lot of folks disappear on the Manchac road," Condon went on. "You wouldn't ever be seen again. Or maybe across the river: there's lots of bones in that swamp."

I closed my eyes against his taunts, trying to think of a plan. But the twin barrels told me I didn't have any plan. I could hope for the thing not to go off, that was all, and that was more like a fantasy.

My body shifted as the van started up a freeway ramp.

He was right: I hadn't been smart. I'd let my temper take over. I'd been upset over Katherine, and so I'd shifted my anger to somebody I didn't feel bad about confronting. The problem was that it had clouded my judgment, and now I was going to pay.

Unless I could find some way out.

The van shifted in and out of traffic, and somebody turned the radio to a rap station.

"Condon," I said, opening my eyes, "people know where I went. If I don't show up again, people will come asking questions."

He stared down at me for a long second and then smiled. "You're lying."

"Am I? Is it worth the risk?"

"Mmm. Maybe so. Maybe it is, to get even with somebody that busts into my room and sticks a gun against me. Not to mention the embarrassment."

There wasn't anything I could answer to that.

For the next ten minutes we dodged in and out of traffic, and I tried to keep track of where we must be. From the gradual turn left, I judged it must be the 610 split, on the parish line. We were going east, toward Manchac, the desolate strip that wound between Lakes Ponchartrain and Maurepas and, coincidentally, led to Calvin Autry's cabin.

"At least you can tell me what it's all about," I said. "Why I'm so dangerous to you."

Condon chuckled, a rich, deep sound. "You're not dangerous, bro. You just a bother, like a blister on my balls. You're not important enough to be dangerous."

"Then why try to kill me?"

He sighed. "How many times I have to tell you I didn't try to kill you." He snorted. "If I'd of tried, you'd be dead now." He leered like a tiger contemplating its meal. "Instead of just the next best thing."

He turned the radio up, and for the rest of the ride I was treated to a combination of rap music and rock. It didn't matter that it kept me from thinking, I couldn't have figured a way out under the best of conditions.

Twenty minutes later I felt us winding to the right, and I knew it wouldn't be long. There was swamp of each side of us now; I didn't have to see it because I knew the stretch well, and I could smell the dank odor of decaying vegetation. The rake of oncoming headlights grew less frequent as the no-man's-land swallowed us up.

My only chance was to run for it. If I caught them by surprise I could make it over the rail while I was still alive. Once in the water I was probably safe—if I didn't hit a log diving in. If I didn't sink up to my knees in slime. If . . .

After another ten minutes the van started to slow, and I began taking deep breaths, trying to prepare myself. The wheels hit the reflectors marking the shoulder, and for a second there was a bumping, then quick deceleration and a jerk as the driver set the parking brake.

The headlights went out. If anyone passed, the van would just be an abandoned vehicle, waiting for the wrecker. The shotgun gave me a cold kiss on the cheek.

"Up," my guard said, and I heard both front doors open.

I rolled onto my left side and the side door slid open. An onrush of cool air hit me in the face, making me flinch. Condon was standing in front of me, his face hidden by the darkness. The shotgun prodded my back and I slid my legs out the door, searching for a hold with my right hand.

Searching . . . My hand touched something metal, and my fingers closed over it. A screwdriver somebody had left on the floor of the van. I dropped my feet to the pavement and stood up, keeping my hand close to my side.

"Now," Condon said, as the man behind me got out, "I think it's time for a little lesson in Christian humility."

It was the other man, the driver, who came out of nowhere. I caught a glimpse of movement on my left, and a split second later saw his fist headed for my midsection. I backed away, into the shotgun, but not before I raised the screwdriver to belly height.

My assailant's fist rammed into the steel blade, and I felt his body shudder. He screamed, jerking his hand back, and I pulled on the handle of the screwdriver, trying to free my weapon, but, too deeply imbedded, it was yanked out of my hand.

Condon frowned, unsure what had happened, and that was when I took the only chance I had: I did a quick spin right, pivoting away from the shotgun, and hooked my right leg behind my guard's right knee. I pushed into him with my body, and he went backward, onto the cement. The shotgun roared, both barrels blasting into the night, and I felt the pellets fly past my head.

I started to run, but the man on the ground grabbed my leg. I stomped his hand and he must have screamed, because his mouth opened, but no sound came out. I yanked my leg away, teetered off balance for a second, and then, with the sound of roaring all around me, I felt a pistol jammed into the back of my neck.

I froze. The man on the ground got slowly to his feet, and I didn't like the look in his eyes. His mouth moved and I knew he was yelling at the man behind me, the man with the gun, who had to be Condon, but no words came out of his mouth, and I finally realized the gunshot had deafened me.

But I didn't need to be a lip-reader to know what the man in front of me wanted to do. The question was why he didn't do it.

And the answer came soon enough: it was because his friend, the one with the screwdriver between the knuckles, got first shot.

Hands pulled me around, and before I could focus, a knee came into my groin, sending waves of nausea shocking through me. I hit the pavement like a sack of cement. Then the one with the shotgun got in his licks, kicking me a few times in the ribs.

And above it all, staring down with the detached interest of a meat-packer, was the Reverend Condon.

Headlights raked over us, and for a second I thought deliverance was at hand, but then the lights passed, and I waited for the beating to start anew. But instead the two bullyboys stepped away, out of sight. There was only Condon, standing over me with the revolver that I'd stupidly brought. I told myself that he was saving the fun part for last.

"I could kill you right now," he said, and I realized I had my hearing back. That was when I knew I was going to live.

"Why don't you?" I managed to ask though the receding waves of pain.

"Because, like I told you," he said, "we're not killers."

He turned and emptied the chamber of the pistol over the railing, so that the cartridges fell into the water, and with a gesture of contempt dropped the revolver onto my prone body.

"Aren't thieves, either. But don't come back. Next time"—he gave a little nod at the railing—"it's for real."

Before I could answer, he was gone. I heard doors slamming. The motor roared, and there was a rush of air as the van pulled away. Suddenly I was alone, fifteen feet above the swamp, in the middle of nowhere at two in the morning, with only the stars for company.

I tried to struggle up onto my knees, and fell back over. My groin ached, but I knew the ache would abate in a few minutes. I was more worried about my ribs. Breathing was painful, and I was afraid some of them had been cracked. But I wasn't spitting blood, so it didn't seem that my lungs had been punctured.

The problem was how I was going to get back. Only a cop would stop for a ragged figure waving his arms on the state's murder stretch at Christ o'clock in the morning.

The little town of Pass Manchac had to be near; there might be somebody there willing to call the sheriff. I tried again to rise, and this time I made it to my knees. I knelt there like a supplicant, trying to breathe slowly. The knife thrusts in my side seemed to be slackening off. Maybe my ribs were just bruised. Maybe I'd be able to walk after all.

I heard a sound ahead of me.

At first I thought it was the wind, and then I realized with a start that the wind didn't make that sound, the quick tapping of shoe leather on concrete, as somebody hurried toward me.

But there were no other cars, no headlights, nothing *human* . . .

The hairs went up on the back of my neck.

My assailants were gone, all the way to the north shore by now. So who was stalking me from the darkness ahead?

I scanned the dark pavement for some kind of weapon, but there was nothing. The steps were only a few feet away now. I could either stay here, like a prisoner waiting for the shot to the back of my head, or I could get up.

With all the strength I could muster, I pushed myself to my feet and faced it.

Twelve

A flashlight blazed on, blinding me, and I threw up a hand instinctively.

"Micah, are you okay?"

It was Sandy's voice, and I felt the tension go out of me.

"Sandy, for God's sake . . ." I lowered my arm and started to sag, but she caught me and kept me from going down.

"It's okay, Micah man. I got you."

"Thank God." I stumbled over to the rail and stared down at the black surface of the water, shuddering at the thought of how close I had come to disappearing beneath it. I began shaking as my system tried to handle the adrenaline it no longer needed.

"It's okay," Sandy soothed. "You just stay here and I'll bring the car."

I blinked, trying to comprehend what had happened. "But how did you get here?"

"All in good time," she said, and started forward to help me.

"No, I can make it." I shoved myself away from the rail and started forward. She knew me well enough to make only token sounds of disapproval.

"It's only about a hundred yards ahead," she said. "I saw you with them when I passed by, but there wasn't anything I could do." She patted her handbag. "This little .25 isn't nothing against the kind of cannons they have. They didn't pay any mind, so I just kept going a ways and then pulled in, turned out the lights, and raised the hood like I'd been here for ages. I was scared, Micah, real scared. I didn't know how I was going to get to you in time."

"But how did you know they had me?"

The beam of her flashlight danced along the roadway, picking up the reflectors, and I followed its circle with my eyes, telling myself it wasn't much further.

"I went by your office and saw you leaving. You seemed in a hell of a big hurry, and I had that feeling you were about to do something not too smart, so I followed. I saw you park under the freeway. That's when I knew you were going to Condon's place."

The light hit something metal, a bumper, a taillight.

"I pulled in a few cars down the street and waited." She giggled. "Micah, you lucky there wasn't anybody out right then. They would've wondered what this white boy was doing dressed up like Jack the Ripper three weeks before Halloween."

I grunted and made my way around the car. Pulling the door open, I collapsed into the seat. All of a sudden my pain faded to secondary significance, and all I wanted to do was sleep.

Sandy got in, reaching across me to pull the door shut. An instant later the motor started, the headlights turned the night into a bright tunnel, and we were rolling.

"Then," she said softly, "I waited while you went around the building tiptoeing like some kind of comic-book cat burglar."

"Don't rub it in," I muttered, but we both knew I didn't care and she could say whatever she wanted, because ten minutes ago I'd been alone in the middle of a swamp and now I was in the care of a beautiful women who was speeding me to safety.

"Of course, when I saw you come out again, I knew something was wrong," she said. "Mainly 'cause they were dragging you. You don't usually travel that way, at least not before ten o'clock in the morning."

"Okay, okay, get in your licks."

"I will. So I followed. 'Course, I couldn't get real close. But they had a broken taillight, so I could keep 'em in sight until the I–Fifty-five turnoff. Then, with a road so lonely like it is, I had to slow down to about fifty-five and let 'em take a big lead. I was scared, but what else could I do? I was about decided to try to speed up and crash 'em—if I could catch up at all—when I saw 'em pulled over.

I had to pass by and hope for the best, knowing that folks don't use this road at this hour except for just one thing."

I leaned my head back and closed my eyes. "It had occurred to me."

"Here," she said, and felt her nudge my hand with something. It was a flask. I unscrewed the top and took a long pull, feeling the whiskey burn down into my guts. It was probably the wrong thing to do, medically, I reflected, but it felt good.

"So what possessed you?" she finally demanded. "Have you gone crazy?"

I took another swig and then sighed. "I was pissed," I said. "I know, I know—it's a lousy reason." I told her about being shot at. "That and getting raked over on TV left me with something less than brotherly love for the reverend."

"I can dig that." Silence closed in on us, and I let my weariness carry me along.

After a while she spoke again. "I was wrong about him, Micah. I want you to know that. I mean, the things he said at first, I could relate to those things. I *feel* for the Augustine boy. But Condon was using him. That's bad enough, but if he's gonna turn out to be a murderer, too . . ."

I let my eyes open halfway. The reflectors in the center made a string of yellow dashes, hypnotic in their regularity. "I don't think he's a killer," I said.

"No?" I sensed her dark eyes on me.

"No. He could have killed me tonight if he'd wanted. And lots of men would have. But he didn't. And that means he was probably telling the truth about not sending somebody to take a shot at me."

"Oh, Jesus," she said. "You think it could have been Calvin Autry?"

A small piece of forever streamed past and I opened my eyes again.

"Calvin wouldn't have taken a shot at me," I said. "Whoever did that was trying either to get rid of me or to warn me off. Same result either way. I'm Calvin's only hope. He wouldn't have anything to gain. And, besides, he's gone to ground."

"Then who?"

I told her about the car I'd followed. "Whoever hires private detectives even more desperate than we are," I tried to joke. "Tell me, what did you find out about George Guidry?"

"My man George," she said in a voice like silk, "handles some interesting corporations. I talked to a friend in the secretary of state's office; she remembers his name and she looked up the corporations. They're duly registered, but they don't seem to do anything, unless you want to count things like 'formed for the purpose of providing management expertise,' or 'for the purpose of providing a resource base of consultants in urban planning.' "

"That's not unusual," I said. "There're lots of dummy companies on the books."

"True enough. But another friend, in the criminal sheriff's office, remembered him taking a case for one of these companies last year. Outfit called Baywater Enterprises. Their plane got seized at the airport after some coke was found inside. Ended up in federal court. George Guidry appeared for the company and claimed the pilot had taken the plane to Colombia and back without authorization, and so it shouldn't be forfeited."

"And?"

"It worked. Mainly because the pilot, a fellow named Armendárez, admitted it and pled guilty on all charges. Plane returned. Case closed."

Oncoming headlights flashed across the darkness for a second and then died away.

"So they paid him to take the fall," I said. "That means they're big time. Five years of a man's life can't go cheap."

"And neither can Guidry."

I tried to force myself to think, but it was difficult.

"So maybe Guidry sicked the hired gun on me," I said, and my words seemed to come out like a record being played too slowly. "That means he was scared I was about to hurt his connection with these drug fronts that call themselves businesses, or else that he had something to do with the Augustine killing."

"Neither one makes sense," Sandy said. "In the first place, you haven't even met the man, and I haven't gotten in his way either. He'd have to have a crystal ball to know you were checking him out."

"Mmm," I agreed, fighting the dreams that wanted to take me away.

"Second, why would he have killed the boy? He didn't have anything to do with Autry except a stupid car repair job. He won in court, so what's the reason for making a career out of trying to frame the man?"

"Who'sthatleave," I mumbled.

"What? Oh, you say, 'Who does that leave?' You tell me, Micah man."

But I couldn't, because I was already asleep.

When my eyes opened again it was dark, but it was the darkness of light shut out rather than the darkness of night, and somewhere nearby I heard the sound of traffic. I reached out for my clock and my hand touched empty space. I waved it in the darkness for a second or two, like a swimmer trying to grab a life ring, and then I drew it back.

I wasn't in my apartment.

"Katherine?" No one answered, and as soon as I'd said it I realized it wasn't her room: the smell was wrong, all vinyl and rug detergent, with none of the soft fragrance of perfume or bath powder that I associated with her.

I pulled myself to a sitting position and a groan forced its way through my lips. I had been killed last night, my dreams made that clear, and I remembered pleading for my life while the three figures in black pajamas debated in Vietnamese what to do with me. I tried to tell them the war was over, had been for more than fifteen years, but they didn't understand. One of them kept pointing to my left arm, and that was when I realized it worked, that there was nothing wrong with it at all, and that meant the year was really 1969, and I'd only imagined the two decades since.

When they shot me I was still trying to figure it out. I felt the bullets go through me, but I was still standing there, and they were walking away, and I knew somehow I was dead and that nobody would ever believe me if I claimed to still be alive.

So it took me a few seconds, propped up against the headboard of the bed, to sort out the truth, and while I was still putting it together the door opened and Sandy came in.

She had some coffee in little plastic cups and a bag that exuded the smell of charbroiled beef. She gave me an indulgent smile.

"I'm glad to see you decided not to sleep the whole day away," she said, flipping the light switch. "It's twelve thirty. Sleep a half hour more and I'm gonna have to pay another day's rent on this place."

"Where are we?" I asked.

"In Mandeville. Can't you smell the pine trees? Call me spoiled, but at three in the morning I just plain didn't feel like taking all twenty-one miles of the Pontchartrain Causeway. And I figured you might be a little bit safer over here, where nobody could find you."

"But—"

"Don't worry. I called Katherine. I told her you and I were out late on a case and everything was okay."

I relaxed and nodded. "Thanks, Sandy. And I guess you put me to bed."

"Nobody else. Motel manager gave me a funny look when I said my husband was asleep in the car, but so what? Wait till he sees we're a salt-and-pepper couple."

"Tough," I said, and swung my legs over the side of the bed. She'd wrestled off my clothes, leaving me in my briefs, and as I looked down I saw a welter of ugly blue marks.

"I've got to get back," I said. "I need to find that—"

"The man who took a shot at you. Right. But just now you better concentrate on not falling on your face. How do you feel?"

"Sore." I touched my ribs with my fingertips. "But I don't think anything's broken."

"You need a doctor to check you out."

"Right. As soon as I get some time."

She shook her head, and reached down to the chair for a paper bag. "Here are some clothes I got for you. Ones you had on aren't fit for the Salvation Army. I'll bill the firm."

Twenty minutes later we were on the causeway, heading south across the lake. I felt better—almost human, in fact—but I knew it would be a couple of days before I had any energy. In any other profession, I could have breathed a sigh of relief because the weekend was coming up. But here it didn't count.

"Villiere," I said finally. "That's who it has to be." I told her about Herman Villiere, and how I'd followed him and gotten my tire slashed for the effort.

Sandy pursed her lips. "Could be," she allowed. "He already knows you're following him, and he may have seen you on the evening news."

"Except that it doesn't leave much time to line up a hit man," I said.

"Hey, if he's into coke in a big way, or hangs out with the pony boys, he may already know somebody. These days it just takes a phone call or two. In my neighborhood there were people who'd kill for a bottle of Night Train Express."

"I reckon."

She brought me in through the gate on Barracks Street and helped me up the stairs. The only person that saw us was LaVelle, but he had seen many things since I'd been upstairs, and my being helped up a step at a time by my assistant wasn't going to surprise him.

I flopped into my chair and checked the answering machine. The only calls were from John O'Rourke, asking that I get in touch with him, and another, oddly, from Scott. I wondered idly what he wanted and decided he would have to wait. I picked up the phone and hit Mancuso's number on the automatic dialer.

When I identified myself he said, "He's not here."

"Neither am I. I'm just passing a message. Micah Dunn says he needs another license run."

"Sure. And I need a man called Autry who bugged out on us. What's this about?"

I told him a man had been following me, which was the truth, up to a point, and described the car I'd seen. "Now if you'll just check the plate maybe I can find out why somebody is so interested in what I do."

"Hell, I don't have to run the plate. I know this bird already."

My heart did a double beat. "You know him?"

"Yeah." Mancuso chuckled. "He's one of your brothers. A small-timer named Eddie Gulch, holds a PI ticket and does cut-rate jobs for jealous husbands. He's got in the way a couple of times. When you described that heap of his and the sticker on it, bells rang. We almost sent a complaint to the DA, because somebody thought he was a cop and he didn't correct the impression."

"Where does he hang out?"

"Last I heard he had offices in the old Maison Blanche building. Gulch Investigations. Around here they call him Dry Gulch. Watch out, Micah, he's strictly half-assed, and that can be a problem. He's too stupid to know when to stop."

"Thanks, Sal."

"Part of the service." He hesitated. "By the way, I saw you on the news."

"Great."

"Take it easy. There's a limit to the number of enemies that are healthy."

I told him good-bye and punched in the number for John O'Rourke.

"Micah, where the hell are you?"

"In my normal place of work," I said dryly. "What's up?"

"That's *my* line. I heard about you mixing it up with Condon." I went cold and then I realized he must be talking about my first, videotaped and televised, visit to the church. "Is there anything I ought to know to protect you?"

"I'm not guilty."

"I didn't think so. It sounded like a setup. But you've got to go easy. That man's politically very astute, and he's as ambitious as hell."

"Yeah," I said.

"I told you he has his eye on a council seat. This kind of thing is grist for his mill. If you get in his way he'll pull out all the stops."

I knew that if I told O'Rourke about my caper the night before, he'd hit the ceiling and read me a lecture about being forced into a corner as my legal adviser. I'd argue that he hadn't been so legalistic in the sixties when he'd broken into the draft board building on Canal with a bunch of protesters, and we'd end up going round and round like a couple of dogs, which wasn't going to do any good, so I kept it to myself.

"But I called the DA's office, and so far Condon hasn't pressed any charges against you for extortion," he was saying, "so my guess is it's all smoke, and he was just using it to get you out of the way."

"I don't think he's implicated, anyway," I said. "At least not directly." Then, on an off chance, I asked, "Ever heard of a small-time PI named Eddie Gulch?"

"Can't say that I have. Why?"

"Our paths crossed, that's all."

"Micah, look, do you know where Calvin Autry is?"

"No."

"Well, I had to ask. He needs to get his ass in here and surrender."

I sighed. "Calvin isn't one of your uptown types. He's a frontiersman at heart. He hasn't got any use for the government or any of its legal machinery. You can count on him staying out of sight till he thinks it's safe to come up for air."

O'Rourke sighed. "Well, I've done my duty as an officer of the court."

"He'll be glad to know. Look, I'll be back in touch. Right now there are some other things I've got to deal with."

I hung up the phone and turned to Sandy. "Okay, where is it?"

"What?" Her eyes were big and innocent.

"You know what."

"Oh, this." She reached into her handbag and brought out the .38 and the clip holster that had been in my pants. I put them on the desk, pulled out a cleaning rag, and rubbed gun and holster all over. I flipped out the cylinder and checked the chambers for obstructions, looking down the barrel at the reflection of my fingernail, the way they teach you in the military. When I was satisfied, I held out my hand for the speedloads I knew she must also have taken from my pants pocket.

She handed them over. I wiped the grime and lint from them and went into the drawer again for some more cartridges and reloaded the gun.

"You're not going after Condon, I hope."

"No," I said. "I'm going to see Eddie Gulch."

"Micah, look at you: you aren't worth a damn right now. Give your bruises a chance to heal, for God's sake. Or were you planning to go disguised as a hunchback?"

"You're a real comic," I told her, and stood up. She was right: it cost me an effort, because my bones were sore and my muscles didn't want to function. Whatever energy I had now would drain away in five or ten minutes like a charge from a battery with a dead cell. But I didn't have much choice.

"He's just in the Maison Blanche building," I told her. "It's not far from here."

She shrugged. "Okay, fool, but at least let me go along for backup."

I knew that if I told her no she'd agree and then follow me anyway. Nodding, I stuck the gun in the holster and thrust the holster down inside my belt.

"Look up his phone number," I said. "I'd like to know if he's there."

She found the listing E. GULCH, INVESTIGATIONS; CONFIDENTIAL, ALL MATTERS. I dialed and after one ring got a recording. It was comforting to know there were others who couldn't afford secretarial help, either.

"Let's go," I said.

It was two thirty when Sandy let me out on Iberville, at the west end of the French Quarter. If Gulch had answered the phone, I would have given him a phony name and asked some bullshit question. But since he wasn't there, it meant that with luck I'd have time to search his office and could be waiting for him when he got back.

I waited for Sandy to return from the parking garage. When I saw her coming across the street, I went inside and headed for the elevator. We'd go up separately, because, after all, this was New Orleans, and a white and black couple was the sort of thing people remembered. I was running a big enough chance just going myself; somebody was likely to see the bruise on my cheek and note that I kept my left arm close to my body. A man with a lame arm doesn't get many shots in undercover work.

I checked the directory in the lobby and went up in the elevator with four other people: a woman on the way to her gynecologist, who kept whispering to her friend just loud enough for me to hear; a man with a Masonic ring, who looked like an insurance agent; and a fellow from the phone company, with a tool belt.

The elevator stopped at the sixth floor and I got off. As the doors closed behind me, I went down the hallway, heading for the stairs. The building was an old one, dating from the Depression, and the doors all had frosted glass panels with the names of doctors and lawyers stenciled on them. There was a brass stand with sand for cigarette butts just beside the elevator, and the hallway smelled vaguely of cigar smoke. I went through the door to the stairwell, glad that nobody else was in the corridor to see me, and down the stairs to the fifth floor. I cracked the door and looked out. The way was clear, and I walked quickly along, counting off the names and numbers on the doors as my feet made slick sounds on the wet floor.

ALVIN TRASKER, M.D.; STEARNS, ROBICHAUX AND HARTNESS, CERTIFIED PUBLIC ACCOUNTANTS; FOLKS AND SMITH, INVESTMENT COUNSELORS; CONFIDENTIAL INVESTIGATIONS.

No name, just Confidential Investigations. I turned the handle and the door opened. Careless, I thought. Or had he returned?

I froze, listening, but there was no sound except the far-away honk of a horn down on Canal. I was in an anteroom, with a desk and a couple of chairs that looked like Goodwill specials. Behind the desk was a door that had to lead to his inner office.

I went through the door and found him sitting in his chair, smiling at me. It was a silly smile, the kind you have when you're caught out at something and don't know what to say.

It didn't take me more than a second to realize he was dead.

Thirteen

*H*is hands were hanging down by his sides, and when I touched his face it was cold. I'd seen smiles like his in Nam, a few hours after death. They weren't pretty. Neither was the red spot on his chest. I bent over to look at it. It wasn't a bullet hole. Someone had jabbed him in the heart with something like an ice pick. Quick, lethal, and silent.

I heard the outer door open and straightened. It was probably Sandy, had to be Sandy. But my hand went down to my belt anyway and closed over the grip of the revolver.

Sandy's face appeared in the doorway, registering a split second of shock at the sight of Gulch. Then her presence of mind took over. "Micah, we've got to get out of here," she said.

"In a minute," I said. "But I need to check his office first."

"But Micah, there was somebody downstairs. He saw us go up."

It was my turn to register shock. I was too tired to be functioning well or I'd have seen him myself. The question was, who was he? "Stand outside in the hall and try to buy me some time," I said. "If it looks like rough stuff, get clear first."

She hesitated, then nodded and vanished through the doorway.

I exhaled slowly, trying to regulate my reactions. I should have been in bed; demanding still more of my body within so short a time was asking for trouble. But I'd been through some rough spots during the war and I knew that long after the physiologists tell you the body is ready to collapse, it has reserves to draw on. The problem comes afterward, with the letdown, but I couldn't worry about that now.

I went through Gulch's pockets quickly and found nothing out of the ordinary, just a notepad with scribblings. The first few pages didn't make much sense, but on the last page I found my office address and a time. The time was about when I'd left for the rendezvous with Taylor Augustine.

The rest of the pages were ripped out, with only the torn tops left.

Next I went through his desk drawers. The only gun I found was a .44 Magnum, a cannon that would knock down a small tree. But it hadn't been a .44 that had been loosed on me last night; the crack had been lighter, more like a .38. So had he ditched the gun?

The drawers also held some old case folders. It looked like he did a lot of skip tracing for loan companies. I shoved the folders back where I'd got them and went to the file cabinet in the corner. It was unlocked, but the two top drawers held only a handful of folders, and the bottom two were empty, unless you counted the office bottle and a stack of porno magazines.

I didn't have much more time. Frustrated, I checked his answering machine.

The message tape was gone. Somebody had called him, set this thing up by leaving a message, and then covered himself by taking it when he left.

I was still standing there, perplexed, when I heard the hubbub outside. A woman screamed, and my belly went weak. Then it registered that it sounded more like hysteria than pain.

Sandy. She was buying me time.

I stepped away from the dead man and was halfway to the anteroom when the office door opened and Fox came in, pistol in hand.

"Freeze," he said.

I raised my right hand slowly, and he barged forward, another cop behind him.

"What's going on here?" he demanded. "Is this burglary or something else?"

"Looks like murder to me," I said, nodding at the man in the chair.

Fox's little eyes went narrow. "Against the wall!" he ordered, going over to the corpse.

"Touch his face," I said. "He's cold. Your man in the lobby'll vouch that I just got here."

"That's right, Lou," said the detective behind him.

"Shut up," growled Fox, but he touched the dead man anyway, bringing his hand away slowly.

"Then why the lookout outside?"

"No lookout," I lied. "I just asked her to wait for me."

"Is that why she pitched a nigger fit?"

I felt my blood rise, but there wasn't anything I could do. Backing away so as not to crowd him, I felt my foot hit something on the floor, something that rustled. I looked down casually. A slip of paper. I put my foot on it.

"Can I tie my shoe?" I asked.

His gun moved to cover me, wavering. "No tricks," he ordered.

A man came in. "I got the woman some water from the bathroom," he said to Fox. "Goddamn mess. Why can't they fix the pipes in these buildings?"

It was enough time for me to slip the paper from under my shoe and into the shoe itself, between my sock and the leather.

Fox looked back at me, his face angry. "Hey, you're wearing loafers."

"Wouldn't you if you only had one good arm?" I asked.

"What?"

He didn't have time to figure it out because they were bringing Sandy in. When she saw me she relaxed and dropped the hysterics.

"Can we go now?" I asked.

"You wise-mouth son of a bitch," Fox snarled, bringing his face only a few inches from my own. "You're coming to the bureau, and you're gonna explain about obstruction of justice and breaking and entering—to start with. Then we'll see what we can do about murder. Now spread!"

I let them search me, the slip of paper still crumpled in my shoe. They took my gun, and Fox pocketed it with a grunt.

"I have a deputy's commission," I said. "Right in my top left pocket."

"Deputy's commission," he muttered. "What'd you do, kick the sheriff a few hundred for his last campaign?"

Rough hands shoved me out through the door, my good right hand manacled in front of me to my useless left one. I knew Fox would rather have shackled both hands behind me, but he figured a one-arm wasn't much of a danger, and he didn't want me to yell about excessive force. The excessive force would come in the continual jabs he was giving me as he moved me down the hallway and toward the stairs.

"Who pissed on the floor?" he demanded, as we tracked water down the hallway.

"I told you, Lou, the john's overflowed."

The door to the stairwell was yanked open, and they pushed me through. I kept trying to look behind me for Sandy, because I knew Fox was a bigot, and he'd take out on her whatever he couldn't on me. But she was behind me with a couple of the others, and the best I could do was catch a glimpse from time to time and hope she was all right.

Halfway to the second landing I bounced off the wall and went flat. Hands jerked me upward, but I'd managed to slip the piece of paper out of my shoe and sneak a look before I crumpled it in my right hand.

The word I saw was PLAYTIME. I didn't worry about the scribbled address, I already knew where it was.

They kept me at the detective bureau for three hours, which pissed them off because it was a Friday and they had to stay into the next shift instead of going home to drink beer. I kept looking for Mancuso, but I knew Fox was keeping this to himself, hoping I'd cough up something so he could get credit.

They took my picture with all the bruises, so I couldn't claim they'd hit me, and then put Sandy and me in two different rooms and came at us in turns. I asked for my lawyer and got the usual bullshit about how I didn't have to worry if I was innocent.

"You know I'm innocent," I told him. "Unless you can figure a way to fuck up the coroner's report and make Gulch die a couple of hours earlier."

"The girl says you were there to go through his shit. That's breaking and entering."

"The girl didn't say anything," I told him. "And I don't say anything, either, without my attorney."

"Tough guy," Fox snarled, and brought his face down to within an inch of mine. I could smell his after-shave.

"What's it with you?" he leered. "You like the dark meat?"

I knew he was goading me to hit him, so I tried to tune him out. He kicked the legs of my chair to get my attention.

"Don't you try to ignore me," he shouted.

"Why don't you ask your man in the lobby who went up this afternoon?"

"You know goddamn well half the city went up."

"Then why were you following Gulch? Who put you onto him?"

His face went crimson. "I ask the questions."

"Sorry. I forgot." But the answer was already bashing its way into my skull. *Of course.*

I looked at the cop standing on the other side of the room. Young, with dark hair and a narrow face, he was narcotics; I'd run into him once a few months before in the station, when Mancuso had pointed him out to me.

"Who beat you up?" Fox asked.

"I fell down a stairwell. A different stairwell," I added.

"Did that nigger Condon have something to do with it? You tried to shake him down, we know that. What did you do, go over there afterwards and hit him with your face?"

Too close to the truth for comfort. "Look," I said, "it's after six thirty. The worst of the traffic is over. You can go home now, unless you want to fuck around like this the rest of the night. If you do, give me a cell and a quarter for the pay phone. And book me for something besides being at a murder scene."

He balled his fist, and I knew if the other cop hadn't been there he'd have hit me, but I was counting on what Mancuso had told me about the other cop: that he was straight and fair, and he didn't take shit or hand it out either. Still, I could tell Fox wanted to hit me, badly, and it was probably only my being disabled that saved me. Sometimes having just one good arm is an advantage.

Fox wheeled, jerking his head at the other cop, who hesitated and then preceded him out of the room. Fox followed, slamming the door behind him. I was left alone in the little interrogation room, with just the big mirror to admire myself in.

They would be on the other side of the mirror now, arguing, and Fox would be sneaking glances, hoping against hope to catch me pulling something out of a hollow heel or the lining of my pants.

Twenty minutes later the narcotics cop came back. "You can come get your things," he said.

Fox watched from across the hallway as they gave me my wallet and my gun. I counted my money and shoved my gun down into my belt holster.

"I'm going to have my eye on you," Fox threatened.

"I know," I said. "But you guys are pretty easy to spot."

Sandy met me in the hallway and we walked out through the front door, conscious of their eyes on us.

"Brrrr," she said, shivering. "Now I know what civil rights workers felt like in the sixties."

"They're not all like that," I said.

It was dark, and I was too stiff to go very far, so we flagged a cab. As we got in I saw the plain Chevrolet pull away from the curb and fall in behind us.

I gave the driver O'Rourke's address on Henry Clay, and tried to relax the rest of the drive.

The lawyer lived in a big yellow two-story dating from the twenties, across the street from the insane asylum. He enjoyed the irony, and right now it seemed appropriate. Of course, I didn't know if he'd be home, but I figured it was worth a chance.

When we stopped at the corner I saw lights on, and I thought I saw a shadow pass in front of the window.

"Wait here," I told the driver. We got out and went through the grill fence and up the walk. I heard the TV playing inside and nodded to Sandy. If O'Rourke had a date, he might not be ecstatic about being interrupted, but there wasn't any choice. I knocked on the door.

A few seconds later he opened it, frowning out at us from behind his glasses, a drink in his hand and his hair tousled.

"Jesus," he said, looking from one of us to the other, "this must be serious."

Sandy went back to pay the cabdriver, and O'Rourke and I waited in the doorway for her. He ushered us in, going to the television and pushing a button on the VCR.

"I was watching *The African Queen*," he said, his tone half re-criminating. "They've just buried Robert Morley."

"Sorry," I said. "We came about another death."

He took a deep breath and sank into his easy chair. He'd been married once, but it hadn't worked, and now, aside from bicycling, his main source of relaxation seemed to be classic movies. He waved a hand at the bar with its decanters and glasses, and Sandy went to fix herself one, but I already had a mouthful of acid.

"So what is it?" he asked, and then squinted at my face. "And who beat the crap out of you?" He frowned. "Was it Condon? Are you holding something back?"

"It's academic," I said. I told him about Eddie Gulch. "So you see, we really just happened to stumble onto it."

"Then you don't have anything to sweat," he said, rolling his glass between his hands. "Unless you picked up something at the scene. And that would be obstruction of justice."

I thought about the little slip of paper, which I'd since gotten rid of.

"Nothing clearly connected with the crime," I said.

"I don't think I want to examine that statement," he muttered. "So now what?"

"Nothing. I just wanted their bird dog out there to see where we'd gone."

"You know," he said, "you're fast establishing me as a mouthpiece for dubious causes." He held up his glass to the light. "Now tell me why they had a cop in the lobby of Gulch's building."

"They were following somebody," I said. "The person that hired Gulch. It's a drug case. They may have figured Gulch was a courier, or, more likely, a hit man."

"Since he took a shot at you, it seems likely," he allowed.

"That's where you come in," I said. "I'd like you to call and make sure they do a gunpowder residue test on Gulch's hands."

"To prove he shot at you?" Sandy asked. "What if he scrubbed?"

"Or wore gloves," O'Rourke said.

"I know, it's a long shot," I admitted. "But let's do it anyway. They might blow me off, but they can't refuse if you ask them. Call one of your contacts in the DA's office."

O'Rourke sighed and reached for the phone. "You might as well go to the icebox," he said, "and get out the lunch meat." He shook his head as he punched the buttons. "They're gonna love me for this."

Sandy and I made a stack of sandwiches and brought them out to the living room, while he took half an hour to track down an ADA named McLemore. I heard him promise everything from Saints tickets to his attendance at the DA's next fund-raiser. When he'd gotten what he needed he muttered his thanks, pressing the receiver back on the hook like a man closing the lid on a basketful of snakes.

"Okay. He'll make the request. It'll take a day or two. Tomorrow's Saturday, and the State Police crime lab's shorthanded, so don't hold your breath."

"Thanks, John."

"Yeah." He gave me a sour look. "Have you ever sat through one of the DA's little after-dinner speeches?" He shook his head. "Since I had to get my man away from the table at T. Pittari's, it's also gonna cost me some tickets I don't have. Micah . . ."

"I know somebody who'll print you up as many as you need," I said, and watched him go green. Before he could protest I had the phone in my hand.

Katherine answered on the first ring. "Micah. Thank God. I've been sitting here worried to death."

"I thought Sandy called you."

"She did. It's not you I'm worried about, it's Scott. I haven't heard from him for two days now. I called his apartment, and he isn't there. His friends haven't seen him and—"

"Whoa," I said. "He called me yesterday. At least, there was a message on my machine."

"You talked to him, then?"

Damn. It had slipped my mind. "No," I admitted. "But he sounded fine."

"Did he say what he wanted to talk to you about?"

"No. But there wasn't any urgency." Or was there?

"Micah, I'm worried. Ever since the other night . . ."

"Scott's a big boy," I said soothingly. "He'll be okay. Probably just studying at somebody's place. I'll check on him."

"Please." She hesitated. "Micah, about the other night, I—"

"It's okay. We'll talk about it later."

"Yeah," she said flatly.

"Katherine . . ." I lowered my voice. "Look, you're his mother. I accept that. I've never had a kid, so maybe I don't know what it's like. But I know Scott, and I think he'll be okay."

"I know," she said in a small voice. "But I'd feel a lot better if you were here right now."

I thought about the gunshot that had missed me, and the beating I'd taken, and then about the dead man, sitting in the chair with a silly smile on his face.

"It's best for me to stay away for the time being," I said. "Until some business matters are resolved."

"You mean the Autry thing. Micah, if you need me . . ."

"Thanks. Right now, though, I need you where you are." I hesitated, looking over at O'Rourke. "I'll be at John's tonight."

"All right. But Micah . . ."

"Yeah?"

"I love you."

For the first time in two days I felt something almost good. "I love you, too," I said. "Later." I hung up.

"The bed's made upstairs," O'Rourke said. "Sandy can have the downstairs. Or you can flip for it."

Sandy shook her head, finishing her sandwich. "Sandy can take care of herself," she said. "And right now she's got some legwork to do."

We both looked at her.

She got up, taking her purse. "Well, I don't know about you dudes, but I'd kinda like to talk to a cat named Taylor Augustine."

Fourteen

The next morning I felt almost human. O'Rourke was downstairs when I got up; I smelled coffee brewing. I went to the window in his bedroom at the end of the upstairs hall and lifted the curtain. The street looked clear, but you can never tell. Fox and his partner might be further down the street, or on Chestnut, the side street that ran alongside the house. Sandy had gone out through the back door, and through the garden gate, and I counted on her ability to slip away into the night. If they were still interested in me, I was going to have to do the same thing, only in daylight.

I went downstairs to the kitchen, where O'Rourke handed me a plate of toast. "I don't eat much on Saturday mornings," he said. "My day to jog."

"Could you do me a favor first?" I asked, and explained what I wanted him to do.

He shrugged. "Why the hell not? I've done everything else." He poured himself a second cup of coffee. "You really think this clears Autry, then?"

"Why would Autry kill Gulch?" I countered.

"I don't know. But you might've just stumbled onto something that's not connected with the Autry business at all."

"If I did, they knew enough about Autry to get Taylor Augustine to call me," I said.

"Yeah, that's true." He pursed his lips. "Well, who do you think hired Gulch, then?"

"My guess is Villiere," I said.

"But what does that have to do with child molesting?"

I shrugged. "You tell me."

"Okay. Try this: Autry was into more than one illegal thing. Dope as well as kids." I started to protest, but he held up a hand. "It's happened to less likely people. His wife left him, he was wrung out . . ."

"Not Cal," I said. But the presence of the young narcotics cop who'd been in the room with Fox argued O'Rourke's case.

Five minutes later O'Rourke went out to his station wagon and drove away. I watched from upstairs, but nobody followed, so far as I could see. I gave it another five minutes and then let myself out the back. O'Rourke would drive around for a few minutes and then return. I was counting on anyone following him, if they were still in place.

I walked down to Magazine, found a grocery with a pay phone, and called a cab. While I was waiting, I looked up Melville Autry's address.

His house was on Oak Island, one of the new subdivisions that formed part of East New Orleans. Something Melville had told me kept coming back to nest in my consciousness, like a buzzard flapping its wings: *Him and me, we've had words, sure, once't I come close to clobbering him, he was so stubborn. . . .*

Maybe Calvin and Melville weren't on such close terms, after all.

My plans called for me to be somewhere at dark; until then I had a day on my hands. Why not? I thought, as the cab pulled up outside.

I had him drive me past the underpass near Condon's church, where I'd left my car two nights ago, but the car was gone. I hoped Sandy had picked it up for me, but I wasn't going back by the office to check, because that was the best way to pick up a tail. Instead I got out at a downtown hotel, where I rented a car, and by ten I was on my way east.

Twenty-five hundred years ago the only people who inhabited Oak Island were a bunch of wandering Indians, whose idea of a feast was shucking clams. The only ones who stayed the year through were the dead, who ended up in the shell heap with the rest of the garbage. It doesn't take a lot of brains to know that land like that goes under whenever there's a good storm.

The streets had names like Expedition and Endeavor, so the suckers who bought houses there should have been warned. But somehow, I reminded myself, looking out at the desolate brown scrub vegetation, suckers never learn, and maybe they'd end up in a shell heap like the ancient Indians.

The house I was looking for was on Founders, a one-story, modern brick affair with a blue pickup in the driveway and toys on the front lawn. I slowed at the end of the street and turned around.

I wasn't sure what I was going to do. I had plenty of time to wait and watch, but this was a neighborhood where there was no cover, just houses on each side of the street, and if I sat there for very long I'd probably get a visit from the law.

Of course, I could just go up to the door and knock. Is Calvin here? Did you ever try to slug it out with him? Did you wind up with a grudge?

I was still thinking about it when the door opened and the question was resolved. It was Melville, dressed in overalls and a plaid shirt, and as I watched he got into the pickup and drove away from me and out of the subdivision.

It was Saturday, so he wasn't heading to work. I thought about letting him go and seeing if Calvin was inside the house. But I could always come back for Calvin. Right now I had time on my hands and could indulge my curiosity. I let him get a block ahead and then followed.

He left the subdivision at Michoud Boulevard and turned right, headed for the interstate. There he curved left, going west toward the city, and I nudged my speed up to sixty-five, keeping him in sight.

There was a wreck on the Intercoastal Bridge, and traffic on our side was bottlenecked into two lanes. I slipped in two cars behind him and saw him get out and stand in the road, trying to see what the holdup was. Our lane soon opened and we set off, Melville weaving in and out of traffic ahead of me. I sped up, aware that I was risking a traffic ticket and the inevitable questioning that would result when I was recognized.

When he turned onto Causeway, it came to me where he was going. Of course, I thought, slowing down to a legal speed. He was heading for his father's house.

I let him lose himself in the traffic. When I turned into the street, his pickup was already in the driveway. I went on past, drove onto a side street, and came back around to park on the opposite side, about five houses down, facing his truck. The lawn beside me had a white sheet with eyeholes cut in it dangling from an oak tree, and a couple of dummy gravestones on the grass. In a few weeks the kids would be out in their costumes, lugging heavy paper bags full of candy. They'd take their candy home and their parents would go through it, looking for razor blades or other signs of tampering. They wouldn't find any, but somebody would know somebody who could swear it had happened to a cousin. It was that kind of neighborhood.

Melville had gone into the house, but I couldn't see what was going on. I wished now I was in my own car, because I keep a pair of binoculars under the seat. Ten minutes later I saw him emerge. He was halfway to his truck when a woman came out of the Bonchaud house next door and said something to him. He threw his hands up in the air, like what she'd said made him angry. She stood her ground, and he shouted something, but even with the window down I couldn't make it out.

The plumber's wife, I thought, and opened my door, undecided whether to break in on them and try to shake something loose or to let them finish and then try to wheedle the truth out of the woman. A minute later they were joined by the plumber himself, but he stood half a step behind his wife, and from his body language it looked like he was trying to arbitrate.

Melville threw up his hands a final time, turned his back on the pair, and got into his truck. The engine roared and he shot backward into the street and squealed away, leaving about a pound of rubber behind him on the asphalt.

I started across the street and caught the couple before they'd reached their front steps.

"You," Virgil Bonchaud said.

"Me again," I said, and hoped I could bluff it out.

"You're not any credit investigator," he pronounced.

"I've seen him before, Virgil," his wife said. She was dumpy, late fifties, with brown curly hair and a doughy complexion. "I've seen you," she repeated, looking straight at me.

"I'm afraid so," I said. "Look, I'm a private detective. I was hired to look into the Autry business. I noticed you were having words with his son."

A dog yapped somewhere nearby, and Virgil Bonchaud spit in the flower bed.

His wife took a step toward me, her eyes flashing. "You hear that?"

The dog was still yapping. I nodded.

"That pit bull's been yapping ever since Cal Autry left. They keep it chained up to the garage door. For burglars, he said. Melville comes over here to feed it every day. That shuts it up for about five minutes. Then, the rest of the day and night, it's yap, yap, yap. You can't sleep, you can't watch TV. I told him just now he ought to take that dog with him or have it put out of its misery. The cops were about to do it, when they came that time to search, but nice guy here went and tied it someplace else." She turned on her husband. "You shoulda let 'em shoot it."

"Mabel's sensitive to sounds, you might say," her husband put in.

"It's all day and all night," Mabel declared. "And the smell, all that dog does is crap."

The plumber nodded gravely. "It *does* stink," he allowed.

"I told him," Mabel went on. "But he didn't want to hear it. Just like his old man. And Marie was nothing but a—"

"Now, Mabel."

"Well," she proclaimed, "you know it's true. And what kinda man would keep a pit bull? The dogs are menaces."

Virgil Bonchaud squinted over at me. "You could of told us who you was to start with," he said. "Instead of all this credit investigator crap."

"I didn't want to stir things up."

He grunted. "What could stir 'em up any more than they are already?"

He had something there. I murmured my apologies and left, feeling their eyes on my back.

Melville had just come to feed the dog, the dog a panicked Cal had left behind. Something about the scenario bothered me, but I wasn't sure what. Not that I didn't believe it; it was something else, something pricking at the edge of consciousness.

I drove back, making a pass by Scott's apartment near Tulane. No one answered the door, and the mail hadn't been picked up. I tried to tell myself that he was just enjoying his independence, but I didn't like the looks of it. There wasn't anything to be done just now, though. I left a note for him to call me and his mother, returned downtown, and stashed the rental car in a parking lot. Then I walked back to my office.

I slipped in through the pedestrian gate, not seeing any watchers. But there was a vacant building across the street, and that was the place I'd pick if I were doing surveillance.

It didn't do any good to worry about it, though; tonight I'd be able to lose them in the narrow streets of the Quarter, if someone really was watching, and then duck back to the parking lot and collect the rental car. I was more worried about my own vehicle.

But I shouldn't have been, because I turned around and there it was, parked in its usual place beside the patio fountain. I breathed a sigh of relief and silently thanked Sandy.

There was something under the wiper on the driver's side, a folded sheet of paper. I unfolded it and read what was written on it.

Sandy hadn't brought the car at all. Shaking my head, I stood staring at the note in my hand: *Courtesy of the brothers and sisters of the Church of the Deliverance. God bless you, Brother Dunn.*

It was three o'clock and I was nodding in my chair, a Brahms symphony from the public radio station lulling me in and out of sleep, when the door opened and I came suddenly awake.

My hand went to the top of the desk, where the revolver waited in its holster, but it was only Sandy, key in hand, and a disgusted expression on her face.

"I can't believe this," she said, setting a paper bag down on the table.

"What?" I asked.

"The price of costumes this year," she said, reaching into the paper bag. "Look at this crap: all plastic and pasteboard." She held up a wand, plastered with stick-on glitter. "Who's gonna believe this?"

"Who the hell are you going to be?" I asked.

"Glenda the Good Witch, from *The Wizard of Oz.*" She shrugged. "I get so tired of being bad-asses."

"Suit yourself," I told her. "So what else is new?"

"Nothing," she said. "Nothing at all. I checked on Brother Augustine. And it's a pisser."

"What?"

"Taylor Augustine, that's what. Man, I don't understand what's going on."

"How so?"

"Well, I went over there expecting some bullshit story, and having to spread some of your bread around to get past the front door, and I found they were all in a state of panic. I asked and that was when they told me, and I believe 'em."

"Told you what, damn it?"

"About the boy's uncle, Taylor Augustine. He's disappeared."

Fifteen

I didn't like the sound of it. From what Sandy had seen of the boy's mother and the other sisters, they were pretty upset. That meant Augustine hadn't told them he was dropping from sight. I tried Mancuso at home, but there was no answer, and I was damned if I was going to call Fox. When Sandy left I tried putting all the facts together, again.

Calvin Autry had had some kind of secret that kept him away from the other boys when he was growing up. A few years later he'd married, though whether it was out of love or to get away from his hometown was hard to say, but after twenty-odd years his wife had run away, dropped him a card from California, and vanished. Calvin had been left with their son, but the relationship between the two had been unstable. At least once they had almost come to blows. Five years after his wife left, Calvin was accused of child molesting. And then the boy he supposedly molested turned up dead.

So much for Calvin. What did I know about the other players in the drama? About the boy I knew next to nothing, though if I could figure a way to get to the Spiderwoman, I might have an outside chance of finding out something. The boy's uncle, Taylor Augustine, could have been used to set me up and then either been bought off or killed. If Calvin was guilty it didn't make much sense for him to hire me and then warn me off the case. And there was no way to forget Eddie Gulch, now the late Eddie Gulch. There was more here than just child molesting, as if that weren't heavy enough.

The phone rang. I picked it up, hoping it was Scott, but instead it was the Captain's voice saying my name, and I thought I could almost hear the waves in the background.

"Hi, Dad," I said.

"I haven't heard from you for two weeks," he said accusingly. "I was wondering if you were dead."

"No, I'm fine. Just working," I said.

"Right," he said, and there was no mistaking the tone of his voice. He didn't think much of my work, never had; I could have done great things, and instead I was following embezzlers and the wayward daughters of the New Orleans country club set.

"I saw Frank Herlihy the other day," he said. "You remember him. He was a plebe your last year at the academy. He retired a couple of years ago, you know, right after he got his fourth stripe."

"Give him my regards," I said wearily. "Look, Dad—"

"So why don't you tell me about it?" he asked. "Maybe I can help."

"Tell you about what?"

"Whatever the hell you're working on that's keeping you so busy. If you're too busy to call, I figure maybe you need my help."

I was speechless. It was the first time since I'd been in the business that he'd shown any interest at all in the work I did. "It's nothing you'd find very interesting," I finally said evasively. "Just a child molesting case."

"Child molesting, eh? That's serious business. You know, we had a few of those in the navy. I sat on a general court once that tried a chief who'd molested five of his shipmates' kids."

I was hearing something new, and I felt my reserve melting. All along I'd envisioned him on the bridge of his destroyer with the spray in his face, and I'd forgotten that there were other aspects to being a naval officer, like serving on courts-martial when called.

"What happened to him?" I asked.

"Thirty years at hard labor," the Captain answered, "and it probably wasn't enough." A pause. "You know, I'd met him once or twice at the PX. He seemed like a pretty nice guy."

"Yeah."

Another pause. "So you want to tell me about it, son?"

Before I could think about whether I wanted to, I was telling him. Now and again I heard him grunt at something I'd said, and occasionally he asked a question. When I was done I felt suddenly naked and vulnerable, a little boy again who'd gone to his parent, only this wasn't just any parent, this was the Captain.

"I guess you could say I'm steering without a compass," I told him, trying to make a joke out of it.

"Yep. But don't forget, son, people were sailing the seas long before the compass was ever invented. They just had to use other ways of reckoning the direction." His voice was soft now, as if the breakers had receded, leaving the lapping of little waves on the sand.

"You have any ideas, Dad?" I finally forced myself to say.

A gentle chuckle. "I thought you wouldn't ever ask. Well, let's start with this Calvin. He's a friend, you can't ever forget that, but you can't let it blind you, either. You've got to look at it as if you were his commanding officer and he was one of your men. You may've been through hell together, love each other like brothers, but there's one thing you can't ever forget if you expect both of you to survive, and that's that you're the boss and he's a member of your command. Only in this case you're not running things because you've got gold stripes on your sleeve, you're running them because you know how to investigate and he doesn't. If he's innocent, then you'll find out, as long as you keep your distance and use your head."

"And if he's guilty?" I asked.

"If he's guilty then you have to do the right thing, because no matter how nice a guy seems to be, no matter how many beers he can pour down when you're sitting around swapping sea stories or how many charities he gives to or how many orphanages have him in their Christmas program, he's still a child molester, and he has to be put away. The chief I was telling you about? He had the Navy Cross and a couple dozen other decorations, plus fifteen years of perfect service. A commendation from the secretary of the navy himself, for some shore duty he pulled at the Pentagon. He was a man who'd give you his last buck. And I guess that all has to count for something. But next to the five young boys whose lives he ruined, it just didn't count for enough. There has to be law in society, boy, and there has to be punishment, or else nobody'll know where they stand. A man has to know he can't get off breaking the code by claiming he gave at the office."

There wasn't anything to say. Of course he was right.

"And in this case," he went on, "we're looking at murder, too." Another pause. "And that's why I don't think your friend did it."

I suddenly felt like a weight had been lifted from me. "That makes me feel better," I said.

"Well, don't feel all that good. Your friend still has to come in. And listen, don't shy from grilling him. If he is your friend, then he'll understand you're doing what's got to be done. Ask him the questions that need to be asked."

"I will—when I find him," I said.

"Man like that hasn't gone too far. He's not at his son's house, of course: the cops will have checked there first off. But he's not too far away."

"Right." The same thought had occurred to me.

"What are you going to do next?"

I told him.

"Son, you be careful. These bastards play for keeps. Damn. I wish I was down there. You could use some help."

The worry in his voice was real, and I felt warm inside. "I'd like to have you," I said. "But I can handle it."

"I know you can. You're a Dunn, aren't you?" He cleared his throat. "Well, look, call me tomorrow, okay? Let me know how it comes out. You got me curious now."

"Sure thing," I told him. We said good-bye and I hung up.

For the first time I really wished he was with me.

It was dark when I went out again. I went over to the caretaker's apartment and knocked on the patio door. Mr. Mamet opened it and squinted out at me, clearly hoping there wasn't something broken that he would have to fix.

"Yeah?" He was a quiet old man who said little to anyone, lived alone, and went about his daily tasks with a perpetual frown.

I reached into my pocket for my checkbook. "Did I pay the rent this month?" I asked.

He cocked his head slightly and then beckoned me inside. "Lemme see." He shuffled through the kitchen, littered with dirty dishes, and into the dining room, where he picked up a big green receipt book and licked his finger.

"Yeah, here it is," he said. "You didn't know you paid?"

"I'm slow sometimes," I said.

"Looks like it." He nodded at my face. "Somebody decked you, huh? What was it, some husband?"

"No," I said, "a preacher."

I went past him and through the living room, which looked like a set out of a fifties film noir, all black and white and chintzy, opening his front door before he could say anything. Like most people, he didn't have a high opinion of my profession, maybe because he associated me with cops, who'd once put him away for killing his unfaithful wife. In the Quarter nobody cared, and, besides, he still had his framed pardon from 1968, signed by Governor John McKeithen, hanging on the wall.

Barracks Street was quiet; on a Saturday night the action in the Quarter would be closer to Canal. Going around a few blocks, I didn't see anybody in any of the cars by the curb. So I went to the parking lot, paid my tab, and collected the rental vehicle.

I was at Playtime twenty minutes later. The parking lot was just filling up, and you could hear the rock music outside. A police car cruised slowly past the rows of vehicles and then left, headed for the next zoo on the list. I stuck the pistol and holster under my belt at the small of my back, in case the bouncer patted me down, and headed for the front door, scanning the cars as I went. But there was no red Ferrari, not yet. And if there was a narcotics stakeout I'd just have to take my chances.

I paid my cover, bought a drink, and took a stool at one end of the bar, where I could catch sight of whoever entered in the big mirror.

It could turn out to be a wasted couple of hours, of course. My prey might blow it off, or decide just to stand outside and do his deal. But a single man standing around outside was too conspicuous, and if I sat in my car I couldn't see everybody who went inside. Which meant I had to go into the hornet's nest, and wait.

The drink tasted like water, which was pretty much what it was, and I only made a pretense of sipping it. After half an hour I managed to quietly spill it on the floor between my stool and the bar. I ordered another and tried to shrink into anonymity. But it was difficult; I'd already been marked as a lone man out to make a pickup, and a girl from the dance floor was headed my way. I'd seen her watching on and off ever since I'd come in. In her early twenties, she had stringy black hair, with a short dress that left too much of her skinny flanks visible. She was a part-timer, I figured, ready to turn a trick on Saturday night for some snort. I'd been safe as long as the stools on either side were occupied, but now the one on the left had opened up, and the girl sidled onto it, giving me a sideways look as she took out a cigarette.

"Got a light?" she asked. The line wasn't original, but then she didn't look like the original type.

I shook my head. "Quit smoking," I said. "Sorry."

"When was that?" she asked, her voice whiny.

"After Nam."

"Oh. You were over there?"

It was asked innocently, as one might ask about an ancient page of history that had flashed past in a textbook she had never bothered to read.

"Yeah," I said.

Her eyes dropped to my left side and lingered. "Something wrong with your arm?"

"Kind of," I said. "It doesn't work."

"Did that happen in Nam?" she asked.

"That's right."

She got some matches from the bar, lit her cigarette, and blew out smoke, trying to look worldly-wise.

"I heard that was bad. I never figured why we wanted to fight the Chinese anyway."

"We didn't," I said. "That was another war."

"Oh. Well, I guess all wars are the same."

"Maybe so."

She sniffed. "If you wanna talk about it, I'll listen. I'm real good at listening."

"Thanks," I said, "but I don't want to talk about it."

"I'm glad there isn't a war today," she said, and I nodded. It wasn't going to do any good to try to drive her away. The last thing I needed was a scene.

"Look, you want a drink?" I asked.

She jerked her head like a reflex. "Yeah. Make mine a grasshopper. I like sweet drinks. Except sometimes I lose track and then they knock me on my ass."

I ordered for her.

"What's your name?" she asked. "Mine is Locksie."

"Don," I said.

"Hi, Don." She frowned then, catching sight of the right side of my face for the first time. "Hey, what happened to you? Did you get beat up?"

"Yeah," I said. "But I'm okay."

"Man, there's some creeps in the world," she declared. "Beating on a guy with one arm." She leaned forward. "Was it about dope?"

"Something like that."

She smiled. "I knew when I saw you, you were into the scene. Hey, it's okay. It makes you forget. I always try to forget too."

"What do you have to forget?" I asked, trying to keep the ragged conversation alive.

"Everything," she spat. "My old man, my mom, Doug Haney."

"Who?"

"My boss. I work at a loan office. He's a creep."

"So quit," I said.

"Look, I only got a GED. There ain't that many places to work in this town."

I raised my right hand to my drink and checked my watch. It was almost nine.

"Hey," she said, seeing me check the time. "You want to get

outta here? If you got some toot, we could go to my place. Play some music, dance some. Whatever you want."

"In a little while," I said. It was too early to give up. I'd stay to ten and then figure my hunch had been wrong.

"You wanna dance, then?" she asked. "Or you want something else?"

She reached over and walked her fingers across my thigh. When that didn't work she ran a finger down my spine. When it got to the small of my back her hand froze.

"Hey," she said. "You've got a gun. Are you a cop?"

"You ever seen a cop with a bad arm?" I asked.

She relaxed a little. "That's true. But look, man, if you're into something heavy . . ."

I thought she was going to split and more than ever I wanted her not to make a fuss, to keep sitting there talking as if nothing had happened.

Because when I raised my eyes to the mirror I saw Herman Villiere walk in.

Sixteen

I watched him make his way over to a table on the other side of the dance floor. The same blonde was leaning on him.

"I have a permit," I told the girl. "Sometimes I carry a lot of money."

"Oh." It took her a while to consider it. "You mean like payrolls and stuff."

"That's right. With just one good arm . . ."

"Sure, that's okay, I understand." She was instantly solicitous. "I didn't mean—"

"It's all right. But I was thinking now might be a good time to leave here, like we were talking about."

"Yeah." She started to get off her stool. "You do have some stuff?"

"No," I said. "That's what I was waiting for. The main man just came in."

"Who?" Her head swiveled.

"Don't look around. Just get up slowly."

We rose together and I led her around the far side of the dance floor, keeping lots of bodies between Villiere and ourselves. When we got to the door and the back of his head was just visible I leaned over and whispered in her ear.

"The man sitting there, to the left."

"Oh."

"I want you to go ask him if he has a red Ferrari parked outside. He'll say yes. Then tell him you ran into it."

"*What?*"

"Just do it. I'll take it from there."

"What is this, a kinda password or something?"

"You got it."

I left her and went outside, making my way to the first row of parked cars. I picked a van to stand behind. A few seconds later Herman Villiere came half running through the door and across the asphalt, with Locksie trailing behind him. He sped through the first row like a torpedo and angled off toward the end of the second row. I followed, going straight across to the second row of cars and then working my way toward the end between the bumpers. He beat me by fifteen seconds, and I saw him staring back at the girl with his hands on his hips, face red.

"Hey, what is this?" He craned his head to look at the side of his vehicle. "I don't see anything."

I stepped out of the shadows.

"It was a lie," I said. "Your car's fine. You're the one with the problem."

"What?" His mouth dropped open.

"Get lost," I told the girl. "This one's out of business."

"But—"

"Get lost," I repeated. When she saw I had the gun drawn, she didn't need another warning.

"Look, you," Villiere tried to bluster, but his eyes went down to the revolver like it was the only thing in the lot besides him.

"Throw me your keys," I said.

He fumbled and came up with a keychain.

"Just slide 'em across the roof."

"Man, that'll scratch the car."

"Probably. Do it anyway."

He did, and I unlocked the passenger door. Then I slid the keys back. "Open yours and get in."

"Look, man, you want money?"

"You wish."

He opened the door, but it took a little while because his hand was shaking, and when I'd slid in beside him, it took him longer to fit the key into the ignition.

"Now," I said, "drive."

"Where?"

"How about Norco?"

"Norco? Man, that's miles. That's—"

"Another parish."

"For God's sake, you wouldn't kill somebody over some fucking tires." It was a statement, not a question: he was too scared to ask because the answer might be yes.

"And don't go too fast," I said. "We don't want to get pulled over."

We got onto the interstate, headed west. Traffic had thinned by the time we reached the airport, and I had him take the off ramp, onto Williams. The airport was on our right now, and a big jet thundered in a hundred feet above us.

"Man," he said, and then swallowed his words when I prodded him with the pistol.

We reached Airline Highway and I motioned for him to go right, passing in front of the airport. We stopped at the traffic signal and I could see his mind working, but in thirty seconds he still hadn't thought of anything better than trying to get out into the traffic. I cocked the gun and he stopped with the door half open, then closed it. The light went green and we started forward again.

It was six or seven miles to Norco, a town built around a chemical plant. The plant made the air unfit to breathe, and a few years before it had blown up and killed some of the workers. But the state was in a depression and there were other workers willing to take their places. As I smelled the acrid fumes, I wondered what happened to the lungs if you grew up in such a place.

Villiere slowed for the light. Ahead was a green sign that pointed the way to the Bonnet Carré Spillway structure. Late in 1927, after New Orleans had its close call during the Big Flood, it was decided to build an outlet from the river to Lake Pontchartrain, five miles to the east. The spillway structure stretched like a low bridge for a mile on the northern edge of the town, across the grass-grown expanse that was the floodway in times of high water. It was a lonely area, with a few cows and occasional fishermen, spanned only by a narrow blacktop crosscut by a series of dirt tracks.

Dead bodies turned up there with monotonous regularity. It was a good place for a heart-to-heart talk.

We came to the levee, and I made him turn right. We were going uphill now, and the dark bulk of the structure rose in front of us. He saw where we were heading and gulped.

"Man, look," he said. "We can work this out."

"I know it," I said.

"If it's part of the action, see, we can fix that. If it's girls—"

"Keep your mouth shut until I ask you to talk," I said.

He licked his lips. "Look, I could run this thing off the bank, kill us both."

"You could. But I think even with the coke you've been snorting, dying doesn't sound like so much fun."

He didn't have an answer, and I was glad, because I'd been taking a chance: if he was high enough, he might not give a damn, feeling like Superman with a snow white cape. But my guess had been that he regularly went to Playtime to score, and that meant he'd been running on residuals, looking for his next hit. Not a fun guy to be with, much less to have behind the wheel of a car, but not yet at the point where he wanted to die, either. That would come later.

We came down off the embankment and into the floodway, with the spillway structure itself on the left.

"Turn onto this road," I said, pointing to a dirt trail on the right. The trail headed off toward the lake, passing under a couple of railroad trestles along the way.

"Man, don't do this," he said.

"You haven't given me a good reason not to," I said. The tires bumped in the ruts, and I was glad it hadn't rained in the last week. "Slow down," I said. "We don't want to get stuck."

The car came to a near halt and crept along the little dirt road, the chassis jarring with each rut. When we were far enough away from the blacktop, I told him to cut the lights and the engine.

"Oh, shit, man," he said, and I could see him shaking in the dark.

"Yeah. That's probably what Eddie Gulch said when he saw the ice pick."

"What do you mean?"

"You forgotten him already? You know who I mean. Eddie, the small-timer you hired to hit me. The man they found dead the day before yesterday."

His mouth came open and he tried to say something, but it took him a couple of tries. When he finally did manage to talk, it was in a near whisper.

"Man, I didn't hire nobody to do nothing to you. I heard the guy was dead, yeah, but it didn't have nothing to do with me. You gotta believe that."

"Why?"

"Because it's the fucking truth. Hey, you think I hired him to kill you? That's crazy: All I did was hire him to see why you came to me with that bullshit story about wanting to buy property. He followed up, that's all. He told me you were some kind of private detective, like him. I paid him off, and that was that. I figured you were probably working for old man Autry. That old fart's had it in for me for a long time, just because I started making him pay his rent on time."

I pressed the snout of the gun into his side and felt him trembling. "Why the hell would Gulch take a shot at me if you didn't order it?"

"How should I know? Maybe he was working for somebody else. I dunno. But I can't see that little asshole taking a shot at anybody, you ask me. I've used him before. Guns aren't his style. The guy's a weasel, I'm telling you."

"*Was,*" I admonished. "He's dead, remember?"

"Yeah. But I didn't do it. I read it in the goddamn paper. I wasn't nowhere around when that happened. I was at my place, asleep."

"In the afternoon, on a weekday?"

"Man, you see the hours I keep."

"And I guess the girl can corroborate it."

"What? Oh, yeah. If anybody would believe that silly cunt."

I lowered the hammer to give him a chance to stop shaking, but his tremors kept on, and I guessed it was all mixed in with his need for drugs now.

"Why would you put Gulch on me to start with? Why was I such a threat?"

He sighed, his hands squeezing the wheel like it was a life ring in a stormy sea. "Look, I got problems, see? I mean, business problems. I owe some money. There's people that are after me if I don't pay."

He didn't have to spell it out, because I'd already pretty much figured the situation. He'd been left a small fortune by his aunt, and in a couple of years he'd managed to squander just about all of it on coke and women. His office was a front, a place where he could claim he worked while he ran around selling off his inheritance. He'd been squeezing Cal because of his own shortfalls, and now he was into some people that didn't like to hear the word *no.*

"You figured I was working for one of them."

"Yeah, sure. I had you figured for some small-time shark, maybe somebody that bought some paper of mine. But I wasn't sure. Look, I've been trying to work things out, like, and it's been rubbing some people the wrong way."

"You've been dealing yourself, you're saying."

"Yeah. Nothing big, see, just a little bit, to try to make back some of what I lost. I buy it at Playtime and then I sell it to some folks I know, only now my contacts won't give me credit. I've gotta have cash. But the people I sell to have been poor-mouthing."

"Got you in a squeeze," I said.

"That's it."

"And by selling you've been moving onto somebody else's turf."

"Something like that. I had some threats, you know? So I had to know who you were working for."

"You ever heard of a man named George Guidry?"

It was a shot in the dark, and he just shook his head. "No. Should I? Did he hire you or something? Look, if it's money—"

"How about a black preacher named Condon?"

"Condon? Oh, yeah. The nig that wants to run the city." He turned his head a little, frowning. "You mean *he* hired you?"

"No." I cocked the revolver. "Well, you haven't been a lot of use to me, Herman."

He flinched and tried to flatten himself against his door, but there wasn't any place to go.

"Christ, man, you don't have to do this. I told you the truth. I don't know what Gulch did on his own time. I never trusted him anyway. You gotta ask *him* if you want to know about all that." A pause while he remembered Gulch was dead. "At least, you gotta ask somewhere else. I swear to God I told you everything."

"You ever have any other dealings with Calvin Autry besides his lease?"

"No, I told you."

"What's so important about the garage?" I demanded. "Why are you holding on to it and selling everything else?"

"Because, damn it, I've taken a beating on everything else I sold. You know how property values are. Now that old Autry's paying his rent regular, I might as well keep it. Besides . . ." He looked down at the floorboard. "I tried once or twice, and couldn't get any takers."

It had the sound of the truth, so I changed my tack. "Who's your main supplier at Playtime?"

"Fat guy called Turk. Cheap bastard. Thinks he's the only source in town. If I'd've known what slime I was dealing with, I'd of never started."

"Get a Life's a Bitch bumper sticker."

He waited, still shaking, and I let him sweat. A car passed a hundred yards away on the blacktop, but we might as well have been a thousand miles from civilization and he knew it. That's why I figured he was telling the truth. The trouble was that the truth I was hearing didn't help much.

"Who would want to kill Eddie Gulch?" I asked.

"How the fuck should I know? Anybody that dealt with him. He was a chiseler, nothing but mountaintop bullshit. He did peeper jobs and delivered packages, whatever paid. He probably got caught in some kind of feud."

"He didn't tell you anything about me that would help?"

"Man, all I got for my money was that Micah Dunn was some kinda small-change investigator who got mixed up in political things sometimes, like that crap with the congressman last year. Said you had one bad arm. Like I couldn't see that myself. Shit, most of what I paid for he got out of the city directory. I paid him two fifty for a day's work, and that's what I got for my trouble. I decided not to waste any more money."

He acted cheated, but that was his problem. Gulch had just done what most PIs do: use their sources. And a PI's best sources are available to the general public, except they don't know where to look.

"So you paid him off."

"I owed him. He acted pissed, but I didn't have it."

"Maybe you killed him to shut him up."

"Over a lousy two hundred and fifty dollars?"

"People have gone to the death house for less."

"I didn't do it."

And that was the bottom line.

"Start up and back out of here," I said. "You bought yourself another day."

Seventeen

*V*illiere pulled into the parking lot at Playtime and stopped.

"Just one more thing," I said.

He gave me a furtive look, as if afraid I might be getting ready to renege.

"You owe me for a tire. I figure it comes to sixty bucks."

He went for his wallet like a fast-draw artist, except that his hand was shaking too much for him to hold it steady. He thrust four twenties at me, peeling them from a roll that was obviously intended to buy coke.

"Is that enough?"

"It ought to do it," I said.

I pulled the keys from the ignition and got out.

"Hey," he yelled after me. "How am I supposed to move this thing?"

Ignoring him, I crossed over to the rental car. I drove two blocks down the boulevard and dropped the keys in a trash barrel.

I don't know what I'd expected from Villiere. Some kind of fumbling admission of guilt, maybe. But his story held together: he'd put Eddie Gulch on me because I'd shown up out of the blue and scared him, and a scare was the last thing he needed. He had no motive to try to kill me. Of course, he could have hired Gulch to miss on purpose, to scare me off, but how would he have known to call Taylor Augustine in order to set me up?

No, damn it, everything pointed to Gulch's acting on his own. Which meant somebody else had hired him. Which was a lot to swallow.

I rolled the window down and let the night wind hit me in the face. I had to rethink things. I was adding two and two, but the answer I was getting was five. That meant there was something else that belonged in the equation. But what?

It was eleven thirty when I parked in front of Katherine's house on Prytania. Her light was still on and I was only halfway up the walk when her door opened and she started out into the night. When she saw me she stopped short.

"Oh, God. I heard the car pull up and I thought maybe it was Scott."

"No word?" I asked.

She came to me, and I put my arm around her. For the first time since I'd known her, I felt her shaking with fear.

"Micah, I'm so damned scared."

"It'll be all right," I said, holding her tightly, but by now the words sounded hollow even to me.

"His car's gone," she said. "I tried all his friends and the professor he works for."

We went in and I closed the door behind me as if somehow by shutting out the night we were controlling the situation.

"Micah, we have to call the police."

I knew about missing persons, and how much attention it would get. I went over to the phone, looking at my watch. This time I connected with Mancuso at home.

"I'm sorry," I told him, "but something's come up. I need your help."

It must have been the tone in my voice, because he didn't come back with a wisecrack but just asked me what it was.

I told him about Scott.

"Well, there's not much we can do," he said. "It's a big city. Young people have been known to try to lose themselves, and it's not hard. Hell, don't tell Katherine, but he's probably shacked up with some girl. I would've been, at that age."

"He'd call," I said. "He wouldn't just drop out of sight."

"Well, give me his description, and the make and license number of his car, and I'll call it in, ask the patrol units to keep a look out. That's about all I can do."

I got the information on the car from Katherine and described Scott for him and gave him the number of his apartment.

"Okay, I'll pass it on," he said. "Hey, what's this about Gulch?" he suddenly asked. "You no sooner ask me about the guy than he turns up cold, and Fox turns up hot as a branding iron. You want to watch that guy, Micah. He's after you now, and I can promise, he won't turn loose till he gets you, fair means or not. *Plus* some ADA starts butting in before Gulch hardly gets to the morgue and starts telling Fox what to look for and what tests to run. If he wasn't pissed before, he's pissed out of his goddamn mind now."

"I'll bet," I told him. "By the way, what's the narcotics angle? Was Gulch dealing or just working for people in the business?"

"You'll have to ask somebody else. They keep those things under wraps."

"Right." I remembered Taylor Augustine. "Have you heard about the boy's uncle disappearing?"

"*What?*"

"That's right."

"I'll look into it," he said. "For whatever that's worth. I don't guess your buddy's ready to give himself up?"

"Calvin? I doubt it."

"Well, I can't say I blame him. If he's guilty, he hasn't got a thing in the world to gain."

"And if he's innocent?"

"I'd hate to have Fox on my ass, either way."

I said good night and turned to Katherine. "He'll put out the word," I said. "If Scott's around, they'll pick him up." My words didn't sound very convincing, even to me.

She came to me and pressed her face against my chest, shaking her head, and I felt the wetness of her tears.

"It'll be okay," I promised. And wished I believed it.

We went upstairs and lay together for a couple of hours, just touching each other, for comfort. I knew she wasn't asleep but was staring up into the darkness, as I was.

I kept running scenarios through my mind: somebody had picked Scott up and was holding him hostage, to get me off the case. But who? And why not make contact?

He had become the victim of a random act of violence, somewhere in the city. But I dismissed that one, because we were dealing with a disappearance, not a corpse.

And I kept coming back to the third possibility, the one almost as bad as the second, because it was a dead end, with no way out. He had blundered into something trying to be helpful, and now he couldn't get loose, either because he was a prisoner or because he was dead.

I cursed myself for not taking him seriously. I could have pulled him aside, given him some little useless, harmless task that made him feel needed.

Except that Scott was a bright kid. Too bright to be fooled or patronized.

"I shouldn't have been that way to him the other night," Katherine said then, and I didn't know if she was taking to me or to herself.

I started to answer but didn't, because I wasn't sure what to say. I felt her stiffen as a car went by in the street outside and I knew we were both listening for the same thing: tires brushing a curb; a door slamming, footsteps on the walk.

More time passed, and finally she shifted onto her side, away from me. I reached over to touch her, then drew my hand back. There wasn't anything I could do, and trying to soothe her wouldn't bring him back.

We were both still staring into the darkness from our separate cocoons hours later when the phone rang beside the bed, sending shards of ice stabbing into my guts.

I grabbed it, hoping it was just a hospital, that he was hurt but would survive: you can't ask for better when the phone rings at that time of night.

But it wasn't the hospital, it was Mancuso, his voice sleep-fogged.

"I told you I'd put out the word," he said. "I asked the shift supervisors to call me if anything turned up—"

"And?" My mouth was dry, and I sensed Katherine's panic as she strained to listen, not knowing who it was.

"I also called the Jefferson Parish Sheriff's Department."

I waited.

"They're the ones who turned it up."

"Turned up what, for God's sake?"

"His car. It was found abandoned on the other side of the river, in Westwego."

I closed my eyes, heart pounding. "Oh, God," I breathed.

"Micah?" Katherine was reaching for the phone now, but I kept it in my hand.

"It's his car," I said. "They found it in Westwego. What else?" I asked into the receiver, scared of the answer.

"Nothing else," the detective said. "It was in the Westwego Shopping Center lot. Must've sat there a day or two before they realized it had been dumped."

I relayed the news to Katherine and heard her inhale sharply. I didn't need to tell her that its being found in the shopping center wasn't a good sign; whoever had taken it had been trying to delay its being found. On the other hand, it showed the kind of foresight you don't find with street crime: Scott hadn't been robbed and killed so somebody could get some money for crack.

"What did you find with it?" I asked.

"I haven't been out there," he said. "I'm just getting dressed. If you want, I can swing by and take you both over."

I thought of red and blue cop lights strobing the night and the crime lab looking for traces of blood, and how it would all affect Katherine. And I knew it didn't matter; she wasn't about to stay here.

"We'll be waiting," I said.

We crossed on the Huey P. Long Bridge, no one speaking, because our fears spoke loudly enough. Behind us the city was a sea of blinking lights. The West Bank stretched out ahead, and I knew that somewhere in the mass of headlights and neons was a small drama about to be acted out by tired cops, who would do their thing and then go home to bed and forget. But Katherine would never forget, and I sensed the distance between us growing.

There were two sheriff's cars, the patrol unit, and the sergeant. No flashing lights, because at three in the morning whatever had happened was history and there was no urgency now.

Scott's white Mustang sat between the two police cars, looking as if he might have just gotten out and gone to search for an all-night burger joint. There was a dent in the right side, but it had been there when he'd gotten the car used, two years ago. He'd always meant to have it fixed, but the money hadn't been there.

Mancuso introduced us to the deputies. He seemed to hunch down into his windbreaker. No, they had nothing to report. They'd found the car an hour and a half ago. The engine was cold and the doors were locked. There were no obvious signs of violence. Had it been here yesterday? Nobody could remember. Tomorrow the detectives would talk to people in the shopping center to see if anybody had noticed.

Mancuso walked around the car like a tiger stalking a tethered goat. I followed, my eyes on the ground, but other than a couple of cigarette butts there was nothing. And the butts could have been left by anyone.

Mancuso gave Katherine a guilty look and cleared his throat. "I'd like to have the forensics people look it over."

The sergeant, a thick man with a red face, nodded. "We'll have to tow it to the yard."

"Right." Mancuso turned toward us, his expression apologetic. He jacked his head for me to follow him and went to the edge of the lighted area.

"We really ought to look in the trunk," he said.

I'd been waiting for it, but it still made my stomach do a flip-flop. I nodded and went back to Katherine.

"Let's walk over this way," I told her, but her hand came out and grabbed my arm like a talon.

"Why? What are they going to do?"

I exhaled and made myself say it: "They want to check the trunk."

She nodded, and warning lights went on in my mind, because her calmness was the kind that you see in people before the full import of a tragedy has sunk in.

"Then let them open it," she said, her voice unusually high. "I can stand it."

Helpless, I nodded to Mancuso, who went back to the deputies.

One of them opened the trunk of one of the patrol units and removed a tire tool. Then he went over to the trunk of the Mustang.

A few seconds, I thought, and everything will be changed; this world of Katherine and her softness and the nights in her arms, and the comfort of having a place to come home to—it will all be gone, or if not gone, then changed so terribly that neither of us will recognize it again. And then I thought of Scott and felt guilty for thinking of myself.

The deputy thrust in the tire tool and pried. The trunk lid emitted a crack and sprang upward. I forced my eyes to stay open, and I tried to sense what the police were feeling by looking at their faces. But there was no apparent change.

"You want to come over here?" one of them asked us.

I took Katherine's hand and we walked over, numb.

"Do you know if anything's missing?" he asked.

I looked down. I saw a tire, some plastic containers of Quaker State oil, and a blanket. Letting out a long, shaky breath, I looked over at Katherine, to see if she was steady. I needn't have worried.

"It looks all right," she said, her voice back in a normal register. "But, then, I don't know what he keeps in there."

The cops nodded at the logic of it and shut the trunk. One of them went to call a wrecker.

"I'll take them home." Mancuso said.

I held the car door open for Katherine and climbed in after her. As we took a left turn onto Fourth, she fell against me and stayed that way for the rest of the ride.

He hadn't been in the trunk, so maybe our luck would hold, I told myself, and then remembered guys who'd thought that way in Nam and gone home in body bags.

Mancuso let us out in front of her house.

"Get some sleep," he advised. "I'll call you as soon as I hear anything." I knew what he meant, of course: *if we find bloodstains or pieces of human tissue inside the car.*

I thanked him and helped her up the walk. Once in, she went to the kitchen and fixed coffee. It was four o'clock, and there was a mist hugging the streets and houses. Another hour or so and it would start to turn grey as another day started. I didn't want to think about what that day might bring.

I took the cup Katherine brought me and tried to think.

There was only one thing I could think of now: Cal. It was Cal who'd started it all.

I turned to face her. "I have to go somewhere," I said.

"What?"

"Trust me," I said, but my words sounded hollow, even to me.

"Micah, do you know where he is?"

"No. But I can't sit here if there's somebody out there who might be able to help."

Before she could protest I was out the door, and heading down the path to the rental car, the anger growing in me with each passing second. Part of it was irrational, I knew, a drowning man's fury at seeing his whole world for the last time before plunging back into the depths. And part of it was resentment at having my concern for a friend turned against me by some force I could only sense.

Action was the only antidote.

I slid through the mist, anonymous, cold, like a shark at the bottom of an ocean, now and again passing another swimmer, whose yellow eyes blinked at me and then were gone. I found the freeway entrance and crept to the top, through the fog, vaguely aware that these were the worst possible conditions in which to be on the interstate. But it didn't matter. I wrestled the rental car off the ramp, swaying just a little as I reached the top, my hand slipping on the unfamiliar wheel. I headed northeast, toward the lake, the speedometer creeping up to fifty, braking as the lights of eighteen-wheelers appeared suddenly in the soup, then overtaking them. Somehow the challenge of it all was satisfying, as if the fog was a foe that I could pit myself against and defeat. It was a dangerous way to think.

By the time I reached Oak Island I thought the fog had lightened a shade, but it might have been my imagination. I don't like the fog: it reminds me of recon missions, squatting beside a trail with my M-16 across my knees, waiting. Hoping that the next movement in the mists would be a shift of wind or an animal, something you could deal with, and not death. The fog had always been the foe.

I found the street and went slowly, having trouble distinguishing the houses. Then I saw the blue pickup and knew I was in the right place. I parked and got out and made my way up the walk to the door, hammering on it for three minutes until he pulled it open and stood staring at me from bloodshot eyes.

"God damn it, Melville, I want to talk to your father and I want to talk to him now. I've got a gun and I'm in a bad mood, and I hope the hell for your sake you won't give me any shit."

Eighteen

*H*is mouth fell open. He started to say something, but I shoved past him, slamming the door behind me and stalked into the living room. There was a fireplace with a gun rack mounted on the wall above it and a coffee table with a house brand of Bourbon standing next to a glass. A bell rang in my mind, but I didn't have time to examine what it was trying to tell me.

"Man," he began, but I had my finger in his face.

"I want you to take me to your father," I repeated. "I know he isn't here because the cops will have looked here first, and they don't build secret chambers in houses like this one. But he can't be far. And I want to see him. *Now.*"

He pointed at the wall clock. "You know what time it is?"

"It won't get easier later," I said, "and I'm not going to go away."

A woman came around the corner into the living room, blond, holding her robe together with one hand. "Melville, what the hell? The kids are gonna wake up."

"It ain't nothing, darling," he said.

"It's plenty," I said. "Now let's go."

He started to double his fist, but my hand went to the gun in my belt. His fist relaxed.

The woman gasped. "Melville, is this about your old man?" she asked, hugging the wall. "I told you this wouldn't be nothing but trouble. For Christ's sake, take the man to him. It ain't worth getting shot over."

"Nobody's getting shot, Lou Anne. This is between friends."

"Friends?" She gave a hoarse laugh and turned on her heel. "Then I'd hate to see enemies," she said over her shoulder. A door slammed down the hall behind her.

Melville flushed red. "You see now? She's pissed off."

"That makes two of us." I could tell he knew I wouldn't shoot him, and too much time had passed for me to maintain the advantage of momentum. I had to use another ploy. I looked up at the gun rack and found it.

"Melville, I swear to God I'll blow a hole right through that Browning of yours, right in the middle of the hand-carved stock."

His eyes went big in horror. *"No."*

I cocked the gun and aimed it at the rifle.

"Shit, man, *no!*" He jumped in front of me. "Okay, I'll take you." He shuffled over to a closet and took out a windbreaker. "He's gonna eat out my ass for this, though."

All at once he was a little boy again, contemplating his father's wrath, and I knew I wouldn't have any more trouble with him. I pulled open the door and pointed out the car, and he went ahead of me like a sheepdog.

We took Discovery Boulevard south, heading for Chef Menteur Highway. The low scrub poked through the fog like skeletal arms.

"I got him at a construction site where I used to work," Melville said. "They were gonna make a subdivision, but the contractor went bankrupt and the whole thing shut down."

I managed a nod. There were plenty of places like that in today's Louisiana, where the good times had stopped rolling in 'eighty-six when the oil glut hit and the economy fell apart.

"Here." He pointed, and I had to brake hard to see the road on my left.

We found ourselves in something that resembled an old movie

set, with ghostly houses whose walls remained propped up by timbers, and cleared lots where nothing grew but gray mist.

"It's down here at the end," he said. "Flash your lights a couple of times so he'll know who it is."

I did as he said and then glided into a driveway next to a two story town house that had been abandoned halfway along.

"There's no watchman?" I asked.

Melville snorted. "There's an old man who checks once or twice a night, but he's too drunk to know where he is half the time."

We got out, and I followed him up the walkway. I had a feeling I didn't like, a sensation of being exposed. Even with the fog we were both good targets, if somebody had a mind to kill us.

But I fought back my misgivings. Nobody was expecting us here, so what was there to be afraid of? Unless Calvin got spooked and started shooting. He still had that .22, and though it wasn't much of a gun, it would do until a better one came along.

"Pop." Melville stood in the side doorway, where the door should have been. I strained to look past him into the dark interior. "Pop, it's me, Melville. You there?"

There was no answer, and my hand went down instinctively to touch the comfort of the .38.

"Damn it, he's got to be here," Melville said. "I brought him dinner at eight o'clock." He stepped into the house and I followed, smelling sawdust and paint. "Hey, Pop."

There was another smell here, faint but still perceptible: the odor of perspiration and old food. The smell of human habitation.

"That old bastard," Melville swore. "I told him not to wander off."

I took the penlight out of my shirt pocket and played it off the walls, going from room to room in turn. There was nothing downstairs but some old wrappers from fast food and a 1988 *Penthouse* with the cover torn away, traces, I surmised, of the last transient that had stayed there. I shot the light up the stairway and tested the first step. It seemed solid and I started up. It was a hell of a place to be, I thought: on a stairway I was dead meat for anybody at the top or bottom.

"Where you going?" Melville called.

"To see what's up here," I said.

"He ain't up there," Melville pronounced, and kicked the floor.

I came to the top and walked down the hallway, whose bare ribs, without the wallboards, made me think of the bars of a jail cell. Melville was right: there was nothing up there.

I started down. Just as I reached the bottom step I heard the movement in the doorway. I dropped my light, my hand going for my revolver, and then I heard Melville utter an oath.

"Shit," he swore. "Don't *do* that!"

A figure flickered in the doorway and then vanished inside.

"How the hell I know who you was?" Calvin Autry shot back. "Weren't no car I recognized out there, so I went out the back way. Who you got with you, anyhow?"

"Me," I said, stepping toward him. "Micah Dunn."

"Micah?" He came toward me, and a flashlight threw glare in my face. "What the hell are you doing here?"

All the anger that had been building since I'd left Katherine's came roaring back.

"I'll tell you what the hell I'm doing here," I said. "You hired me to help you and I did my best. You paid me back by running away, making yourself look guilty, whether you are or not. And leaving me out on a limb."

"You wasn't out on no limb," Cal said. "It wasn't your hide."

"You're wrong about that," I said. "I've been shot at, brought in by the cops, and shown on television trying to pass a bribe. And now somebody I care about is missing and may be dead. So don't you fucking tell me I don't have any stake."

Calvin backed up a step. "I don't know about none of that," he said.

"No? Well, why the hell don't you tell me just what you *do* know? I'm tired of games, and I want some straight answers."

I could sense him shrink back in the darkness. "I told you the truth," he said. "Did you check out them people I told you?"

"I checked 'em, everybody but NOPSI, and your're right, they're some pretty shady types, but they didn't do this."

"Why didn't you check NOPSI?"

"Because," I exploded, "the goddamn New Orleans Public Service doesn't have to shoot and kidnap people to get paid, they just cut you off, that's why!"

"But I wrote my congressman about 'em."

"See?" Melville said under his breath. "See what I mean?"

"See what?" Calvin demanded. "You shut up, Melville. I'm your old man, and I'm still big enough to knock shit outta you."

"Both of you shut up," I said. "Calvin, I want to know what you were so sensitive about when you were a kid that you wouldn't take showers with the others in high school. I want to know what you got into a fight with another boy about; what made you so mad you damn near killed him and had to leave town?"

Melville took a step away from his father. *"What?"*

"So you raked all that up, did you?" Calvin asked, his tone a mixture of hurt and anger. "You had to go poking into things forty years old."

"It's my job," I said.

"Your job is to get me off the hook, 'cause I'm innocent. That's your job."

"Answer the question," I said.

I heard him breathing hard. For a second I thought he might rush me, and I tensed, but instead he just exhaled heavily.

"Okay, I'll answer. But I want you to know what I think about you. I counted you my friend, and I trusted you. The way I see it, a friend don't go suspecting another friend. But I see now how it is. You ain't my friend. You think I did it. That's why you're here."

"That's not true," I said. "But I need to know everything."

"Everything," he snorted. "You and this boy of mine are about the same, the way I see it. Ain't neither of you worth a shit."

"Pop," Melville started, but I cut him off.

"I want the answer," I said.

He nodded. "All right. You'll get your goddamn answer." He spat on the ground and kicked the earth. "Where I grew up it wasn't like the goddamn city," he said. "Out there people said what they had a mind to say. People wasn't kind to you when they talked. They told it the way it was. If a kid was different, he got told so, right out. I remember this little fat kid in our class. He had a name, Everett P. Kittridge. But he was just called Fatty. That's how it was. You didn't get no chance to like it or not. . . ." His voice trailed off.

"It ain't easy to be told when you're twelve years old you're gonna be different the rest of your life," he began again after a long silence "But I didn't have no choice. It was the accident, see."

"The accident?" Melville said. "I never heard of no accident."

" 'Cause I didn't tell you," Calvin said. "I didn't tell nobody, except your mother. And that hurt enough."

"What kind of accident, Calvin?" I asked him.

"Fell on a pitchfork. Ripped me right here." He clutched his groin. "Doctor said wasn't no good to try to save it, a man had two of 'em, only needed one. Sewed me back up. But there was a scar. And you don't keep things quiet in a little place like that." He squinted over at me. "How would you like to be called names?" He coughed. "Oh, there was a lot of jokes. I was growing up then. I couldn't stand the things they said."

"What did they say?" I asked.

"All kinds of crap. You name it. I ought to join the priesthood, I should stick to farm animals. I ought to try boys cause I wouldn't never satisfy no real woman. I—"

He halted, suddenly conscious of what he'd said.

"But I didn't, damn it. It didn't make no difference. You coulda asked Marie. She was satisfied with me. While we was together, we was happy. She said I was a real man, as much a man as anybody she ever met."

"You said you argued," his son said.

"But not about that, damn it."

"Then why did she leave?" Melville persisted.

"Goddamn it, I don't know why she left. She didn't say. She just said she was leaving. A one-line note, it was. Hell, maybe I didn't make enough money for her. Your mother had rich blood, boy.

She didn't think too much of me running a damn garage. She always talked about California. So I reckon she finally just up and went there. People . . ." He spat again. "You just never know what's in their minds. No matter how well you think you know 'em."

I stood there, feeling the morning cold creep into my bones, unsure whether to laugh or cry. It was a good story, but something still bothered me, something I'd seen in Melville's house. I was trying to summon up the image when we all heard it at the same time: a noise from outside.

Cal was at the door in half a second, gun in hand.

"What was it?" Melville asked.

It came again, only this time from behind us, in the kitchen area. I went for my flashlight, but before I reached it the room exploded into burning daylight.

Running footsteps pounded the hard earth outside, and I heard somebody yell for everybody to freeze. Cal uttered an oath, and in the split second before he fired, my eyes met his and I flinched at their accusation.

A volley of shots answered Cal's challenge, and I saw him fly backward against the doorframe. I started toward him but something slammed me to the dank earth floor.

I tried to rise, but a foot pressed me back down, and somebody yanked my good hand behind me and I felt the cold bite of handcuffs. I tried to pick out Cal's voice, to convince myself that what I'd seen had been distortion, that they'd really missed, but all I heard was Melville pleading, yelling for them not to shoot, and cop voices telling everybody to stay where they were and somebody else saying to get an ambulance and somebody else saying not to worry about the ambulance, to call the coroner.

Fox's voice.

Nineteen

The weight lifted from my back, and I managed to get to my knees. Fox was staring down at Cal Autry's crumpled body, a grim smile on his face. The cop next to me yanked the handcuff to keep me back, and I let out a curse.

Fox looked over in my direction, his eyes half hooded like those of a predator after a meal. "Let him go," he said, his voice suddenly silky. "He did what we needed him to. We need him again, we can always send the street cleaners."

Grinding my teeth, I looked over at Melville. He was cowering in a corner under a cop's shotgun.

"What about this one?" one of the cops said. "Harboring?"

Fox shook his head. "Nah. I got what I want." He gave Cal's body a nudge, and that was when the man on the ground groaned.

Fox drew back his foot as if it had been bitten and several of the men uttered oaths.

"Damn you," I yelled, "he's alive." I started toward him, but hands reached out and held me. A detective stooped down and turned Cal over.

"We better call the meat wagon, Lou."

Fox bit his lip, chagrin showing all too plainly on his face. "Yeah, okay." He turned around and walked back through the empty door-way into the mist.

"Let me go to him," I begged, and the cops holding me released their grip. I went over to Cal and knelt down beside him. "Cal, can you hear me?"

His eyelids fluttered and his eyes wandered over to focus on me.

"Cal, we'll get help. I promise."

His eyes narrowed slightly and his lips struggled to form a word. I leaned close and waited, and after what seemed an eternity it came out, barely audible, but with all the force of a Magnum bullet: "*Sellout.*"

The ambulance arrived fifteen minutes later, and I watched them huddle over him and then strap him to a stretcher and slide him inside. The ambulance roared away, its lights blurred by the fog, its siren wailing like the cry of some prehistoric creature. Men came with cameras and took pictures, and the original detectives pushed us aside, and only after what seemed an interminable period did somebody come forward to take our statements, one at a time.

The detective hadn't been present when the shooting had happened, and I guessed he was part of the shooting team that would ultimately make a recommendation about whether the force used had been necessary or excessive. I told him the truth, too tired to worry by this time. I'd like to have stuck it to Fox, but the truth was that Calvin had pulled his gun, and there was no way to get around the fact that the cops had shot an armed fugitive. I couldn't hang Fox for his smile or the look on his face when he'd found Cal was still alive; the best thing I could do was lamely complain that no attempt had been made to ascertain his condition until at least a minute after the shooting, and I knew that was small potatoes.

Then the detective threw in the spanner: "What about the cocaine?"

Melville was standing ten feet away, looking miserable, and I tried to read his features, but there was nothing in them I could make sense of.

"What cocaine?" I asked.

"The search team found a bag of crack cocaine in the back of the house."

"I wouldn't know about that." I thought for a minute. "Maybe somebody who was here before left it. Maybe the house was a stash place for drug deals."

The cop grunted and told me I'd be expected downtown to sign my statement. I told him I was dead on my feet; that I'd been shoved face down into the dirt and I felt like vomiting. He was unimpressed. So I followed them downtown in the rental car with the gray sky now giving way to burned orange behind us in the east, and the fog congealing into wisps.

The cocaine didn't make any sense. But I was tired, too tired to think, and there were a lot of things that didn't make any sense, things like Eddie Gulch's killer walking across the lobby under the eye of a watching cop and not being seen. But now I remembered what I had seen in Melville's house that had troubled me: it was the whiskey bottle that had been on his coffee table. My mind told me *that* made sense, but right now I was too far gone to understand where it fit in.

It took another hour at the detective bureau, and then they told me to go home and warned me not to leave their jurisdiction. I got into the rental car and drove back to my place.

It was just after seven in the morning when I got home. I looked back over my shoulder at the car as I went inside; after I'd gotten some sleep I'd go over it inch by inch for coke or anything else Fox might have planted to get me off the case. But I guessed there was nothing, or they'd have pulled a search earlier.

Cal had been set up, though why was beyond me. I stumbled into the front room and dialed Katherine's number. She answered, as I'd known she would, before the end of the first ring.

"It's me," I said wearily. "Everything's okay. No news. I'll get back to you as soon as I can."

"Micah, what happened? Where did you go?"

"I'll explain tomorrow," I said, realizing dully that it was already tomorrow. "Promise."

I hung up and went into the bedroom, where I fell onto the bed without taking off my clothes.

They must have had Melville's house staked out, I thought as I drifted toward unconsciousness. Ordinarily he would have driven around, shaken them, before going to where his father was. But I'd scared him too badly, and he'd led me straight there. Cal thought I'd set him up. It hurt like an open wound, knowing that there was no way to explain, to tell him I hadn't. Because in a real sense I *had*: by demanding that his son take me there in the middle of the night I'd thrown caution to the wind, and I hadn't paused to think about what Cal's response would be because I was too worried about Scott. Thanks to me, an innocent man had been shot.

Well, you can't have everything, a little voice said inside me.

Yeah, said its companion, but you've been screwing up by the numbers. First Condon, and now Cal. What'll you do next?

I don't know, I told myself.

Yes, you do, said one of the voices. You know where to look. Only don't fire all barrels this time. Cunning. That's what you need.

Cunning, the other voice said. Take a lesson from Condon. Condon?

I awoke at eleven, feeling drugged. A mishmash of dreams sorted themselves out and I tried to make sense of them. Mouth dry, I got up and went to the refrigerator for some milk.

I hadn't any liquor and yet I felt drunk. Almost as if I'd had the bottle instead of Melville.

The bottle. Of course.

The label had been a house brand. But not a common one, like K&B, which was sold at all the Katz and Besthof drugstores in New Orleans, or Schwegmann's, which was sold by the supermarket chain. It was one I'd only seen once, several days ago, while walking among the racks in a converted house on Magazine, not interested in alcohol, my mind anywhere but on the rows of bottles in front of my eyes.

The bottle on Melville's table had come from the wineshop owned by the Spiderwoman.

A wave of nausea swept through me. I reached for the milk carton and downed half of it.

Katherine would be half crazy by now, and I wasn't helping her. I hoped she knew that the only good I could do was by following things on my own. But she also knew it was my profession and my having lapsed by talking over my case in a social situation that had brought matters to this pass.

Maybe, days from now, when things were resolved . . . But I didn't dare think about it. The future was never, and all that mattered was now.

My phone rang. I stared at it and lifted the receiver slowly, afraid of what I might hear.

"Yes?"

"Micah?" It was Katherine's voice, and a shiver passed over me.

"What is it? Has something happened?"

"It's Scott," she breathed, in a voice almost too low for me to hear. "He just called."

"Called? You mean he's all right?"

"Yes—no. I mean, they're holding him. That's what he said. 'Mom, they've got me. Tell Micah he was right.' And then it sounded like another voice and a scuffle of some sort and the line went dead. Micah, for God's sake—"

"I know," I told her. "But at least he's still alive. If they haven't killed him by now, they probably won't." There was no basis in fact for that, but she needed to hear it.

"But what can we do?"

"I'll take it from here," I said. For a few seconds I debated calling Mancuso and asking for a warrant on the wineshop and on the Spiderwoman's home. But I didn't know where she lived, and Scott hadn't implicated her directly. If she had pull, a friendly judge might delay signing long enough for her to dump Scott. If she lived out of the parish, she might be able to call on local authorities for help: Plaquemines and St. Bernard parishes were about as famous for good government as New Orleans.

No, there were too many ifs in dealing with the legal bureaucracy. This would have to be extralegal.

I hunted up my telephone directory and found the number I wanted. When a voice answered, I asked for the Reverend Condon and gave my name.

The voice didn't respond, just left me in silence for five minutes. Finally I heard a shuffle of footsteps, and Condon's voice came on the line.

"Mr. Dunn. You're the last person I expected to hear from. You aren't going to threaten me, are you?"

"Not this time. I called for your help."

Half a heartbeat. "Are you serious?"

"Why not? You wanted me out of the way because you have

interests to protect. I have interests to protect too. I think the same person's threatening us."

"I'm listening."

I told him about Taylor Augustine. "I've got to know if you have him stashed somewhere," I said.

"Just a minute," he said. I heard muffled noise, and I imagined he had his hand over the mouthpiece. A minute passed, then two. Finally he spoke again.

"I asked my people, to see if anybody got too enthusiastic on their own. And the answer is no."

"Then somebody's grabbed him," I said. "The same person that shot at me, and the same person that killed the boy."

"Your main man: Calvin Autry," he said.

"Calvin would have had to have been everywhere," I said. "All with the cops a step behind him." I told him about where I'd found Cal early this morning, and what had happened. "And now somebody else is missing," I said.

He listened while I explained about the wineshop and its proprietress.

"I've got a feeling Taylor Augustine knows something about all this and that's why he's been gotten out of the way. But I have to find him: if he does know something, it may be the only way to get Scott back, if they're holding him."

"Sounds like your white boy got himself in a peck of trouble," the minister said.

"That's right. But he may not be the only one."

Silence. Then, "You want me to find Taylor Augustine," he said.

"If you can. I know I can't, and maybe you can't either. But maybe his sister saw something, or he told her something, who knows?"

"All right. You got it. Is that all?"

"Actually, no." I told him I needed a couple of his men.

"A robbery?" he asked, when I'd finished explaining. "Okay, man, you got it," he said again. The phone went dead.

I stared down at the desktop. The Spiderwoman. Francine Le-

Jeune. That was all that made sense. Scott must have blundered into her operation, and she had snatched him.

I'd gone after Cal to see if he knew her, and a bottle of whiskey had told the story: if Cal didn't know her, his son did. That left only the LeJeune woman herself now. It was too late to get anything out of Cal, and I didn't have any more time to fool with Melville. I'd have to approach her cold, which is what I should have done to begin with. Would have done, if I'd been thinking clearly, had been less angry, less certain Cal would cave in when he saw me and tell me about her operation.

My Polk's directories for New Orleans and the New Orleans suburbs listed no Francine LeJeune for the city or the suburbs, but there were plenty of LeJeunes. I put the books away and tried to decide which way to go. It was Sunday, and the government offices were closed, which meant no access to property books. That only left one way.

I washed my face, combed my hair, and then went down the outside steps to my car, parked beside the rental machine. I wasn't worried about being followed now; I'd pretty well botched that part of the operation. Fox was happy, he had his man, and he'd be too busy trying to hang Gulch's murder on Cal to be thinking about me. I took Esplanade to Claiborne and Claiborne to Napoleon. From there it was a straight shot south to Magazine and only a few blocks to the wineshop.

I drove slowly past, checking the single car in the driveway. It was a red Caprice with a New Orleans plate. Not, I judged, the kind of car Francine LeJeune would drive.

I made the block, trying to blink away the sand under my eyelids. My mind kept fading whenever I tried to focus. Finally I gave up. There was no other way. I had to do it.

A few blocks over was a fastfood place, and I got a burger and coffee to go. While I was waiting I called Condon and told him to send his troops and when I hung up I knew there was no going back. I drove back to the wineshop and parked across the street.

I watched customers come and go. The big rush was on Friday and Saturday nights; Sundays were slower, so much so the place shut down at two in the afternoon. The clients now were mostly upscale couples, in to get wine for lunch or dinner, coming back out with their bottles in plastic carrying bags. By one o'clock I had counted fifteen customers, with an hour left before the shop closed for the day. But the Spiderwoman had yet to show up.

There had to have been an easier way, I told myself.

Too late to worry, I argued back.

At one twenty a police car drove up, and one of the cops went inside. I went cold all over, cursing them for their laxness. They weren't being paid to buy tonight's six-pack on city time; hadn't anybody told them that?

But finally, an interminable seven minutes later, the cops drove off.

It was a felony, no matter how you looked at it. The last thing I needed was to compound it with a shootout.

Why the hell didn't she come? It would all be so simple then: take her license number, get it run for an address, go there . . .

At one forty-five two black men opened the door and went inside. I put my head back against the seat and closed my eyes. Six minutes later there was a shot, followed by three more in quick succession. I felt something inside me spasm, and I knew this had been the worst idea I'd ever had.

Twenty

The door of the store flew open, and the two men came running out, their guns in their hands. I watched them vanish down the sidewalk and heard a powerful engine start. Three minutes later the first police car swung into the driveway, its blue flasher going, and I wondered if the same cop I'd seen before would get out, but these were two different ones. They ran inside, guns drawn, and a few seconds later another cruiser pulled up, blocking the street behind me. One of the first cops appeared in the doorway of the wineshop and yelled something I didn't catch.

For the next half hour it was a circus. The detectives came, a pair I'd seen around but didn't know well enough to speak to. But it wasn't the cops I was interested in. It was the gray-haired woman getting out of the maroon Lincoln, walking toward the front door, stopping to talk to the policeman, and going inside.

She was wearing pearls, high heels, and a fur piece and I wondered if she sat around the house like that or whether she'd dressed just to come to a robbery.

I could imagine the scene inside right now, with the white-faced clerk explaining that it had all been very weird, the two black men had drawn pistols, made her lie on the floor, and she was sure it was a robbery, but even though they pulled the cash drawer out there didn't seem to be anything missing, and the shots had only damaged some bottles on the shelves. They'd made a mess of course, spilling things off the counter and even ransacking the office in the back. Maybe that's where they thought the real money was. And Francine LeJeune, her face tight, would go to the back office and look around at the clutter of papers all over the floor and the over-turned chair and realize it was impossible, just now, to know what was missing, if anything was.

It would only be hours later that she would be sure that the address book was gone. Or the card file. Or whatever medium might be used for keeping such information. If they had found it. As they were supposed to.

Except that now I wasn't sure I needed it, because the so-called robbery itself had done the job, drawn the Spiderwoman here, and as she climbed back into her Lincoln, I knew it was only a matter of my following, and I was glad I had my own car now, to wrestle in and out of traffic.

She probably wouldn't expect to be followed. Holdups shake people, and her mind would still be on what had happened at the shop—if she was an ordinary person. But that was an assumption I couldn't make, I reminded myself. She wasn't ordinary; she was the Spiderwoman, and what ran in her veins was colder than ice.

So I hung back, letting her get four cars ahead on Magazine and speeding through a yellow light as I followed her left onto Louisiana, hoping there were no cops nearby.

It could be a wild goose chase, of course, but it was the only chance I had. The two "robbers" had also been looking for Scott, and they obviously hadn't found him at the shop.

She was headed for Claiborne and probably the expressway. I had gotten her license number when she went past, but I didn't want to wait for it to be run. Still, if I lost her, at least I had something.

I cursed myself for not having a car phone. The damn things were expensive, and very little of my work involved instant communications; I used a handheld radio when I needed to contact somebody on a stakeout. But right now I could have used a telephone on the seat next to me. Well, it didn't do any good to wish.

She was on the interstate now, and I followed, rising above the city, the Superdome falling behind on the left. But she surprised me, leaving the freeway after a couple of miles for Claiborne again where it headed east, toward the Ninth Ward and the Inner Harbor Navigation Canal.

I followed her, weaving my way through the old Holy Cross district, an assemblage of shotgun houses tenanted mostly by blacks. In one of the houses, I rememberd vaguely, Fats Domino had been born, and a thread of the old tune "Walkin' to New Orleans" popped up in my brain.

At the St. Bernard line, where the parish of Orleans ends, Claiborne changes abruptly to Judge Perez Drive, which says something about relative views of greatness. Claiborne was an influential governor in the last century; Perez was a segregationist despot in this one. He'd ruled Plaquemines Parish with an iron hand for about thirty years, and they'd thought highly of him in neighboring St. Bernard Parish, as well. He'd threatened to run an electric fence along the parish line, to keep out blacks and feds. For his trouble he was excommunicated by the Church, but when he died in 1968, he got a requiem mass, because, some suggested, in Louisiana even God takes bribes.

Why did I think the Spiderwoman and Judge Perez might have been political allies?

We were in Chalmette now, not far from the place where Jackson had defeated Packenham in 1815, with the help of a bunch of trappers and some pirates. The British had made the mistake of advancing over an open field, against musketry and artillery; I hoped I wasn't about to make a mistake just as bad.

She took Paris Road south, to Highway 46, which ran alongside the river, all the way to Poydras, site of a succession of levee breaks that had helped save New Orleans up until this century, when the government finally built the spillways. You only survived along the river at somebody else's expense. I thought: his broken levee was your good luck, because it gave the surging waters somewhere to go besides your own land. It was a dog-eat-dog attitude, and I wondered idly if it might not have something to do with the way some people still operated.

We were well out of Chalmette, almost to Meraux, the first in the series of small communities that lined the river, when ahead of me she turned in. I slowed.

It was a plantation house, set back two hundred yards from the road, with a lawn shaded by pecan trees. I saw her car winding its way up the drive and noted the two-foot-high brick wall supporting a wrought iron fence, reflecting as I drove past the already closed front gate, that she must have an automatic device to open and shut it.

I went another half mile, found a farm road, and turned around. From here I could see the big house, set off by itself, with the wall running completely around the property. It was the kind of wall you put up for ornamentation, or to divide your property from somebody else's, not the kind that effectively keeps people out. I wondered if there was an alarm for that.

Two ways in, I thought: the front or through the fields. There wasn't any cover in front, but the fields were thick with cane, almost ready for harvest. That pretty well decided it.

I went on to Meraux, found a pay phone, and called Sandy. "I need some backup," I said. Then I told her what I was planning to do.

"Micah, you're crazy," she said.

"I know. But I can't think of anything else."

"You're gonna get caught, and that'll be it, man."

"If Scott's in there, it's worth the risk."

"You may not be dealing with Gabe Condon this time; did you think of that?"

"I know I'm not. Look, can you come?"

"Wouldn't miss it for the world. Should I bring a black mask?"

"No. I'll do the dirty work. I just want you for stakeout and backup."

"*What?* You planning to be the first one-armed cat burglar?"

"Something like that," I mumbled. Then I told her what to get at my office.

An hour and a half later she met me near the pay phone. I'd been back a couple of times, cruising past to ensure nothing had changed. More than that I couldn't do without arousing suspicion. We only had two more hours until dark. I got the phone book and went through the *Ls* but there was no LeJeune listed for the area.

"Call Directory Assistance and get the number of the wineshop," I said to Sandy. "My guess is they're still open, so call whoever's there and tell them you're with the insurance company; that Mrs. LeJeune reported a robbery earlier and you need to call her back. Make sure you get her home number."

She nodded and put a quarter in the phone, and a few seconds later I heard a very concerned insurance adjuster asking for information. Sandy, I had learned, could be anybody, anytime the occasion demanded. She said once that it came from being invisible in our society; that a black person trying to survive had to be able to play a multitude of roles.

After she'd made the second call she hung up and handed me a slip of paper. "Here. May I ask what you plan to do? Invite yourself for cocktails?"

"Hardly." I smiled. She shrugged, knowing my mind was made up. Maybe it would work, maybe not. We'd see.

We made another next check of the house in her car, Sandy driving while I hunkered down in her back seat. Maybe, I told myself, when this was over, I would have a chance to sleep. A hundred years from now.

God, let Scott be there. . . .

"Micah, there's more cars there now." Her voice shook me out of my lethargy. "Looks like a little party or something. Must be expecting more, 'cause the gate's open."

I prayed that the party wouldn't break up until after dark, until I'd had my chance.

There might be a contact alarm on the brick wall, but I didn't think so, just as I didn't think there'd be infrared beams on the lawn: too many false soundings from squirrels and birds. You could rig up a computer to screen them out, but it was expensive, and no system is perfect. No, the alarm system would be at the house itself. And if that was the case, it didn't matter much, because all I needed to do was get close enough and then all hell would break loose with my blessings. I was more worried about guards, because they were less predictable, but I hadn't seen any. Which meant they were probably inside; a little room off the entrance, with a peephole out onto the lawn, like in the governor's mansion at Baton Rouge. And somebody sitting in a chair by the kitchen door.

We changed drivers on a side street and this time I made the swing past the plantation while Sandy drove all the way down to Violet and turned onto Highway 39, because in a small place like Violet you couldn't stay in one place for very long without people noticing. Nothing had changed on the River Road except that there was less light. Good. Sundown couldn't come quickly enough. This time I went all the way to Poydras, letting the air thicken into dusk, and swung east to where the highway met Judge Perez, where I turned north again, this time passing half a mile behind the house, which was a barely discernable blot now against a darkening sky.

I met Sandy at Cypress Point Shopping Center in Mereaux. We

locked her car and got into mine, because if the cops found hers parked there, they'd revert to the usual stereotypes about blacks, especially when Sandy told them it had broken down. If they ran my plate, though, they'd get my name and profession and know something was up.

We went back the way I'd come, and she pulled over at the edge of the cane field, behind the big house. I got my equipment: a flashlight and the items she had brought, the latter stowed in my knapsack, as I had asked her to do. With my right hand, I put my left arm through one strap and drew the strap up to my shoulder. Then I slipped my good arm through the other strap and started my lonely trek.

I kept the sugarcane on my left, skirting the planted area, confident that I could duck into the thick rows of growth if anyone saw me. My feet slid on the ground barely dry, and once or twice I stepped into a puddle, feeling myself sink into the goo.

They call it gumbo mud, and before the levees it was deposited with the yearly floods, bringing fertility to the land. Now the floods are a thing of the past, but the mud is still there, though presumably some day its potential will be exhausted.

It was a strange thing to be thinking about, the problems of floodplain agriculture. But it was a more pleasant subject than the one at hand.

I was halfway there when I heard the movement behind me. I froze, and my hand went down to the butt of my gun.

Footsteps. Dogging my own, gently crunching the fallen cane stalks. Too light to be human.

I turned slowly, letting the gun butt fill my hand.

The dog stared at me, head lowered, it eyes fixed on my own. It was a mongrel, part hound, part something else, maybe forty pounds. And it was growling.

I took a slow step backward and saw its haunches start to quiver. It was lean to the point of emaciation, probably living off whatever it could forage. Maybe somebody in one of the houses within a mile or so thought of it as theirs, but if it were found flattened in the road tomorrow nobody would grieve.

And if it launched itself at a stranger in the cane fields, nobody would give a damn, either.

I thought about the times I'd killed dogs in Nam, when their silence was the price of my life in some hamlet twenty miles from the nearest allied troops. I never enjoyed it, but I was a realist: I valued my own life more than I did a dog's.

But if I shot now, I would be risking a mission that was already questionable at best. Maybe somebody would figure a hunter was in the fields, jacklighting, but not if they stopped to think about it: the sound of a short-barreled pistol is too different from that of a shotgun or rifle, and it was too early to be hunting at night.

I didn't have much choice: forty pounds of hound is nothing to take lightly, and with only one good hand I was already at too much of a disadvantage. Unless . . .

Moving my right arm slowly, I pulled down the strap over my left shoulder and shrugged off the knapsack, letting it slide to the gound behind me. The dog's lip lifted, revealing its fangs, and it snarled at my movement. I tried making friendly noises, but the growling only increased: it sensed I was an interloper, and even if this territory didn't belong to it, it knew it damn sure didn't belong to me.

I was reaching for the pack when it launched itself, a blur of gray that caught me off balance, giving me barely enough time to swing the pack between us. It snarled in frustration, and I rolled, trying to keep the heavy canvas between us as a shield. It tried to launch itself again, but this time when I swung the pack I caught it alongside the head, sending it rolling. It was up in an instant, but not before I made a hammer motion, clouting it between the eyes with the gun butt. It yelped, and I used the few seconds to reach into the sack, letting my gun go as I touched the object I wanted. I drew it out, flipping it on just as the animal flew toward me a third time.

There was a flash and a sizzling sound. The dog uttered a choked bark and fell like a dead weight. I waited a few seconds, catching my breath, but it only lay there, whining. It would be another couple of minutes before it was able to get back to its feet, and my guess was that it would head for the road with its tail between its legs.

For the first time in my life I was greatful for a punk called Sammy Short, who'd tried to use the stun gun on me once and gotten clipped on the head for his trouble. My first impulse had been to throw it into the river, but then I thought it might one day come in handy. It never occurred to me that I'd end up using it on a dog.

I brushed myself off and put the stun gun in my belt, within easy reach. Then I picked up my revolver, shouldered the pack, and started forward again.

It took me fifteen more minutes of walking before I reached the rear wall. I halted and pulled out my binoculars and trained them on the back of the house.

All of the windows of the big house were lit and I searched each one in turn. The party seemed to be downstairs, if party it was: at any rate, I caught glimpses of men in evening clothes and a couple of women in frilly dresses. I moved my sights to the second story.

At the left end of the house there didn't seem to be any movement, just pale light behind gauze curtains. But on the right I caught a shadow passing in front of the window like a spirit. I waited, my binoculars focused on the single square of light. The shadow appeared again, from the other direction. I waited. Three seconds later the shadow came again, retracing its steps.

Somebody upstairs was pacing.

Odd, while the celebration went on below.

I checked my watch. I had two minutes left before Sandy called. I flashed my light along the brick wall and then along the wrought iron bars, but there was no trace of an alarm system. Stepping up onto the low brick wall, I swung first one leg and then the other over the iron railings. Then I jumped down into the yard.

There were floodlights near the house, but the lawn was dark. I ran hunched over, heading for a giant elm that would provide cover. Once there I strained to listen; all I could hear was the distant sound of glasses clinking and an occasional high-pitched, woman's laugh.

I looked up at the second-floor window at the right of the house and felt my muscles tense: the shadow had stoped pacing.

Was there a phone upstairs? Had the shadow gone down to advise the Spiderwoman? Then I saw the shadow again, moving past the window.

Except this time it stopped midway. As I watched it was joined by another shadow, and I saw heads and hands move, as though a discussion were taking place. I searched the back of the house with the binoculars until I found the circuit box. Then I reached down into my pack and took out the gas mask, fitting it carefully over the lower part of my face. Taking the canister from the bottom of the pack, I wedged it into my belt, took a deep breath, and ran straight for the house, bending low.

I was under the lower left-hand window, what I judged to be the dining room, and I could hear their voices clearly, through a faint strain of orchestra music. I went cold, as the enormity of what I planned to do struck me. If it had seemed foolhardy before, now it seemed insane. I edged along the wall to the corner and the electric breaker box. They'd been careless, leaving it unlocked, which meant I wouldn't need the bolt cutters, just the small padlock Sandy had picked up on the way to meet me. I opened the box, flipped the master switch, and slammed the cover shut, fastening the lock into the projecting tongue.

The house went dark, and I heard voices raised in dismay.

I ran for the back door at full speed, stun gun in hand. Taking the steps three at a time, I jerked open the screen door.

His mouth was half open and he was reaching for something when he saw me, a beefy black man who probably served as a combination major domo and bodyguard. I thrust the stun gun against him and he gave a yell and fell backward. I stuck the instrument back into my belt and pulled my penlight from my shirt pocket. Then I shoved through milling bodies, disregarding the cries of protest.

My penlight beam picked out the stairway, just to the right. People were lighting matches now, and somebody in front of me held up a flickering flame.

"Hey," he said. I knocked the match from his hand and went past, hearing him curse.

I started up the stairs, colliding with a body as I went. A woman gasped, and I felt her breasts brush past me.

"Francine . . ." It was a man's voice, old, quavery, from the top of the landing. "Francine, what's the matter? What's going on?"

They were coming to their senses downstairs, and I heard the back door slam as somebody started out to check the breaker box. Then I heard a scream, and somebody was saying Albert had been knocked out, and I knew they'd tripped over the guy I'd stunned.

"Somebody went up the stairs," a man said. "I saw him."

It was time for the canister. I droped the penlight back into my pocket, pulled the metal cylinder from my belt, armed it, and tossed it down the stairs. I heard it rolling, and there was a stifled "What in hell?" from below, then more frantic noises.

"My God," somebody yelled, "it's a bomb!"

There was a full-scale stampede for the back door, and I turned back to the old man at the top of the steps.

"Francine," he called again. "Are you all right?"

I reached him in two steps, just as I heard the pop of the grenade downstairs.

"Who are you?" he asked, seeing my shadow before him. "What do you want?"

"I want the boy," I said, my voice hollow through the mouthpiece of the mask. "And I'll kill you if I don't find him."

I felt the first fumes now, harsh and irritating on the bare skin of my arm. People pushing toward the door below were already starting to cough and choke.

"What's going on?" the old man demanded. "What's happening?"

"What's happening is that I've come for the boy," I said. "What's happening is that you're a dead man if I don't leave here with him."

"I—I don't know what you mean," the old man said, his voice quaking.

I spun him around with my hand and headed him down the hallway. "You were up here pacing," I said, hoping my deduction was correct. "Francine got a phone call and came up to talk to you."

"I—how did you know?"

I shoved him into the dim doorway and shut the door behind me, falshing my light around until I found the phone. I yanked the receiver off the hook; when I heard the dial tone, I knew I had gotten to it in time: nobody would be using the phone downstairs now until the receiver of this one was replaced.

Then I shined my light around the room, playing the beam on filing cabinets, a desk and a chair, a computer terminal. I was in the office. I shoved the old man toward the chair and heard him sigh as he sank down into it. There were some computer disks on the table, beside the console. I flashed the beam on them and read the labels: CALIFORNIA REDS, 1970–; YUGOSLAVIAN VINTAGES; CHILEAN.

My adrenaline high began to give way to a cold feeling, the kind of feeling you get in the bottom of the ninth, seventh game of the Series, two out, and you're watching the first strike sail past you, wondering why you didn't swing.

Only I'd swung. As if it mattered.

"Do you want money?" the old man asked. "I'll give you whatever you want."

I swore to myself. He really didn't seem to have any idea.

"I'm looking for a boy," I told him, knowing it was my last chance, and that in the time left all I could manage now was to scoop up some records and run. "Five eleven, blond, twenty years old."

The old man didn't say anything, and I yanked open a desk drawer, almost dropping the penlight as I tried to keep it in my hand at the same time. The drawer seemed to hold nothing but business records. I left it open and headed for the door.

The tear gas was everywhere now, a thin, biting vapor that clung to the skin and clothing. I heard more coughing downstairs, but the house seemed to have largely emptied. I started for the stairs, trying to decide which would be the easiest escape, the front door or the back.

Then I saw the door on my left, the door to the room at the other end of the hall. What the hell, I thought, and kicked it open.

I gave myself three seconds. In that time my beam picked out the bed, a mirror, and a chair, but no human inhabitant. Strike two.

I left the room and started for the stairway—I was halfway down when I heard footsteps above me.

Something warned me, but I turned around anyway.

A flash hit me in the eyes. I blinked, barely able to make out the thin figure at the head of the stairway.

"Put your hands up and stand still," the old man's voice said. "I've got a gun."

Strike three.

Twenty-One

I had a fleeting notion to wheel and run down the stairs, and then I heard the hammer click back to full cock and knew the moment was past.

"You wouldn't have a chance," the old man said as if reading my thoughts.

There was movement beside me, and the light moved a fraction, coming to rest on an angry pair of eyes, set into a round, elderly, woman's face.

"You've got him," the Spiderwoman said with evident satisfaction, holding a handkerchief demurely up to her eyes.

"Stand aside, my dear," the old man said, discreetly suppressing a cough. "I think I should shoot him right here."

"What a good idea, Dalton," the woman said, brushing a wisp of gray hair out of her eyes. "But I want to see what he looks like first."

A talon reached out for my mask, jerking it away, and the full force of the lingering tear gas hit me.

"Where have I seen you before?" she asked, sniffling from the fumes.

I didn't answer, and she pulled away in disgust.

"All right, shoot him now," she said, her face a death's-head leer.

The flashlight lowered a fraction to center on my midsection, and

I tensed. Then there was a thud and the old man slid to the floor, the flashlight falling to the rug and bounding down the steps toward us.

"*Dalton!*" the woman shrieked.

I didn't have time to think about causes and effects, I just shot an elbow into the woman's side and felt her fold like a deflated balloon. Something dark hurtled down the stairs toward me, and I threw up my arm to protect myself.

"Micah, let's get out of here."

It was Scott's voice, and all of a sudden I felt alive again. The woman was moaning behind us on the stairs as we half slid, half jumped to the bottom. The air was biting and tears streaked my face. Beside me, I dimly saw Scott put a hand to his mouth, gagging.

"This way," I said, choking, and guided him toward what had to be the front. I slammed into a coffee table and sent it sprawling with myself atop it. I felt Scott's hand pull me upright. I fumbled for the penlight in my shirt pocket, switched it on, and found the open front door.

The woman was screaming behind us now, and I knew they would hear her outside. We started across the empty living room but froze as a man's figure appeared in the open doorway.

"Francine? What's going on there?"

"In here," I called. "We need help."

When he came through the living room I dropped him with a chop to the neck. Then, with Scott behind me, we rushed out onto the lawn.

People were coming around the side of the house. A man and woman approached, fear in their eyes, but I waved them away.

"It's a bomb," I croaked. "The whole house is going to blow."

The woman gave a little squeal and I heard cries of "It's a bomb!" and "Explosives!" as we trotted down the driveway to the open gate.

My skin felt like it had been rubbed in pepper and my eyes were on fire. I heard Scott coughing behind me.

We reached the road and I flicked my penlight a couple of times in the direction of the cane field, hoping nothing had kept Sandy from positioning herself. I heard an engine roar into life, and a few seconds later the dark form of my car arrowed toward us like a cannonball. Tires screeched, and the door on the passenger side shot open. I pushed Scott forward and turned in time to confront the bodyguard, who looked like he was ready to kill. I threw the penlight into the car and drew my pistol. The bouncer halted in his tracks. Then I fired twice, quickly, into the air, and saw him flinch. Behind him, I knew others would be hitting the ground instinctively. I took the few seconds of grace and jumped into the car after Scott. Five minutes later Sandy was pulling up beside her car.

"When you get back," she called, "you better get a car wash for the mud on your plates."

I watched her drive away. Grateful to have Scott beside me, I started home.

Back at my office, I had a stiff drink and listened to Scott explain to his mother on the phone. He was in good shape, considering they'd held him for four days and kept him tied up most of that time. He handed me the phone, flinching. I took it wearily.

"Micah, I want to see him," Katharine said.

"It's not a good idea yet," I said. "I'd rather stash him someplace with a guard. It won't be for long. I think we're about to finish this up." I hoped I was telling her the truth.

"Micah . . . " Katherine said, and then was silent. I understood, because I didn't know what to say, either.

"Later," I whispered and hung up.

Scott gave me a sorrowful look. "Sorry about that. She's a hard lady."

"Yeah."

"But look, do you really think we're close? I mean, do you figure the LeJeunes are the ones?"

I shook my head.

"They didn't kill anybody, or they'd have done away with you when they had the chance. All they were willing to do was dump your car and make it look like you'd been killed while they tried to decide what to do with you."

"Maybe so," he said ruefully, rubbing his wrists where the bonds had been. "And I thought I was being so smooth when I went in there and did my pervert act. How was I supposed to know they'd have the place staked out that night with Gargantua?"

"You mean you tried to break into the shop?" I said.

"Yeah. And I was almost successful. I didn't see the alarm on the door. I thought I was stealing a march on you. There I was, in the private office, going through the notebooks full of kiddie porn photos and thinking how I was going to serve them up to you the next morning and, bam! Lights out."

"Bad luck," I said sarcastically. But it didn't help to berate him; he'd learned his lesson.

"She wanted to kill me, you know. Especially after I got loose and managed to call Mom." He was shaking now, as the delayed reaction took over. "But the old man, Dalton, kept saying they needed me as a hostage, they could use me to call you off. I think the idea of murder scared him. So I kept trying to work my hands loose again. When you kicked the door open I was almost free. I was on the floor on the other side of the bed. I thought they were coming for me then. That's when I picked up the ashtray and went out to the hall. And I saw Dalton with the gun." He gave a shaky little laugh. "It made me feel good to finally be able to do something beside lie there."

"It made me feel even better," I said, remembering my close call.

We'd been over it a couple of times already, but he needed to talk it all out.

He went to shower and I tried to put the rest of it together. Somebody had called the first day he was there, and afterward he heard Francine and Dalton arguing over it in the room next door. I looked down at the pad where I'd written down what Scott remembered of the conversation:

FRANCINE: I told him not ever to call here. He killed that boy. We can't afford to be involved.

DALTON: I quite agree, my dear, but he knows about our little business. We can't alienate him.

F: He wouldn't say anything. He's got more to lose than we do.

D: You know how that kind of person is, Francine; it's a sickness and it does no good to try to reason with them.

Scott came out and I took my own shower, scrubbing hard to get the stinging residue off my skin and washing my eyes out. I was dressing when I heard steps coming up the patio stairway. I reached for the revolver, relaxing when I saw Sandy.

"Done like champs." She smiled as I slipped into my shirt. "We should all be burglars."

I gave her a weak smile, remembering how close it had been. It was only luck that it had turned out to be a rescue instead of an aggravated burglary.

"Where to?" I asked her.

"I've got a friend that's gone for the week on business," she said. "I just happen to have the key to his house."

We went out, using the patio stairs, and took the rental car, with Sandy driving. It wasn't likely the LeJeunes would press charges, but if in fact they were tied in with the officials in St. Bernard, I might get a visit I didn't like. And right now I was too tired for a legal hassle.

The house was on Bayou St. John, a modernistic Spanish-style place with a swimming pool where the patio ought to be and, best of all, a protective wall around the back. Sandy pointed out the bedrooms and a bar with a full stock of bottles.

"He must be a pretty good friend," I said.

She winked.

I went over the checklist in my mind: the car was off the street, nobody knew our location, Sandy would stay awake the first part of the night and keep watch.

I went into one of the bedrooms and lay down to rest for a few minutes, but all I could do was turn things over in my mind.

If the LeJeunes hadn't killed Arthur Augustine, they almost certainly hadn't killed Eddie Gulch. Eddie Gulch had been killed by an invisible murderer.

But why had Gulch been killed? Because the killer had hired Gulch to get me and the murderer didn't want to be tied to him? Or because . . .

The thought stamped itself on my consciousness. I sat up in bed. Of course. . . .

Coincidence. That's what it was. Blind coincidence. And bad luck for Eddie Gulch.

But who *had* killed him?

There'd been a cop in the lobby. But this wasn't some kind of locked-room mystery: cops can leave their posts, sleep on the job, and lie afterward. So it didn't mean much that the cop *said* he hadn't seen anybody suspicious. Or he may have seen the killer and it hadn't registered.

Because I kept thinking of what one of Fox's detectives had said standing in the hallway, outside Eddie Gulch's office: he'd been complaining, and I hadn't thought anything about it at the time. Now, though, it suddenly made sense.

The invisible man.

The kind of man you don't notice when you're standing in a lobby, or a hallway, or even in an elevator. . . .

The elevator was falling, and I was reaching out. Katherine was beside me, watching me with a quizzical look, as if she didn't understand. But I understood and I knew that within ten seconds we'd strike the bottom and that would be the end. And I wanted her to understand and not be angry anymore, to forgive. . . .

Sunlight was streaming into the room through the drawn curtains. My God, had I been asleep the whole night?

I sat up on the edge of the bed, aware of the smell of bacon frying. My watch said seven thirty. I padded into the den to find Scott sprawled on the rug, watching *Today*. Sandy appeared from the kitchen, a bandana around her brow and a tray in her hand.

"So the Sleeping Beauty woke up," she said. "I came in there at twelve thirty, but you were dead to the world, so I let you be. Figured somebody as old as you needed your rest."

"Thanks," I said, rubbing my eyes. I sat down on the sofa and I accepted a plate of bacon and toast, suddenly realizing I hadn't eaten in a day. When I'd wolfed it down Sandy served me some more, accompanied by fresh orange juice, and I began to feel a little more human.

There was one thing I had to do.

I got up and went back into the bedroom to use the phone. Katherine answered almost immediately.

"Look," I told her, "I want to explain."

"You don't have to explain," she said. There was a hint of frost in her voice.

"Yes, I do. I feel pretty bad about the whole thing, and what you've been through. I just wanted you to know I felt it, too."

"I know you did." Was there a suggestion of softening?

"Scott's a good boy. He was just trying to prove something. Granted, it was a crazy thing to do, but he meant well."

"He was almost killed," she said tonelessly.

"Yes," I agreed. "He was. But please don't go too hard on him."

"Why not? Who should I go hard on?" The question hung between us.

"I can't change what I do," I told her. "It's my job, and I think it has some value, at least sometimes."

"Getting child molesters off? Dealing with pornographers?"

"It's the world we live in," I said, and didn't think it sounded very convincing. "Look, we need to talk."

"Yes," she agreed.

There wasn't any more to say, so I hung up, feeling hollow. Then I dialed my office, using the number code to activate my answering machine. There was a message from a man who said only that he was from the church, and he asked me to call. I did.

After I'd identified myself, Gabriel Condon came on, his voice mellifluous over the wires. "We couldn't find Brother Taylor," he said. "His sister says he went out to get a cigar the other night and never came back. So you aren't going to find your white boy that way."

"I already found him," I said. I told him about the raid on the house in Meraux.

"But you don't think they kidnapped the boy's uncle, too," Condon said.

"No. I think Taylor Augustine is never going to be found. Or if he is, there won't be enough of him left to identify."

"Who killed him?" he asked, his voice deceptively smooth.

"The same person that killed Eddie Gulch," I said. "And dumped Arthur Augustine's body on the levee."

"You know who that is?"

"I know *who* to look for," I said. "But I still don't know *why*. I was hoping Taylor could help me."

Condon sighed. "Maybe he can."

"What do you mean?" I asked, surprised.

"His sister, Cherisa: she saw a man come by and pick him up once last week. Man in a van. She didn't think about it. But when Taylor turned up missing she remembered."

"Can she identify the man? Was he white?"

"It was almost dark, and she didn't see anything but the van."

"Well, that's better than nothing," I said.

"Maybe. Now you just got to go through all the vans in five parishes. Shouldn't be more than, say, ten thousand."

"I'll get back to you," I told him.

"Hold on. You said you know who it is. So talk."

"No, I said I know who to look for. I meant, the kind of person, not his name."

"And?"

"If I tell you, you may find him first and kill him. I want him to confess."

He grumbled something and was in the middle of making a threat when I hung up. It wouldn't make much sense to tell him that the kind of man I was looking for was invisible.

I called O'Rourke and got him on the second try, at his office. Before he could say anything I told him about my escapade with the Spiderwoman.

"There'll probably be something in the paper about an armed

robbery," I said. "They won't say anything about holding a college student upstairs for half a week. I don't think they'll do anything about it, legally. My guess is they're busy burning all their records right now."

"Shit," said O'Rourke. "Do you know what would have happened if—"

"Yeah," I said. "Look, is there any word on Autry's condition?"

"I hear he'd holding his own. The bullets missed all his vitals. His son came to see me, begged me to stay on the case. What could I say? He said his father was going to sell some property, swore I'd get paid. I tried to tell him tactfully that the property was already gone, with the first shot. I don't think he understood."

"That's Melville," I said, and suddenly it all made sense, appalling, mundane sense, the kind of logic that obtains when a fourteen-year-old mother confesses to killing her child. You'd rather it was something else, a serial killer, someone obviously demented, because there she is, all the time looking sorrowful, weeping real tears.

"Oh, and I checked with the crime lab in Baton Rouge as soon as I got in; they worked through the weekend. Eddie Gulch didn't fire a handgun for at least forty-eight hours before his death, unless he scrubbed awfully hard. But I told them he probably wore gloves."

"No," I said. "He didn't wear gloves. They're right."

"What?"

"Do you read Father Brown?" I asked.

"What? You mean Chesterton's detective? Some of them, sure. Alec Guinness played him in the movie. I don't have it on tape, but—"

"There was a story called The Invisible Man," I said. "Do you remember it?"

"Not offhand. Should I?"

"Look it up," I said. "I think that's what we've got here."

"Don't be obscure."

"Look it up," I said. "And while you're at it, read Doyle's Silver Blaze."

"Huh?"

"I've got to go."

Because it held everything together: the wire used to tie the boy, the motive—God, the motive . . .

It was time for me to see a man and find out if I was right.

Twenty-Two

The man, whose name was Hap Silverman, worked out of a lab at the University of New Orleans, doing contract archaeology for private firms seeking wetlands development permits from the Corps of Engineers. He was a gnomish, balding little fellow in his late thirties, in love with his work. I'd met him a couple of years before, through Katherine, who knew most of the archaeologists in town. He'd never rise higher than instructor, because he only held a master's degree, but so long as he had his lab he would be satisfied. Some people went out with shovels, he explained, leading me around his little room and pointing to rusted agglomerations of metal, and some people worked with augers. But none of that for him: he was high tech. He went to a cabinet in the corner and drew out some multicolored maps. I'd seen the same sort of thing in Nam, but the technology, he explained, had come a long way since then.

"Landsat," he said. "We get 'em from the Space Center in Gulfport. The whole Mississippi River delta. And with side-looking radar we can even do even more. Indian mounds that have been buried by sediment, for example. Well, that's only theoretical, but it ought to be possible."

"But all this high-tech stuff is pretty fallible," I said, "just like radiocarbon dating."

He drew back, offended. "Is it any more fallible than some yuk with a shovel who gets his artifact bags confused? Look, I could tell you horror stories about some of the old-timers."

I patted his shoulder. "Just kidding, Hap. Actually, I need your help. And maybe your high-tech stuff as well."

He smiled, mollified.

"I thought so. What is it, Micah? A dead body? No. Something bigger than that, right? Detectable through remote sensing."

"Hap," I said, "you're dead on."

I set it up for that afternoon and went back to my office, feeling worn out. If I was right, it would be over soon.

All along I'd been looking for the wrong person. I'd been looking for the killer of Arthur Augustine, and then the killer of Eddie Gulch. But there was somebody else I should have looked for first. Because if my hunch was right, that was the key to the whole business.

I turned my thoughts to Katherine. I needed Scott for one more thing. I could only hope she would eventually understand. But first I had to tie up a loose end.

I called O'Rourke and he listened in horror.

"Jesus, Micah, are you crazy?"

"Probably. But I have to get clear on this. I can't get stopped for questioning."

"That's not the reason. You just want to get even."

"Yeah," I said. "Maybe so. Will you do it?"

"But I can't get a warrant."

"You don't need one. Get a dog. You know the people at customs."

"And I know the people at the DA's, one of whom I owe my soul for something that didn't matter to start with."

"Believe me," I said. "This matters."

He sighed. "All right."

We drove over to Scott's place and got his equipment. At twelve thirty we picked up Hap at the university and headed for the Pontchartrain Causeway. Hap told us his kids were looking forward to Halloween. I thought we were about to have it a couple weeks early.

It was dark when we got back. I passed up dinner, feeling slightly nauseous. Scott was on an adrenaline high, though, and I knew it would take a long time for him to come down: he'd redeemed himself, and that was important. I dropped him at Katherine's and watched her fly into his arms, half admonishing, half soothing. Her eyes touched mine for an instant, and I nodded to let her know I understood and then got back in to my car.

All the weariness of the last few days seemed to have descended onto me at once, and I wished I could go back, tell her it had all been a dream, and curl up beside her on the sofa as if nothing had happened. But something *had* happened, to other people and to ourselves. And there would be no time to look for comfort until it was over.

I went back to my office, where the red eye of the answering machine stared accusingly. For a long time I sat in my chair in the dark, staring back. Finally, my hand weighing a ton, I picked up the phone and punched in Melville Autry's number.

"You," he said.

"Yeah."

"You got a hell of a lot of nerve."

"Shut up, Melville. I've got something to talk to you about, and I want you to listen."

It must have been my tone of voice. He listened. I replaced the phone and resigned myself to wait. But waiting was too difficult, as tired as I was: my eyes couldn't meet the red light, and I kept finding I needed something in the kitchen, first a soft drink, and then some snack crackers. Finally I gave up and went down the inside stairs and out onto Decatur.

Across the street was the brooding old Mint building, now a museum. In 1862, when the federal troops landed to occupy the city, a local youth named Mumford pulled down the stars and stripes from the building. General Benjamin Butler, determined to assert his authority, hanged Mumford from the flagpole on the Mint's front lawn. Today bums congregate along the iron fence outside, and Mumford would be given a misdemeanor summons if he were caught at all. But it is unlikely he'd be caught, because the police are busy with more serious things, like protecting the tourists in the

French Quarter, who tend to get shot, robbed, and raped at a disconcertingly frequent rate.

In my years in the Quarter, though, I've never been molested by street thugs. Maybe it's the impression I convey, or maybe I don't look worth the trouble. I wouldn't have advised anybody to fool with me at that moment, because I was in a mean mood.

The motive for it all had been so petty.

Then I thought about the professor who'd been shot dead by a holdup man a few blocks from here: the motives, I reminded myself, were usually petty. When you're twisted, it doesn't take much.

I made my way through the thin crowd. It was Monday night, and the usual denizens of the Quarter weren't into the spirit of things. They piled up on street corners like dirty laundry, eyes dull and without enthusiasm. Even the tourists seemed chilled, as if the sixty degrees on the thermometer was a lie and the real temperature was below freezing. At the corner of Chartres and Dumaine a wino started in my direction and then veered away, as if he saw something he didn't like. I made my way back toward Jackson Square and stood in front of the cathedral. A woman with a kerchief on her head went in through the big main door and, without thinking, I followed. I watched the woman head for one of the confessionals. The air smelled of incense, and I thought of something I'd read once, about the medieval cathedral being a model of the cosmos. It was a comforting thought, to have everything set out and measurable. Heaven was one way, hell another, and mankind was in between.

I'd never been religious, but I thought I knew about hell and it wasn't under St. Louis Cathedral. I was sure of that, because I'd seen it today.

I left the church and walked back to my rooms. Two hours later Melville called back.

It was just after ten when I reached the cabin. I used a picklock to open the back door and went in, the bare wood floor creaking under my feet. I thought about Cal's grandchildren, Melville's kids, and how Cal had wanted to have this place for them, so they could go swimming off the pier he was going to build. The thought stirred my stomach, and I forced it away. I took out my penlight and swept its beam over the counter, the bedrooms, the big living room, but everything seemed as I had left it the night I'd spent there with Cal. Wrapping my blanket around me, I took a seat on the couch and waited.

Maybe it wouldn't work, but I thought it would. There was too much for the killer to lose.

I didn't like being there alone, though. Even with my revolver in my hand under the blanket, I still felt like a staked goat. I just hoped my timing was right; dawn would be a better time than midnight or the hours just after. All I had to do was see who it was and it would be enough: there was no other reason for that person to be here.

Eleven o'clock came and went. An owl took a perch on a limb outside the window and chilled me with its eerie *hoot-hoot-hoot*. A couple of times I thought I heard the sound of tires on the gravel, and I got up, holding my blanket about me, and went to the front window to look out, but there was nothing but darkness.

The cabin smelled of dust and pine needles. I wondered what it had smelled like that day five years before. Or had the thing been done outside?

Twelve thirty.

My limbs were getting stiff. I still had bruises from my encounter with Condon, and my exploits at the LeJeune house hadn't helped any. I wanted to get up and pace, work my muscles loose, but if I did that I might miss the all-important noise and change myself from hunter to hunted.

One o'clock.

It was times like this when the memory was always the worst: waiting by the trail for Truong, knowing they'd be just as glad if I took him out, because he'd thrown a bomb into the village school and killed fifteen kids. But the orders weren't to take him out, because nobody wanted an assassination coming back to haunt them at a court-martial. The orders were to attempt to capture him, but to take no chances. None at all.

When he'd reached the spot where I was hiding he'd stopped, nose quivering like a hunted animal's. I knew he probably smelled me, and so I stepped out of my hiding place then, my silenced .22 pointing straight at his head. For a second we looked at each other, and then he reached for the knife at his belt and I shot him. He was still looking at me as he fell.

It was self-defense; I hadn't assassinated the man. And back at the base they asked no questions, just scratched out one code name and closed a file. They even bought me drinks. Nobody mentioned the killing, there was just the usual men's talk, as if nothing had really happened.

But something *had* happened. They didn't issue you a .22 with a silencer for routine missions. I'd made a pact with them by accepting it, and I'd honored the pact with myself by giving Truong a chance to go for his own weapon, to be sure he couldn't be taken alive. But he'd never really had a chance, because if he'd surrendered, it would've been out of my hands, he'd have been handed over to the interrogators, and they weren't nice people. So he'd done the only thing he could.

Afterward I refused that kind of mission. But I still remembered Truong and the light fading from his eyes as he went down, looking at me.

A twig crackled outside, and I came instantly alert.

My heart started to pound. I tried to ignore it, to focus all my attention on the sounds of the night, because maybe it was just a pine cone falling from a branch, or a dog rooting in the pine needles.

There was a swish, like a piece of cloth brushing the side of the house. I'd been wrong. I'd expected him at dawn and he'd come early.

The back step creaked, and I heard a faint jingle of keys as someone fit one into the lock. *He was coming into the cabin.*

I gathered my blanket and stepped softly back to the big closet, closing the door behind me.

The hinges creaked as the back door opened, and I heard footsteps in the kitchen. From the crack in the closet door I could see flickers in the darkness as the intruder's penlight searched the room. Then the darkness folded back over everything, and I knew he had gone into the bedroom. I thought of tiptoing out, catching him from behind, but it would take five seconds, and in that time he could be out and facing me. Even as I made the decision, the floorboards groaned again and the beam of light darted back into the kitchen and then resolved into a single eye, looking straight at my hiding place.

For a moment my blood froze; I was sure he'd seen me, but then the light streaked off at an angle and came to rest on the wall opposite. It painted a stripe on the wall that moved methodically from one corner to the other. When the light was thrown on the wall directly across from me and I knew his back had to be to me, I stepped out.

"Put both hands in the air and kneel down," I said.

The figure seemed to congeal into a darker mass against the night, as if my words had shrunken it, causing it to solidify in the gloom. I took a step forward, pistol cocked, edging my way toward the light switch by the front door.

He made his move before I got there. The light spun at me like a rocket, catching me in the forehead. I fired once, but the shot went wild, and he grabbed my legs, sending me crashing backward against the wall. I brought the gun down hard where I thought his head should be, but it only caught him a glancing blow, and I heard him grunt. Then something hammered my face, and the darkness seemed to flash red. I raised my hand but something hit my forearm, sending arrows of pain through it. I still had my legs, but he was too smart for that. He was bigger than I was and used his bulk to pin me. Something else hit my head, and this time my entire body went numb. The darkness began to spin slowly, as if I was drunk, and as consciousness fled I knew I had underestimated him and was going to die.

I was on the floor, my back propped against the wall. When I tried to move my right arm I couldn't. At first I thought it was still numb, but after a few seconds I realized it was tied to my body. I bent my head so that my chin touched my chest, feeling something cold and hard: wire. He had tied me up with wire, the same way he had the Augustine boy.

I'd been stupid. I'd thought he would come at dawn, because that's when I'd told Melville I'd be here, but the killer had been smarter than I'd given him credit for. He'd come early, to wait for me, just as I'd come to wait for him.

The floor creaked, and I saw the light flashing in the kitchen. There was a strong smell and I recoiled at the recognition of what it was.

Gasoline.

The light hit me in the face, making me flinch.

"You shouldn't of never come here," the killer said. "Now I guess I got to let you burn with the place."

I didn't say anything, just kept trying to think of something to do and kept coming back full circle to the realization that there wasn't anything to be done.

"Just one thing, though," he said, and I heard the springs of the big chair across the room squeak. "I'd like to know how you got on to me. Was it that bitch, Francine?"

My throat was dry, but I managed to make my vocal cords work. "No," I said. "It wasn't Francine. It was you."

"Me?" He managed a short laugh. "What do you mean?"

"You killed Eddie Gulch," I said. "And you probably killed Taylor Augustine. The only reason I could think of for killing Gulch was that you were trying to kill me that night, and he saw you. He saw you and you saw him. He could identify you, so you tracked him down. You went into the lobby of his building with a cop standing there and went up in the elevator to his floor and went to his office. But he wasn't there yet, so you did something else while you were waiting. People saw you, but they didn't pay any attention. When he came you dropped what you were doing and went down to his office and killed him. Then you took the message tape with your voice on it and walked out as easily as you'd come in."

"How did you figure all that out?"

"Because it made sense, and because of something I saw on the elevator, going up."

"What?"

"A telephone repairman," I said. "I'll bet if I'd have asked the cop in the lobby he wouldn't have seen him, either. You made a real mess in the men's room."

"Pipes were old. I just wanted to make like I was working on 'em in case anybody came, but the drain was rusted. I got the wrench on it and it crumbled. Damn water went all over the floor."

"I noticed," I told him.

"You're a smart bastard," my captor said. "I'm going to feel a hell of a lot safer when you're gone."

"It won't do you any good," I said. "People know. I've told them."

"Maybe, maybe not. Seems to me if all those people knew, you wouldn't be up here all by yourself."

"It's a flaw in my character," I said. "Just like murder is a flaw in yours. They'll find her, you know. And the trail will lead right back to you."

"They won't ever find her," he said. "The water's at least fifteen feet there, and I've already made an offer on this property. Nobody'll come here then."

"They'll come here because I've already found her," I said.

"How?"

"It's called a magnetometer, sort of a supermagnet you hang on a boat. It picks up things under the water, like steel shipwrecks— and automobiles. When we got a suspicious reading we sent a diver down. He saw it. The police will be here in a few hours to haul it out. I just wanted to be here first."

"You're full of bullshit," he said. "I don't believe you."

"You believe me," I said. "That's what's got you scared."

"Shut up!" He got up and started to light a cigarette, then sniffed the fumes and put it away.

"When they find the same kind of wire on me that they found on the Augustine boy, that'll help cinch it."

"Shut up, I said. I gotta think."

"And then," I said, trying to keep him rattled, "there was the van. Cal Autry has a van. But vans are used a lot by other kinds of tradesmen. Electricians. Locksmiths. And plumbers."

"I knew from the first you weren't any goddamn insurance man," Virgil Bonchaud said. "I should of killed you then."

Twenty-Three

*H*e spat on the floor. I tried to stretch my legs, to see if they were bound, too. I found I could move them a few inches, and I wondered if he could see the movement in the dark.

"I should have figured you from the first, too," I said. "The next-door neighbor; you were a natural. I thought it was funny about the wire in his garage."

"What?"

"So convenient. It's a lot easier to get into a garage than a locked house. He didn't even have a lock on it. Just a barking dog. That was the other thing: that dog wouldn't let anybody close. Anybody except you or Melville. It knew you. You could walk right by it."

"Yeah, that's right," Bonchaud said. "You got it."

"Just like the liquor I saw in Melville's place," I said. "I remembered seeing that label in Francine LeJeune's wine shop. For a little while it threw me. I thought Melville or Cal had bought it there. But then I thought, what if neither of them had? And it came to me that sometimes neighbors exchange gifts. Melville probably got the bottle from Cal, but Cal probably had it from you."

"Smart. Yeah, I give him a bottle for Christmas every year."

"And the boy: you tried to make a good case for how Cal met him when he came by to do yard work. But the boy's house is at least three miles away, and the kid only had a bike. He wouldn't come all the way to Metairie to cut lawns. And if Cal was innocent, who could come up with a frame like that? Only somebody who had the experience to make it stand up. Somebody who knew a boy who could be expected to make a false complaint for enough money, because he did other things for money too. You got the boy through Francine LeJeune, didn't you? He was on her list. You were the child molester, not Cal."

There was a long silence before he spoke.

"No. You missed there, by a mile. Did you think I was into little black boys?" He laughed. "You think I'm a pervert? It was always girls. Francine handles them, too, you know. That's what I went to her for to start with. Young girls. Fresh meat. Unspoiled. Expensive, but God, worth it. It was only after I was using Francine for a while I found out she kept lists of boys, too. That's when it came to me to use one of 'em against Cal. Because he was talking about building that damn pier, and I couldn't let him do that."

"No," I agreed. "He would have found the car when he tried to sink the pilings. So you had to figure a way to make him have to sell the place instead. I checked with the owner of the subdivision; he confirms that you called a couple of times about buying Cal's lot if it ever got put on the market."

"I offered him good money for it, too, just like I offered Cal over the years. But he never would take it; always gonna hold onto it for a vacation place. Didn't matter, so long as nothing was done. But this year, when he started talking about the pier, I knew I had to force his hand."

"And the best way was a criminal charge that would make him have to come up with money quickly."

"Sure. Lawyers ain't cheap."

"Why did you kill her?" I asked. "Was it just a fight?"

He grunted. "You never seen nobody like Marie Autry. Always coming on, always touching you, throwing herself at you. Couple of times the old lady and me come up here with 'em, and all the while Marie was looking at me, giving me them eyes. Finally one day she came over from next door and asked me if I wanted to go for a ride with her. I said what the hell, and we come up here." He chuckled again. "It ain't never as good as you think it'll be, but it was good, I'll give her that. But afterwards I couldn't get loose from her. She was always after me, always asking for things, presents and money. She had a big mouth. I was scared she was gonna say the wrong thing to Cal. We come over here that day, it was in December. She'd had a fight with Cal, said he was being cheap with her. She said she wanted to get away from him, told me she even left him a note saying she was fed up. All of a sudden I realized what she was setting me up for—like I was going to run away with her, leave my business and all. I knew I had to cut it off while there was time. But she cussed and cried and threatened to tell her old man. I grabbed her, tried to shake sense into her, and . . ." The boards creaked, and I sensed that he had turned away at the memory.

"So you put her body in the car," I said, "and drove it to the edge of the lake and pushed it into the deep water. And walked back out to the highway and thumbed a ride, I'd guess."

"Yeah. That's what I did. And it was pretty damn near perfect. I found some letters in her purse, and I copied her handwriting on a postcard and had somebody mail it from California. One of those remailing services, you know. Far as Cal or anybody else knew, she just run off. And good riddance."

My legs were numb, the circulation cut off from the way I'd been sitting. There was no chance of my making a fast move.

"Why did you have to kill Taylor Augustine?" I asked, trying to keep him talking.

"The kid's uncle? Hell, the uncle found out about the kid. The kid talked. The uncle called me, asked if it was true, like he expected me to tell him. That's a dumb nigger for you. I told him it was all lies. Then one night he called me back, told me you'd been by and he was going to talk to you. So I went out there first and picked him up when he left the house. Put a gun to his skull and made him tell me where he was supposed to meet you. Then I killed him and took his body with me when I went to meet you. Too bad I missed."

"You dumped his body later that night, I guess."

"Where they won't find it." He sighed. "But they'll find yours. There just won't be much to see."

A match flared in the darkness. I tried to shrink away, but it came sailing toward me like a shooting star, landing between us. A sheet of flame sprang up from the floor. For an instant I saw his face, wavering like a death's-head on the other side of the flames, and then he was gone.

I rolled away, toward the wall, as the heat breathed death at me. The fire was everywhere now, except for my little island, where the gasoline hadn't flowed. Finding strength somewhere, I lurched halfway to my feet and then collapsed onto the couch. The hair on my head was already singed, and I knew it was only a matter of a couple of seconds before the fire reached me. I raised my legs and kicked at the curtains that hid the big glass window. The glass shattered and I felt the flames leap toward me, drawn to the fresh oxygen. I used all my willpower to force myself upright and then dove through the curtains, away from the inferno.

I landed on my shoulder and rolled, the smell of burning cloth in my nostrils. Looking back, I saw bits of the curtain still afire. The cabin itself was a mass of hissing flames. I rolled some more, trying to get as far away as I could, finally coming to a stop against something hard.

A tree. I turned my head, trying to get my bearings.

And the tree moved.

"You've got more lives than a cat," said Virgil Bonchaud. "But I think you're about out of 'em now."

The reflection of the flames glinted on the pistol, and I heard it click as he cocked the hammer.

"Good-bye, Mr. Dunn."

The shot cracked like a piece of green kindling, and then the cabin behind us collapsed into sparks. Virgil Bonchaud swayed slightly, letting the pistol fall to the ground. He got about two steps and then sprawled flat on his face. Footsteps emerged against the crackle of the fire.

Melville Autry stared down at the body of his father's neighbor. Then he squatted down and went to work on my bonds.

"We got to get Mama out," he said. "I can't stand the thought of her being down there."

Epilogue

*I*t was midmorning before they got the car out of the water. I stayed because it seemed fitting to be there at the end. Melville stood apart, slightly hunched, hands deep in his pockets. At first they'd cuffed him and put him in the back of a police cruiser, but I'd intervened, and with Sal Mancuso's pleas added, they agreed to free him, though a deputy was always two steps behind, as if they still half expected him to run.

It was a big production: three cops in a skiff and a couple of divers, and the high sheriff himself, who knew a good story when he saw one and figured this was a way to double-trump both the New Orleans cops, who'd been dead wrong about the killings, and his predecessor, who'd been sheriff five years ago and had had a body left under his nose. There were crews from all the New Orleans stations, and when the wrecker cable snapped the first time, I half suspected it was part of the show.

But finally they got it hooked up right and the diver's head popped to the surface. He gave the thumbs-up, and the sheriff walked over to the brink and that was the sign for all the cameras to roll. The wrecker's engine raced, and the cable went taut and I smelled something burning, and for a second I thought it was going to happen again, a no-go, but the cable moved, and then it moved a little more, and I heard somebody say, "Here it comes."

Two seconds later there was a boiling of water as the hood of the old Caddy broke the surface, and I wished Scott were here to see what he'd only glimpsed under the murky waters.

Somebody said, "I see her," but I think it was imagination, because the car was being hauled up the bluff at about a forty-degree angle, nose up, and the body inside would have been thrown back against the seat. But maybe it was just my own mind at work; maybe I didn't really want to see her. I'd seen enough dead bodies already for one lifetime.

And after five years there wouldn't be that much to see, anyway.

They got the car to the top of the bank and it rolled forward onto the lawn, and immediately the deputies and newsmen swarmed forward, craning to look in the windows.

But even as they jostled for a view, someone must have said something, because they parted again, making a place for Melville. He stood beside the rusted hulk, staring down through the window, and he was still staring when I turned away.

"Shit," Mancuso said. "Well, I guess he has the right."

"I guess so," I agreed.

"I talked to O'Rourke," he said, as if to take our minds away from the macabre drama going on a few feet away. "They found the white stuff where you said it would be."

"Good," I said.

The detective chuckled. "I'd like to have been there to see Fox's face. Here he gets this anonymous tip to raid your apartment—and you're somebody he'd love to stick it to. So he grabs a packet of coke from the trunk of his car, to plant in your place in case he comes up dry, and as soon as he's out on the sidewalk a damn sniffer dog comes up and starts barking, and the DEA asks him to step over and explain a few things. How the hell did you know he'd try to plant something?"

"Because he did with Cal. There was no reason in the world to try to plant cocaine on Cal after that shootout, but Fox is the kind who always tries for overkill. I knew he'd been the one, and I figured he wouldn't miss the chance again. I figured he was always prepared."

"You know he'll find some way to talk his way out of it. Then he'll come back with both barrels."

"Let him. At least he'll get a few days off without pay."

"Oh, by the way: O'Rourke wants to know what the crap about Father Brown and Arthur Conan Doyle was all about. He said to tell you he doesn't have time to go to the library."

I smiled. "Tell him to read *The Invisible Man*. The killer was the mailman, only nobody saw him because they weren't looking for somebody in uniform."

"And Doyle?"

"In *Silver Blaze* the dog didn't bark because he knew the person who went past him. Cal's dog wouldn't let anybody close—except people he knew: Melville and Virgil Bonchaud."

"Okay."

We turned at the sound of steps behind us. Melville had seen what he needed and had walked away from the crowd to light a cigarette.

I made my way over to him.

"I guess I owe you one," I told him. "But I didn't expect you to come out here."

"I knew I had to come," he said. "As soon as you told me you wanted me to go to the house and mention to Virgil how the case was going to be all wrapped up, because you were going to have the lake dragged at daylight. I went to the hospital and asked my old man what he thought you figured was down there. He knew right off. He knew it had to be Mama. So I had to come."

I followed him out in my car. An hour later we were standing next to Cal's hospital bed. I let Melville talk, because it was his place, and because I didn't need to tell Cal what Virgil had said about Marie's intending to leave him. When Melville had finished, Cal just nodded grimly.

"You done good, son," Calvin said, and I saw Melville stand up a little straighter. "Your Mama and me may have had our problems, but she shouldn't've been killed."

"No," Melville agreed.

"I'm still gonna have to sell the property," Cal said. "And I'll have to fight for my business."

I didn't say anything, because it was true. Getting justice doesn't mean having things come out right.

"But I was thinking while I was laying here with nothing to do that even if I can't afford to stay in the garage, I can make it. I'll find some other place. And I got some good customers, who won't give a damn about all this. I ain't gonna quit."

"Good for you, Cal," I said. "You know you'll get my business."

"Yeah," he said, and gave me his hand. "I know that. Thanks, Micah. I'm sorry if I said things to you."

I looked away. "Don't worry about it, Cal."

"Come see me when I get out of this place."

"Sure."

I went out the door, feeling ashamed, because I'd wondered about him, and it would take more than just dismissal of charges to put things back the way they were. It was the ancient conflict between law and equity, what was legal and what was fair. The law had been upheld, but an honest man had been deprived of his livelihood, while a crook named Morris Frazier continued to cheat customers at his filling station on Esplanade, a shyster lawyer named Guidry stayed fat and happy sucking the teats of crooked judges and clients, and the Sam DeNovas of the world went on welshing on deals.

I was so absorbed in my thoughts that when I turned a corner in the corridor I didn't see the other man until his arm reached out and caught me.

"I hear there was some excitement," the Reverend Condon said, a bodyguard standing comfortably close behind him.

"Oh?" I asked.

"Come on, Dunn, I got ears everywhere, especially on the New Orleans police force. I hear a fellow name of Bonchaud did it."

"Then you heard right," I said. "Look, Condon, you helped me out at the wineshop; I figure that squares us, after the beating I took."

Condon rumbled a deep laugh. "Not hardly, Ace. You had that beatin' comin'. On the other hand, I was wrong to try to set you up."

"Well, write a letter to the newspaper," I said. "Nobody'll read it, but I figure everybody's forgotten that story, anyhow. You know how it is with TV: a half-life of three hours."

The laugh again. "I got to do more than that. Matter of my *credibility*, understand?"

I started away from him but turned back as an idea struck me. "You really want to make amends?" I asked.

"Within reason."

"There's a strung-out white boy named Villiere who's fixing to take a dive. Won't come up again for five or six years. I figure he's going to need every cent he can come up with for his defense."

"So?"

"He owns a garage off Esplanade. You may know the place."

The minister's eyes narrowed. "What have you got up your sleeve?"

"I figure he'll dump it for a song. I also figure it would be a good deal for somebody to pick up cheap. Especially since there's a paying tenant. Tenant may have to pay a little less than he's paying now; business reverses and all. But the property will go for next to nothing. I'd call it a damn good investment."

Condon snorted. "You want me to bankroll that old redneck?"

"Let's call it an experiment in brotherhood," I said. "Anyway, you asked, so I told you what you could do."

Condon turned to his bodyguard. "This white boy has got some balls." He seemed to consider for a second; then he nodded.

"Okay. We'll see what happens. But I ain't taking any shit."

"I think the pair of you will get along just fine," I said.

I went out into the parking lot, feeling a little better. Maybe it would work, maybe it wouldn't. But I'd done what I could, what I had to. Because my own relationship with Cal had subtly altered, and it might never be the same again.

I thought about it all the way back on the causeway; how relationships change, not because of anything either of the parties do, but because of events.

When I reached Katherine's house, I sat in front for a long time trying to decide what I would say. But after a while I realized that there were no words, just as there hadn't been anything for Cal and me to say to each other about what had happened.

Finally I made myself open the door and go slowly up the walk to the door and knock. It was a long time before it opened, and then I was staring into her eyes and she was standing back a little, as if she weren't sure what to do.

"You didn't have your key?" she asked finally, her voice trembling.

"I guess I left it," I lied.

She stood aside and I came in and collapsed onto the sofa.

"Is it over?" she asked.

"It's over," I said. "Finally."

"You look like hell. You have soot on your face. Have you been in a fire?"

I nodded. "Yeah."

"I'll get you a drink. Have you had anything to eat?"

I shook my head. "I just want to sleep for a couple of years."

"Then I'll draw a bath."

"Maybe I ought to go back to my own place," I said.

She halted, the whiskey decanter in her hand. "It isn't necessary. Unless you want to."

I felt like telling her that what I wanted was for none of it to have happened, but it wouldn't have done any good, so I didn't say anything.

She handed me the drink and stood watching, just out of reach. The whiskey felt good, a slow burn that loosened my muscles and brought me to the edge of sleep.

Katherine reached forward, taking the glass out of my hand before I could drop it onto the carpet. She sat down beside me.

"Micah, I've done a lot of thinking. I don't blame you. I really don't. But you've got to understand: I'm not just one person, I'm two. Part of me is the Katherine you know who loves you, but the other part is Scott's mother. That can't ever change. And it may be the part that's dominant. You may have to learn to live with that."

I forced my mind back into focus and nodded. "I know," I said.

"And?"

"I don't know if I can live with it or not."

"An honest answer," she said.

"We'll talk about it tomorrow," I told her. "Things will look better then."

"Yes," she said. I felt my head going back against the cushion of the sofa, and then I felt her removing my shoes.

Yes, I told myself as I drifted into comforting sleep. There would be time for everything tomorrow.